Calista's Court

SUSAN HULCHER

DISCLAIMER

This book is a work of fiction. Names, and character descriptions in this book are solely the product of the author's imagination and any resemblance to a real person is purely coincidental.

Cover art by: selfpubbookcovers.com/DiversePixel

Copyright © December 2013 by Susan Hulcher
ISBN-13: 978-1494849948
ISBN-10: 1494849941

All Rights Reserved. Except as permitted under current legislation no part of this work may be photocopied, stored in a retrieval system, published, performed in public, adapted, broadcast, transmitted, recorded or reproduced in any form or by any means, without the prior permission of the copyright owner.

:

DEDICATION

Dedicated to my mother who, not only spent days on initial editing, but was forever encouraging. More importantly, she taught me to question everything. Thank you to my children who remind me every day why it's such an important lesson and for being the reason for me to strive.

ACKNOWLEDGMENTS

Ask and it shall be given, and so you came. In early stages, knowing there was still much to learn, I asked the universe to send me teachers. Magically, Dean Sault, Sue Sault, and Sass Cadeaux appeared. One day I hope to repay them for their support, time, and knowledge, but if for some reason I cannot, I will return by giving to another. As they would want me to.

CALISTA'S COURT

CHAPTER 1

A filthy, stinking hand slipped over my mouth. It reeked of stale smoke and motor oil. His arm reached around my waist. It was Max, my foster parent's sleaze-ball friend. I tried to shout and kick, but was powerless. My heels burned as they dug into the carpet, trying to prevent him from taking me anywhere. It was useless, but I kept thrashing in his grasp.

"Sophia," little Jackie cried out from my bed where she was laying with the other children. "What's going on?"

It was too dark to see. Jackie must have been awakened by the scuffle.

I knew exactly what this repugnant creature was thinking, and it was outrageous to me that, with all the "adults" carousing in the living room, nobody knew what was going on back here. If only I could bang a wall or squeak out a sound.

Tightening his hold, a belt buckle dug into the small of my back. With one last heave, he shoved me into the bathroom. Lit only by the twin's princess nightlight, my face was pressed against the wall. The door slammed shut.

"Pretty, pretty girl," he sang, "where have you been hiding?"

Metal clinked at his waist.

Did he unfasten his belt?

A jagged breath caught in my throat. In my mind I screamed, *Don't touch me!*

"I love that sound you make," he panted at my neck. "You've been on my mind all night."

Pounding came to the door.

Help me!

"Hurry up. I need to take a piss," a man yelled from the other side.

Muffled pleas would surely be unheard, so I kicked the wall. Max immediately clamped my legs with his.

"Does that mean you're going to be a while?" the man questioned from the hallway.

No. He's got me trapped. He's going to hurt me! I screeched inside my head.

"Sheila, is that you in there, baby? I've been looking all over for you. Listen, what you saw earlier was nothing. That chick doesn't mean jack."

Don't care who you think I am. Just help me. Please!

Even though Max was bigger, restraining me with only the support of one leg would have set him off balance. It was enough to let me thrust forward, if only once. I threw my head into the wall.

I became dizzy.

"Sheila, let me in baby! Are you hurt?"

Bust in please!

Max forced me on the floor, suppressing every inch of my body with his. My throat felt raw from screams that strained to rip through his fingers.

"Sheila left an hour ago, Larry." Max called to the man.

"She did?" the drunken dumbstruck fool questioned.

"Yeah, took one of your credit cards," Max explained. "Said she was going to teach you a lesson."

It's a lie. Don't believe him!

"That bitch." Larry struck the door.

"Better go after her," Max hollered. "Carol hid your keys in the microwave."

"I'm going, Max." Larry slurred in drunken boldness. "You really are a great friend."

Don't go. Don't go! Don't leave me! Please.

"Now, where were we?" Max twisted my head and licked my neck. His clasp on my face relaxed.

It must have been repulsion that compelled me. I bit his hand. The taste of blood, sweat and grime filled my mouth.

Hearing him shriek was almost worth the backhand across the cheek. Unfortunately, ringing in my ears, combined with impaired vision caused my awareness to falter temporarily. It was enough of a reprieve for him to wrap his belt around my throat.

Pulling it tight like a noose, he said, "Don't try that again, you little bitch."

My gasps for breath indicated his point was made. I did not dare scream. It would take only a flick of his wrist to end me.

Kids!

Time and state became a blur as fears drifted to the children, Cara, Jackie, and Caleb. My door was left open. What if someone went after them, too? They were so innocent. I began to cry.

Someone please help them.

The appeal was made to anyone who could hear.

Is anyone listening?

At first it sounded like a bomb blast. Then I realized the front door had been kicked in.

"Police! Nobody move!" The deep voice seemed miles away.

Max leapt off me.

I shot up, threw the door open, and ran straight into a lady cop who was about to open the bathroom door.

She embraced me immediately. Tears streamed down my face.

Over her shoulder, illuminated by the kitchen light, another savior, a man angel holding a gun, stepped into the hallway and flipped on the light.

"I didn't know she was underage." Max held his hands up in defense.

"What has he done to you?" The fair haired lady cop took the belt from my neck, while digging her glare into Max. "There's a slum in hell calling your name."

"He's just lucky we're in a room full of witnesses." The gun welding policeman stepped past us to the bathroom.

A third officer ushered the children from my room to Mrs. Tifton, a downstairs neighbor, who was waiting in the hallway.

"Caleb." I reached out to my foster-brother. His eyes were wide with terror.

"You'll see them soon, sweetie," the police woman assured. "I just need to ask you a few questions." She took me to my room.

Consumed with concern for the children I regarded as under my charge, I relayed the day's events on auto-pilot. The only thing I remember saying was, "Can I see them yet?"

Eyes red and glistening, the angelic officer replied, "Yes, Sophia. You've told us everything we need to know."

The officer's emotional response puzzled me. Surely she had seen similar scenes in her line of work. I hoped this was not like my other space-out episodes, where I'd absently rattle off wild stories about munchkins who made me tiny clothes and tucked me in at night.

Nah, that can't be. Those weird incidents only happened because I got little sleep which made me dreamy, and I watched too much Wizard of Oz as a kid.

The apartment was no longer a dank, base-pounding party house. It was somber, with murmurs of police questioning idiot drunks.

Ignoring them, I raced out the door and down the apartment's steps.

Stopping at the top of the second set of stairs, I saw a social worker guide Caleb toward the main doors.

"Where are you taking him?" I questioned.

Caleb turned back with a bewildered expression. The woman hurried him outdoors before he could speak.

Enraged by her dismissal, I flew down the steps after them.

Tossing open the doors, I shouted, "Hey!"

After tucking my foster-brother in the backseat of her sedan, the mousy woman mustered some nerve to face me. "I suggest you calm yourself, young lady."

Her statement seemed ludicrous.

Calm myself? I was just attacked by some sicko and the only person I've ever loved was being taken away from me.

All I meant to do was blast her verbally, but a male officer standing near-by must have thought something different. Maybe the way I collided into his arms after he seized me proved he was right.

"No." I thrashed in his hold. "You morons can't protect him. None of you can."

The woman bumped into her car as she backed up. Startled by impediment, she slid along the side and scurried to the driver's side.

The woman cop who questioned me came to my side. I could tell she was trying to comfort me, but her words never absorbed.

Caleb's tear-soaked face met mine, and they drove away.

Cops arrested my foster parents, and that vile gutter-slug, Max. Red and blue lights flashed from parked police cars and acted like a beacon to draw out every curious neighbor on the street. A cold and queasy feeling enveloped me as realization came. I was trapped in this hellish world, and too young to do anything about it.

Is this my life? I know I'm not worth much to anyone, but do I deserve this? Oh God, couldn't you have warned me that this was going to happen? I could have done something . . . I don't know what . . . but there must have been something. This must be my fault.

CHAPTER 2

Shivering in the late night chill, I could not help thinking about my life.

What did I do that was so wrong?

This morning began like every other day. "Why do I put up with you, woman?" Keith yelled like clockwork at seven-fifteen, awakening the entire house before slamming the door behind him as he left for work.

He neglected to broadcast his grievance, so I am not sure what made him so mad this morning. Normally though, it was because, while either in a drunken or hung over state, Carol forgot to make his lunch.

Occasionally, he got clever or downright ridiculous, depending on how you looked at it, and came up with something new. Yesterday, he bellowed, "There's a sticky mess in the pocket of my workpants, and you wasted another perfectly good pack of gum." One time when Carol was not able to wash away the cigarette burn in his jacket, I thought he might implode.

Keith had his own drywall company, and Carol stayed at home and did some sort of telemarketing. In addition to their own twin, ten-year-old girls, Cara and Jackie, the Larooses fostered two other children. The unwanted yet financially needed fosters were a ten-year-old boy named Caleb, and a twelve-year-old me.

Skin was often stone cold in the morning due to the twins taking my blankets during the night. I could not blame them, though. We were all cold. Gas to heat the home was considered a "want," while cigarettes and beer were revered as "needs."

Breakfast and lunch were luxuries that Caleb and I normally had to forgo. There never seemed to be enough. Fortunately, Mrs. Tifton, a neighbor in the downstairs duplex, took pity on us. She must have waited at her window each morning for us to leave for school.

"Children!" she would call from her red door, hair in curlers and still in her pink bathrobe. Rushing down the cement steps, she met us on the sidewalk. "Wish I had more for you," she would say as she slipped an apple or a homemade muffin into our coat pockets. We would thank her, and she patted us on the shoulder saying, "Off you go to school now." As we continued down the street, we could hear her grumbling under her breath about those drunken so-called caregivers.

After dropping Caleb off at his elementary doors, I would head to my entrance at the opposite side of the school. Crossing the basketball courts prompted me to pray that I would not run into Nicki and her evil minions. But, like Mrs. Tifton, I think they waited for me. Only they did not wish to give me baked goods.

Nicki and her cronies lived to torture me. I was an easy target. Not particularly smart or pretty, no family or skills to speak of. I was simply white trash that nobody really loved.

When Nicki followed behind me, calling me names like "flat chest" or "greasy-haired beanpole," I quickened my pace, hoping they would not notice my eyes welling up.

I hid in the back of each of my classes until lunchtime. When the heavenly noon-bell rang, I would take off across the street to find Caleb waiting for me in the city park. We were not supposed to leave the grounds until after school, but we knew we were practically invisible here anyway. A winged statue in the adjacent park was the only witness to our act of rebellion.

On one particular average, insignificant day, I placed my science textbook on the base of the statue and hopped up to join Caleb who was waiting for me.

"How was your morning?" I asked Caleb as I pulled out Mrs. Tifton's pumpkin-cranberry muffin from my coat pocket.

"It blows goats," Caleb replied, taking out his muffin and carefully peeling away the paper wrap. He had a funny habit of waiting until I took my first bite before he would take his. "How was yours?"

"Let's see." I dramatically flipped my sight to the sky and tapped my lip in mock contemplation. "Nicki and company decorated the front of my locker with condoms this morning, and in social, they tied tampons to the back of my chair. That was especially fun."

Most kids Caleb's age would not know what a tampon or condoms were, but there was a certain enlightenment that came with being a foster. We were exposed to a plethora of age inappropriate sights, sounds, and living conditions. It's funny. If it were not for TV sit-coms, we might think everyone lived the same way we did. Maybe it would have been preferable not to know.

Lowering his muffin, he looked up at me with sad brown eyes. "That sucks. Sorry Phia."

Chilly breath of an October wind scattered fallen leaves and sent them skidding along the paved path. A red leaf flipped up and caught on the hood of Caleb's grey, hooded sweatshirt. Reaching around him, I brushed it off and knocked him with my shoulder.

"So, how did you do in language arts today?" I did not want to spend too much time on the cruel pranks subject. It hurt Caleb terribly when people picked on me.

"Okay, I guess." The boy shrugged. "The teacher asked us what we wanted to be when we grow up."

"And, you want to be a rock star?" I joked.

"Yeah." He took a bite of his muffin. "But, then I thought being a fireman would be great. Do you think I could be a fireman, Phia?"

"Of course you can, silly. You can do anything you want. Why do you want to be a fireman?"

"I want to be a hero." Caleb broadened his shoulders momentarily before slumping back down as if someone had let the air out of his body. "Only, I'm kinda small. Keith says I'm so weak that Mrs. Tifton's terrier could take me down."

"You're ten. You're supposed to be small, and Keith is a bully. Don't worry, you'll grow. One day, you'll be as big and strong as this gargoyle."

I looked up at the statue towering over us. I had seen it many times before, and had grown to think of it as a strong, silent uncle of sorts. Arms crossed over a chiseled stone chest, he stood tall, as if vigilantly waiting to do his duty. Perhaps it reminded me of a cartoon I used to watch.

Caleb followed my gaze to the stone man we rested beneath. A faint smile appeared on his face. "You think so?"

"Of course." I popped the last bite of muffin in my mouth before digging hands deep into my pockets, and feeling a rip as fingers caught on a tear in the bottom.

That's what happens when your clothes come from the thrift store, I thought.

He grinned. "What do you want to be when you grow up, Phia?"

"I don't know, maybe a cop or a vet. I like animals."

"That sounds cool. You could definitely do that." Caleb nodded and shifted down into his all-too-common, sympathetic, serious face. "Did you have that dream again last night? I could hear you crying."

Shuddering, I shook my head. "Yeah. It always starts out so beautiful, and I keep praying this time it will end differently, but it never does." I tucked a messy tuff of blonde hair behind my ear. "Hope I didn't wake you."

"Nah, I was already awake. What do you dream about that makes you cry?" He asked with more distress than any ten-year-old should have to know.

"I dream of a beautiful, golden-haired woman with shimmering wings. She has soft skin and bright green eyes. She seems to love me. When she kisses me on the forehead, her teardrops fall onto my cheeks, and it makes them all warm and tingly." I touched a hand to my face as if I could still feel traces of her emotions. "A wind blows up, but it's actually warm, and the air smells like . . ." Eyes closed, I took a breath, trying to remember the scent. "I don't know . . . chewing gum and perfume.

"Then, the golden-haired lady turns into a wrinkled old woman and looks so sad. I cry and reach out to touch her face, but she disintegrates into a pile of sparkling ash. The wind stirs up her ashes, and blow back into my face."

Covering my mouth, I coughed. My chest tightened, like in the dream, when the ashes drift through my nostrils and coat my lungs.

Poor Caleb jumped with a start and began patting my back in an attempt to sooth my spontaneous coughing fit. "Are you alright, Phia?"

Taking a deep breath, I remind myself, *It's just a dream. Ashes didn't really fly into my face.* But, it felt so real.

"I'm good." I paused and cleared my throat before turning to Caleb. "And, then I wake up."

"That's a creepy dream, Phia." Caleb's teasing woke me from my somewhat altered state.

I jumped down. "We better get back to school."

Averting his eyes, he slid down the statue.

"I was just kidding, Phia."

Obviously, he thought he had hurt my feelings. Half laughing, I pulled the brim of his hat over his eyes.

"I know. Don't worry about it. You're just a kid."

"Sophia," a deep voice rumbled from behind me. "You forgot your book."

"Right. Thanks for the reminder." I retrieved my text from the foot of the statue, then returned to Caleb.

Wait a second. Where did that voice come from?

"Who are you talking to?" Caleb asked.

Flipping back to the statue and seeing no one else around, I stammered.

Caleb waited for my response.

I scrutinized the stationary stone body and then its head.

Get a grip Sophia, I told myself. *You're too old for imaginary friends anymore.*

Eyes shifted on the stone face. It was only a tiny movement, like he was checking out my expression, but I saw it.

As our gaze locked, his rock jaw lowed. He looked petrified. But why? I was the one who was supposed to move. It was my right to be scared.

The school book slipped from my hands. It m[ade a] crack-and split-open sound when it crashed on th[e ...]

"Did you see that?" I gasped.

"See what?" Caleb looked up to where I was [... Of] course, it had returned to its previous state.

"Oh no." My text book distracted me. I bent to pick up. "The seam's busted. The school's going to make me pay for this. What am I going to do?"

A piercing voice shrieked from a few yards away. "Miss Templar and Mr. Winters."

It was Ms. Viden, the assistant principal. She had just rounded a thick assembly of trees, and was charging in our direction. At any moment, her accusing boney finger would be flicking out like a talon.

"Quick, hide it in my pack before she sees it." Caleb thumbed toward his backpack.

After slipping the busted book in his bag, I fumbled to zip it back up. Straightening, I held my breath and answered, "Yes, ma'am?"

I do not know why the woman scared me so much. It is not like she could actually cause me physical harm. No adult could hurt you . . . at school, at least.

"You are both off school grounds." Ms. Viden scowled while wagging a finger at us. "Do you think the rules don't apply to you?"

"No, Ma'am." I positioned myself ahead of Caleb, and clutched his tiny hand behind my back. "We'll get back right away."

I attempted to walk us past Ms. Viden.

"Not so fast!" She grabbed Caleb's shoulder.

I felt him cringe as he lowered his arm to unhook himself from her clawed grip.

"What were you in such a hurry to hide?"

She was so close, the smell of coffee and antiseptic mouthwash on her breath blew in my face.

"Nothing, Ms. Viden," Caleb lied.

The Vice Principal did not look convinced. She roughly unzipped Caleb's backpack while I anxiously rolled my eyes at him. I did not want to watch.

My foster brother wrinkled his face.

With a disappointed purse, Ms. Viden demanded, "Is there a reason you need a child in grade four to carry your books, Miss Templar?"

I looked at the science book. It was perfect, no broken seam, not damaged in the slightest. I was speechless.

"I offered to carry it, Mrs. Viden," Caleb answered while hiding his confusion.

"That's Mizz, not Misses, Caleb! And, I'll thank you not to--"

Her speech was interrupted by the ba-lang, ba-lang sound of the school fire alarm. It was probably another drill.

"Quickly, go line up in the court with your classes." She sent us away. Relieved and perplexed, we raced out of the park and back into the schoolyard. Once at the basketball courts, Caleb and I separated and took a place in our respective class line-ups. The broken book and stone man scenario raced in my head.

What happened? I wondered.

CHAPTER 3

"It was broken wasn't it?" I questioned Caleb as we walked home.

We traveled through an old area of Gettysburg, known as The Pond. More specifically, we were walking down Swan Street. It was once a vibrant entertainment hub, but you would not know it today with the cracked sidewalks and graffiti. There were a few boarded up buildings mixed in with a vacuum repair shop, tattoo parlor, bar, and a lone burger joint.

The old movie theater became a textile factory. Remnants of the red paint somehow felt grey and dingy.

Sometimes, I observed young Asian girls being guided into the factory from a blue van that sat out front. A girl, about my age, caught my attention once. She looked as if she wanted to run. As our eyes met, I had a bizarre sense she was declaring defeat. It was also mixed with a warning to stay away from this area. Even though, I wondered why she would choose to work at a place that treated her so poorly, I heeded her warning, and made sure to walk on the opposite side of the street.

"It looked broken to me." Caleb adjusted his wire-rim glasses, as he sidestepped a mess of broken glass on the sidewalk. "Maybe aliens came down, stopped time, and fixed it for you."

"Yeah, that's probably what happened," I joked uneasily.

Or maybe the rock statue was really an enchanted creature with superpowers, and he fixed it. That's about as likely.

I chuckled to myself. Sometimes my imagination was the only thing that kept me going.

I'm probably dehydrated.

I heard in health class that not drinking enough water could cause hallucinations. Of course, I always drank a lot of water. It helped temporarily with the constant hunger ache in my stomach.

"Hey, Sophia," Cara, one of the twins, called from in front of us. "Mom said you're supposed to wash the dishes and clean the bathroom before you get to work on your homework."

The girl's mother, Carol, told them to stay close to me, and I was to look out for them. Cara and Jackie considered themselves far too good to be seen with the likes of a government throw away, so they remained a safe distance ahead of us.

"Right. I know," I answered dryly, while doing a mental eye roll.

Those ungrateful brats should consider their butts lucky they had parents, and never had to live in an orphanage. They would not last a day with their superior attitude. You had to either show no fear, or keep off everyone else's radar.

Sophia-style was a bit of both, mingled with a hint of humor to get me out of sticky situations. For the most part, it was a winning strategy, when dealing with kids anyways. Adults followed a different set of rules. I often found them more irrational. I offered my point of view to Mrs. Tifton one time. She advised me that I was hanging around the wrong kinds of adults.

Jackie lifted from the teen magazine she was reading only long enough to say, "And, she wants you to clean out the fridge too. It's grocery day."

"Okay," I breathed. Carol believed it was terribly important to have a nice clean fridge to store their beer in on grocery day

Mrs. Tifton waved through her front window as we approached the steps of the duplex. I waved back.

She must have been a pretty lady in her day, I thought, holding the door open for the kids.

CHAPTER 4

A familiar blue haze of cigarette and pot smoke welcomed us as we entered the front door to the kitchen. The party must have started earlier than usual this Friday afternoon.

Jackie poked her head around to the living room to see who was with her mother. Stepping back, she gasped and came up behind me as I headed to the sink to start dishes.

"What is it Jackie?" I put the stopper in the sink and flipped up the handle to run water.

"Nothing. I just wanted to help you," she answered in a whisper while she added a bit of dish soap to the running water.

That's odd, I thought. *Jackie and Cara never lifted a finger to help me with anything.*

"Jackie, Cara, look who's here for a visit," Carol's drunken voice screeched as she traipsed into the kitchen wearing a shabby jean skirt and tank top. The strap of her bra had slipped down over her arm but she made no attempt to correct it. "It's Uncle Max."

In dirty jeans and a red plaid shirt, a slight man rounded the corner after Carol. His greasy, slicked-back hair matched his dark sunken eyes and generally unkempt appearance.

Cara and Caleb were digging through the fridge looking for something to drink. They swiftly closed the door and took a step backward. Jackie quivered as she pressed against me.

"Aren't you guys going to give Uncle Max a hug?" Carol almost demanded after a short silence.

Jackie looked at me as though pleading. I did not know what to do. Reluctantly, she went to the unfavorable man and hugged him around the waist.

Smoothing his hands along Jackie's back, he pressed her against his mid-section. From where I stood, I could feel a low groan that emitted from the back of his throat. He then set his sight on me and released Jackie. She promptly stepped back against Caleb and her sister.

"And who do you have here, Carol? I've never met this young lady." His eyes bore into me.

"That's Sophia." Carol sent a dismissive wave, before taking a drag from the stub of a cigarette, which was close to burning her fingers. A painful pleasure swept her face as she inhaled the poison, as if it was her last breath of air. "She's one of our foster kids."

"It's nice to meet you, Miss Sophia. Aren't you a pretty little girl?"

Taking my hand, he pressed it to his lips. I could smell the stink of beer and smoke on his breath as he raised his head to examine me.

"You can call me Uncle Max."

"Nice to meet you, Uncle Max," I managed to get out without vomiting.

I had heard in school that you should be cautious of strangers. Even somebody who seemed nice and trustworthy could have plans to harm you. That was not the case with this guy. He did not seem even a little trustworthy. Every muscle in my body wanted to run as far away as possible. If crawling out of my skin to get away was an option, I would have.

Inching closer to the sink, I turned to Jackie and instructed her, with an intense glare, to take the kids to my room. She understood and went immediately.

A knock sounded at the kitchen door, and then it opened.

"Hi guys," Carol called out, and tossed her cigarette butt in the dishwater before stumbling towards the door to greet her new guests.

One of the men from the group bellowed a vulgar greeting, and they all laughed. Max asked the man for a smoke. I took the distraction as my cue to head the other way to check on the children.

I opened the door to my bedroom and the kids jumped with a start. They relaxed when they saw it was only me. Diving into the room, I pressed the door closed.

Jackie sat at the edge of the bed clutching a pillow to her stomach. Her reddened eyes looked up at me. The tears she meant to withhold suddenly exploded.

Rushing to her side, I cradled her in my arms as though she was a little doll. She shook physically and could not bring herself to return my embrace, but I knew she did not want me to let her go.

Cara and Caleb did not say a word as they crouched on the floor against the wall. I suppose there was no need to say anything. The revolting situation was obvious to anyone that was not a slobbering drunk like Carol, although, it was hard to believe, that even in her state, the signs would not be clear.

What the hell is Carol thinking? My anger grew. *How can she bring that vile human into the house with her children?*

CHAPTER 5

As afternoon rolled into evening, the sound level outside the safety of my tiny bedroom got louder and wilder. Knock after knock at the living room door brought another group of half-cut undesirables, followed by a measurable increase in drunken babbling.

Smoke stench, thick and stinging to the eyes, crept in through the cracks around my door. Caleb yanked on the small window beside the head of my bed. It had been painted shut but Caleb was not giving up. He managed to raise it an inch. The fresh air that rolled in provided a welcome relief.

Stealth-like, I snuck out to forage for food for the four of us. An opened pizza box sat on the kitchen table, and I was able to snatch it up before a longhaired man boosted the girl he was making out with onto the table. Empty beer bottles that had once been on the table shattered on the floor as the couple wildly thrashed over each other. The pair hooted at the momentary distraction before getting back to their business of groping and slurping.

Later that evening, we were all able to creep out to the bathroom to brush our teeth before bed. The party was still in full swing. I did not dare let either of the twins or Caleb out of my sight.

Caleb turned his back while we all used the toilet. In any other circumstance, it might have been uncomfortable to pee in the presence of a boy, but we were in survival mode and in no position to be picky.

Slipping back into my room, I locked the door behind us. "Let's try to get some sleep guys," I said to them.

Together as if oysters in a can, we crammed into my twin bed. Noise from the party became a drone that we were able to tune out. We had lots of practice. Eventually the kids fell asleep, and my eyes closed shortly after.

Persistent rattling came from the knob of my bedroom door. I shot up, not knowing what time it was, or how long we had been sleeping. Noise from the living room, however, told me the party was still going strong.

The children lay peacefully in my bed as the door continued to rattle. I did not want the sound to wake them. They had been so on edge all evening. It was probably a sex-crazed couple looking for a place to fool around. I went to the door, ready to tell whoever stood on the other side that they should have a little class and travel onward. There were children sleeping, for heaven's sake.

In a stupor of exhaustion and rage, I whipped the door open to blast whoever was rattling the handle. The sick look of craving on Max's face froze me. That was when he grabbed me.

~

While standing in the cold and watching the police sort out the party drunks, I thought, *nope, even I can't find a way to blame this one on me.*

A form of sadness washed over me. I looked up and saw Mrs. Tifton standing in her front window, with a pity-filled expression. She nodded and waved goodbye. I waved back, knowing that it was she, who called the cops.

Does she know she saved my innocence?

Perhaps there were angels living among demons after all.

CHAPTER 6

On my thirteenth birthday, I got placed with Elka and Edwin Gordon. I had no idea when the social worker dropped a worthless young me off at the screen door, of their yellow ranch house, that home had finally arrived.

"Time to wake up, dear," a sweet, elderly voice whispered from across the room. "Good gracious, Sophia, your ivy is attacking me again."

Sitting upright in my bed, I saw Elka, my foster mother, brushing a fallen ivy vine away from her face. Giggling, I hopped to the floor.

"Sorry, Mrs. G. I thought it would be pretty to let the ivy grow around the door. She seems to have a mind of her own though."

Scooting my vanity chair over to the loose vine, I re-hooked it to its proper place above the frame.

With her hands on her hips, Elka watched me and said, "It must be my imagination, but that ivy looks as if it's grown a foot overnight. Did it?"

"I've been busy." I shrugged. "Haven't paid much attention. Ivy's are supposed to grow fast, aren't they?"

"Not for me, apparently."

She scanned the rest of the room. Two mint-green ferns hung on either side of the vanity, and a family of bamboo plants sat in the corner.

An old-fashioned desk rested in front of a window in the middle of the next wall. The window on the side of the house gave a full view of the barn. Sometimes, I allowed myself to get distracted from homework by Kris, the hotty, part-time farmhand. Cowboys did not necessarily draw me, but he sure could wear a pair of Wranglers.

Lofty windows framed either side of the headboard of my queen-sized bed. I had never had a bed so large before, and perhaps, if the space had not been a guestroom before my arrival, I would not have been so fortunate.

A small, glass lamp with jeweled tassels sat on a bedside table. Besides that, I had another row of plants, and a nine-drawer dresser with an attached mirror. The new guitar I got for Christmas a week before sat in its black case next to my bed.

Elka's eyes rested on the bedside table, and she squealed with delight, "You brought my African violet back to life!"

"You can take her back now, but Miss Mauve does not wish to return to the kitchen window." Leaping to the table, I picked up the plant and handed it to her.

"Oh?" Elka grinned and waited for my response.

"She would prefer to be in the living room window behind the sheer curtain."

"That is good to know." Elka turned her attention to the plant. "Have I been mistreating you, Miss Mauve? Now that your wishes are known, I will certainly oblige. Breakfast is almost ready," she called back as she was leaving, but did not wait for a response.

Taking a seat at the dressing table, I roughly braided my long blonde hair. Mrs. Gordon made a point of having Mr. Gordon bring the dressing table out of the attic four years ago when I came to live with them. She said, every lady needs a place to tend to her beauty needs. They had plans of sanding and re-painting the vanity, but to date, it had not been done. I did not mind either. The handsome frame and ornate carved features were that much more beautiful with all of the wear from time.

Elka told me her father built the vanity set for her mother on one of their anniversaries. Her mother loved it dearly. She loved it, not only because her husband made it for her, but because she said it made her feel like a queen when she sat down. There was no time in my life, when I ever felt like a queen, but I was incredibly blessed.

Reflected in the mirror, a scar on my right shoulder caught my eye. It did not look raised or ugly the way some scars could appear. It was more of a silvery-white imprint in the flesh. There was a definite design in the mind of whoever branded me. It was a triangle with kind of an X in the middle, which was encircled by a ring.

When I was seven, I overheard Beth, one of my social workers, talking to the secretary at Twin Oaks orphanage. Beth said anger could be an issue with me, because one of my previous abhorrent foster families let their sociopathic son abuse me. She said, when the government finally removed me from that home, my skin was covered in burns and welts where he had tortured me with cigarettes and other white-hot instruments.

All the other burns, along with memories of that event, long since healed and faded away. And to my knowledge, I have never had any anger issues, relatively speaking.

The mark is actually quite pretty.

I shook my head at myself every time inner approval voiced itself. It seemed sadistic to admire a wound that someone had inflicted on me, because they were evil, or whatever.

When I first arrived with the Gordon's, I was scared to let them love me, and fought them at every turn. Not the actual rude kind of fight, rather, I just found it hard to return their affection. They were so patient with me. My brain found this suspect. It made me want to run even more.

One day, after I had been with them for about a month, Elka came to me. She told me she understood my hesitance to get comfortable with them.

She said, "Sophia, darling, the walls you put up can shield you from some pain, but they also prevent you from feeling joy. I would sooner feel a day's worth of love, to a lifetime of loneliness."

That made sense to me, and perhaps I was looking for a reason to let them in anyway.

After pulling on a pair of jeans and a simple, yet feminine, blue knit sweater, I cleaned up in the bathroom and went downstairs. Edwin was seated at the kitchen table reading yesterday's newspaper and sipping coffee. Elka stood at the stove making sausage and eggs. The savory scent filled my nose, and my mouth began to water.

"Isn't it an oatmeal day today?" I joked to Elka, taking a seat next to Mr. Gordon at the table.

"You know, it is dear, but when waking this morning, I thought to myself, 'eggs would really be great.' And, why should modest pleasures be denied, simply because it's the wrong day?"

Elka crossed the kitchen and put a tender hand on my shoulder.

"I hear ya, Mrs. G." I patted her hand.

"Did you get that book report finished last night?" Elka asked.

As she returned to the stove, she nodded toward the toaster. It was a silent request, asking if I wanted any. I shook my head, while taking a sip of juice, then tilted to the pitcher that sat in front of me. She lifted her coffee cup outward before taking a long enjoyable sip. Smiling, I set my drink down.

"I did finish the report, and it's definitely an A plus paper."

"I don't doubt it," Mr. Gordon spoke from behind his paper. "You take after me in that regard."

"Edwin." Elka laughed and swatted him, before placing a plate full of food in front of me.

I made a conscious effort not to ravage my food like a starving animal, but my plate always seemed to be cleared before everyone else's. Even after the long stint of abundance, I still feared that if I did not eat immediately, someone would take my food away.

"You look tired, Mr. G," I commented while cutting a piece of sausage with the side of my fork. Edwin had lovely, sun-bronzed skin that often hid dark circles under his eyes. Today, they were noticeable.

Edwin opened his mouth to speak, but Elka took over. "That's because he was up all night watching Star Wars."

Her growl was mixed with amusement.

Edwin looked up at her with apologetic eyes, but it was not needed. Elka was not really mad. Edwin often had trouble sleeping and his wife understood. That did not stop her from teasing him, though.

If only I could have been born to them, I thought. *If only my whole life was spent living with them, and not the six other so-called foster families, one home, being worse than the next. No*, I quickly told myself. *I will not waste time wishing to change history. We are together now. The horrors of the past are a distant memory, while the glory of the future is waiting.*

That is what Edwin always said.

Edwin and Elka married at twenty-five and never had children of their own, which was really too bad, because they were the most fabulous people. Edwin was a farmer turned lawyer, who turned rancher after retirement. He was an excellent speaker and negotiator, not that I would have known unless I had been told. Mr. Gordon did not talk that much. He was not a wallflower by any stretch, but his tendency was to sit back and ponder a situation. Analyze things from every angle before expressing a definitive opinion on anything.

Edwin's wife, on the other hand, was very much the center of attention at any social gathering. She never demanded the spotlight, perhaps not even wanting it. People just wanted to be near her. They felt good merely standing in her presence.

Elka told me they tried to keep themselves busy after retirement. They bought a couple horses and trained them. Edwin joined a lawn bowling club and took up fencing. Elka had to begin creating jobs for her husband to keep him busy.

One day, Elka decided she needed to have fresh organic chicken eggs, instead of the nasty store-bought kind packed in Styrofoam. It took no time at all to convince Edwin that he needed to build her a chicken coop. Her plan worked splendidly. After a week and a half, she discovered a brand new chicken hotel next to the horse barn. He even painted it in her favorite color of teal.

I came to them a few months later.

"Sophia, we have a little bit of an early birthday gift for you," Elka said across the table. "It's in the barn. Do you want to see it now or wait until later?"

"It's in the barn? That sounds scary." I laughed. "But, I'll chance it. Can I see it now?"

"Why don't you go take a look? We'll be right behind you," Edwin said with a grin.

After bolting from my chair, stopping only to pull on boots, I raced to the big, red barn door. It took a great deal of effort to heave it open, due to heavy snowfall that accumulated over night. Darting inside, I expected to see a horse or a puppy, but nothing was visible with the brand new silver Acura in the way.

"Oh! My! Gosh!" I backed away and dashed out to the yard almost running into Elka and Edwin. "You're not telling me the car is my present, are you? I'm sure it's not, but it's in the way." I rambled, clearly unable to stand still in one place.

They laughed.

"Well, you passed your driver's training test," Edwin said, "and your mechanics course. You've kept your grades up in school, even with your part-time job at the animal shelter." He proudly listed my accomplishments on the fingers of his hand.

"The thing is, Sophia," Elka interrupted. "I've joined a new pottery club, and we meet early in the morning. I honestly won't have time to drive you to school anymore." Elka lied beautifully and held her hands open, as if the gesture would validate her claim.

"It's unbelievable! Thank you, thank you!"

I danced about and then threw my arms around them both. "I think my knees are going to give out."

I giggled breathlessly then folded over to catch a breath of air.

Edwin tried to contain his excitement, but little bits of delight curled around his eyes and lips.

"Want to take it to school?" he asked.

"Take it . . . today?" I replied excitedly.

"It's yours," Elka said.

Edwin dangled the keys in front of me. After accepting them merrily, Elka handed me my coat and backpack.

"See you this evening Sophia!"

They waved good-bye.

"See-you!" I hugged them again, waved back and darted into the barn to get acquainted with my new baby.

Turned the key in the ignition and tires quickly splashed through driveway slush on the way to the main road. I could barely maintain decorum. A not-so-light touch on the accelerator, once out of earshot of home, shot me into my future.

Switching on the radio, one of my favorite songs sang back to me. Feet and legs reacted to the music as I danced my way to school.

"See you later, baby." I kissed my hand and set it lovingly on the door.

Breezing through the parking, I headed into school. I might as well have been walking on air, that is, until tripping on a crushed, disposable coffee cup, lying haphazardly three paces from the garbage can.

That's a whole new level of lazy, were my thoughts while tossing the litter into the garbage can.

Floating to the center of the classroom, I took a seat next to my friend, Cindy Smith. English Lit was the only class we were able to get together. It would have scared the old Sophia terribly to be without the protection of a best friend in each class. This new Sophia, however, was okay with it. I found many friends to spend time with, and often longed for the solace of my own company.

Schoolwork became much easier now that I slept more than five hours a night and had food to eat each day. Then again, maybe it became easier because of the people rooting for me. The Gordons never put any pressure on me to excel. They merely refused to let me believe that the infinite was not entirely possible.

Mr. Manu began our class reading a poem about a woman who walked a path that was smooth and then it turned to thorns. I had zoned out when Cindy handed me a note. It read, "Logan Donavan wants to ask you out, but he's scared you'll say no. He asked me to find out what you think of him, but I'm not supposed to tell you he likes you. So, what do you think?"

Chuckling inside, I tried not to show too much emotion. I had a crush on Logan for weeks, and he happened to sit two rows behind me. He was sure to know that the note Cindy handed me was about him. I was about to write my response when Miss Merriday, the school guidance counselor, came to the door. She appeared flustered when she whispered to Mr. Manu. They both looked at me.

"Sophia, could you come with me," Miss Merriday asked with a gentle urgency.

Gathering my book and bag, I followed her out into the hallway.

"What is it?" I asked.

"It's the Gordons. There's been an accident." This was all she could get out before she burst into tears.

"What kind of accident?" The walls were closing in on me.

She shook her head. "A car accident. They're gone, Sophia."

CHAPTER 7

Lying on my bed back at Twin Oaks orphanage, I replayed those three words over and over in my mind.

They're gone, Sophia.

The Gordons had been on their way to the courthouse to finalize my adoption. It seemed a little unnecessary to have them adopt me one year away from my eighteenth birthday. They wanted to do it years earlier, but were waiting on me to be okay with it.

Elka planned a special surprise dinner, and had invited a few neighbors to be part of the celebration. Slushy gravel roads and a drunk driver running a stop sign brought about a permanent change of plans.

I had almost forgotten how much I hated Twin Oaks. The dormitory had not changed much in the last few years, yet it seemed much worse than remembered. Blankets were still scratchy, and walls remained a depressing, pale green. I covered my head with a pillow to mask the scent of must and Pine-Sol. I pleaded, to anyone who could hear, for sleep.

Grant me a few moments of peace from this nightmare.

Focus kept shifting to the door. Vera was on my mind. She was an old friend who always seemed to be on the same "between foster homes" schedule as me. Vera's presence brought me great comfort. I tried to stop myself from questioning why she was always here when I was. It was awful to think it could be because she was never placed anywhere. On second thought, depending on where you were located, the orphanage was the lesser of plights.

Vera was so different from other girls in the system. She had an undeniable authority about her that resided below her effervescent personality. We spent most of our time together meditating, and she taught me how to protect myself against tormentors.

Her training techniques were strange. She told me to use the meditation to connect with forces and elements around me, and become the water, or become the lion in the jungle. Most of the time, I stared at her with my mouth open. She would laugh and say, "It'll come to you when you need it."

Vera ended up saving my butt on several occasions. One was a vicious fight in the dormitory involving a switchblade that one of the other girls had stolen. The disturbed girl went to slash, and Vera knocked me out of the way, getting her arm cut in the process.

Come to think of it, that was the last time we saw each other. While she was taken to get stiches, the social worker tucked me under her arm, and off we went to the Gordons.

Vera's movements were precise and forceful, especially for her age. Although she was not much older than me, I kept getting the feeling she was actually restraining herself. One time, I asked her where she learned to fight that way. She told me her Grandma taught her. That is certainly a grandma one would not want to get on the bad side of.

Sometimes, I would watch her . . . she was so striking. Vera's curly black hair surrounded warm, ebony skin. Her delicately featured face and green eyes were as bright as her smile. In my head, I thought of her as my little African angel, even though she was taller than me.

She probably would not be here today. I prayed it was because a loving family, worthy of her spirit had adopted her.

~

The Gordon's funeral came four days after the accident. Mr. Harold, the new social worker assigned to my case, was kind enough to pick me up and take me to the service. We sat in the first row of the church with Elka's brother, Carl, and Edwin's Aunt Adana. The rest of the church was packed with friends and neighbors of the beloved couple.

It was so unsettling. I had known most parishioners as the daughter of Elka and Edwin Gordon, but now, I might as well have been a stranger. Everyone offered me their condolences, but it seemed more of a courtesy rather than genuine sympathy.

The Gordons never wanted their funeral to last longer than an ordinary church service. They hated the idea of people driving all the way to the cemetery to watch a body being lowered into the ground.

Elka once said, "It is simply pointless to have people freezing their tuchus off when they could be in a warm reception hall having a drink and toasting how wonderful I was." Elka surmised that most people died in winter.

After the service, everyone made their way to the fellowship hall located in the church basement. Feeling completely lost and overwhelmed, I went, instead, to the viewing room. I wanted to have one last good-bye before they took the bodies to the cemetery.

"Are they still here?" I asked a man standing in front of the door.

"They'll be taking them shortly. You can go in now," he answered gently and opened the door.

Two shiny black coffins stood on either side of the small, tastefully decorated room. I was taken aback by the sight of Mr. and Mrs. Gordon in their respective resting places. They were not frightening. It was just that seeing them in that state was so surreal. The bodies resembled my parents, but it was apparent they were no longer there.

Their faces looked terribly painted, although you could hardly blame the mortician. Make-up is only meant to be a temporary mask. You cannot hide death.

Elka's face was still. It reminded me of a long forgotten dream. I reached out to touch her cheek, but something stopped me. It was as if the body itself emanated cold. I pulled away. This was not Elka anymore. Softly, I closed the lid, then crossed to Edwin's casket and closed his.

Adagio Cantabile from Beethoven's Sonata 8 played in my head. It was Edwin's favorite song. Slowly, the melody that danced in my thoughts, filled the room. I could actually hear it.

Am I going crazy?

Before getting too distressed, wondering where the music had come from, I noticed a CD player under a small side table. It was not plugged into the wall.

Must have batteries in it. That's a nice touch. Those funeral directors thought of everything.

No longer able to look at the coffins, I set one hand on the doorknob and spoke as if they were actually behind me.

"Thank you for loving me. I am truly honored to have known you." Swallowing was hard. "I don't know what I did to deserve you, but with everything in me . . . I love you both. And I'm so sorry I could never bring myself to tell you. Please tell me you always knew."

Eyelids closed, releasing multiple drops that trickled down my face.

"Goodbye."

Warmth suddenly filled the room and embraced me. My heart raced.

Tiny flecks of sparkles fluttered overhead and onto my shoulders. I watched in awe. Grief had surely overtaken me, but I did not mind. The delusion was beautiful.

A voice inside me said, *pull yourself together, Sophia.* I might have even said it out loud.

As the song ended, the flecks disappeared.

Wiping my eyes, I shook off the hallucination and went outside.

Mr. Harold sat in the lobby, waiting, as I carefully closed the door behind me.

"Are you ready to go Sophia?" he asked.

"Yes, we can go," I said, looking out the window at the snowflakes that began to fall.

"Miss Templar, I was looking for you." Mr. Harold and I turned to the voice of a man coming towards us. The tall, sandy brown haired gentleman was dressed in a well-tailored black suit and he appeared to be in his late twenties. "I'm Terrance Grant, Edwin and Elka's attorney."

"Yes, I remember seeing you a few years ago at the Gordon's Christmas party."

I recalled he had enjoyed a few too many alcoholic beverages at that party, and accidently dropped a ring inside Elka's famous cranberry-boomerang punch. I was the only one around when he stumbled back and fell onto one of the dining room chairs. The distraught look that stretched across his face was heart wrenching.

If he were not drunk, he would have easily used the ladle to scoop out the ring. In this scenario, however, he was completely unable to fathom a solution. I fished it out for him and asked why he would wear a ring that was too big for his finger. He told me it was his brother's ring, and it was on a chain in his pocket. The chain must have caught on his pen when he was reaching for it, and it slipped out.

Embarrassment, ever so slight, crossed Mr. Grant's face.

"That's right," he said. "I wasn't sure if you would remember. You sure have changed in the last few years."

He shook my hand and smiled genuinely. "Anyway, there will be a reading of the will next Friday, at one, at my office. Someone from the firm can pick you up, if you need."

Tugging at my skirt, I struggled to compose myself. "I'm sure I can find a ride."

"Okay, if you're sure." Terrance reached into his briefcase and pulled out a card. "Here's my business card in case you have any questions."

"Thank you, Mr. Grant." I slipped the card into my purse.

"Sophia, I'm sorry but we have to get back," Mr. Harold said, standing by the door and clasping his watch. He was trying to be understanding, but I'm sure had many other appointments to get to.

"Of course," I replied. "It was nice seeing you again, Mr. Grant." I shook the attorney's hand and left with Mr. Harold.

On the car ride back to Twin Oaks, I mentally mapped out my imminent future. No foster parent would be willing to take a near adult into their care, so the next year would be spent at Twin Oaks. I would dorm with nine other girls, and be awakened several times a night by the pangs and screams of the distraught.

My belongings? I might as well them give away, since they will be stolen anyway.

Brawls would be daily, if not weekly. Girls were particularly territorial in asylums. This was probably because boundries of an unseen turf were the only things the forsaken could hold on to.

On my eighteenth birthday, I would be cast out to fend for myself. Maybe I could acquire a job at a fast-food establishment, and get a small apartment with a few people.

Roomates would probably be young-- my age, or a bit older. Their friends would constantley be over, smoking pot and doing who knows what else. There would be parties with stumbling drunks traipsing around, touching my stuff. It would be the same as living with the Larooses. My muscles tightened.

I can't go through that again!

Maybe I could run away. Twin Oaks was terribly overburdened. They would not even notice me gone. Sure, they would send someone to look for me, but they would give up after they put in the required minimum amount of effort.

Where will I go? Maybe I can hitchhike to California where it's warm all the time. Maybe a few odd jobs could buy me a tent, and I could camp out in the woods. It will be like that book Mrs. Tifton read me when I was a kid–The Box Car Children. What if I run into muggers? Or killers . . . or pimps . . . or gangs! Nah, the chances of that are slim. Right now, I would sooner take my chances with the unknown, rather than the absolutes of life at the orphanage.

After pulling into a visitor stall in the parking lot at Twin Oaks, Mr. Harold shut the engine off.

"Thank you, again, for taking me to the funeral, Mr. Harold. It was good of you," I said while stepping out of the car.

Meeting me at the passenger side of the vehicle, he said, "Don't mention it, Sophia. I'm very sorry for your loss. I can't even imagine what you must be feeling right now."

The slender man looked upon me with pity and whispered under his breath, "You had everything."

CHAPTER 8

Books and magazines lined a shelf that overlooked the register at Red Henry's convenience store. Arriving early outside Terrance Grant's office, and seeing they were still closed for lunch, I had decided to bide time with some trashy gossip magazines.

I thought going to the reading of the will was the real waste of time, mind you. I do not know why they had to make such a formal production out of telling me that I was returning to my former post as ward of the state.

Did I really need to come down here for them to declare that all my so-called possessions, including my new car, belonged to the estate, and would be sold at auction? What a joke. Perhaps I should consider myself lucky that I got to miss out on school for the afternoon.

I was growing tired of people whispering in the halls, acting as if broken glass surrounded me.

Four kids—three boys and a girl—tore in through the front door of the convenience store. They roguishly shoved each other.

Howling pack of wild dogs, I thought.

It surprised me that Mr. Henry, the store owner, did not hear them carrying on. Normally he would have shuffled out with his cane, telling them to zip it. Course, he was hard of hearing and had slipped away to the back, probably to take a few puffs of his cigar.

Inside, I was shaking my head at them. Their behavior made me mad. At first, I figured it was because they were acting like a bunch of street punks, and then realization came. It was jealousy.

They appeared happy, if nothing else, and I missed that. The skin on my face felt heavy and worn. There did not seem enough water in the world to replenish the tears wept when no one was around.

I used to cry freely with Elka and Edwin, and was unashamed. But, safety no long belonged to me.

Oh God, forgive me for being selfish, but I miss that the most.

The boys disappeared into the potato chip isle, while the girl in ripped jeans and a fake leather jacket wandered around to my side of the rack. I could feel her looking at me as she pretended to search among the titles. I wondered what she wanted. She was starting to piss me off.

"Hey," she greeted with an I'm-a-mafia-chick vibe.

An answer might have been polite, but I was not in the mood. Instead, I grazed my eyes across her to let her know she was nothing, and returned to the story in the magazine about Leo and Kristen, the new power couple of Hollywood.

She took a pace towards me, running her hand along the shelf. Leaning into me, she got dangerously close to invading my personal space, and said, "You go to my school."

"What's your point?" I replied.

"I've seen you there. You kind of stand out," she continued.

Yeah right. I totally stand out. I've never been visible anywhere, except with the Gordons.

I felt a sting on the bridge of my nose as the thought of my parents came back. Quickly, I scolded myself.

That's enough Sophia. Stop being such a baby! It's not like you didn't know you would lose them in the end anyway.

"Fascinating," I said. "Why aren't you there, instead of here, harassing me?"

I flipped past several pages.

"I'm taking a mental health day. What about you, princess? Aren't you supposed to be in school?"

"I've been excused to meet with my parent's lawyer," I answered.

"Oh," her tone was scornful, "and since we share the same accommodation at the five star hotel de Twin Oaks, am I to assume that you're having parental issues? Perhaps daddy has some night blindness and mistook your bed for his own."

Wrathful thoughts did not even have time to formulate before my fist hit her face launching her backwards into a vertical stand of gift cards. Her buddies scampered out from the chip isle when they heard the clatter.

Instead of helping her off the ground they laughed. One of them said, "Whoa dude that sucks."

I think they were stoned.

Cupping her jaw, she snorted in more of an impressed, slow-moving fury. "You're tougher than you look, princess. I underestimated you."

Why the hell does she keep calling me that? I'm the government throw-away that nobody wants.

"Most people do," I replied.

Since situations such as these were once common, I knew she was going to lunge at me. Of course, it had been a while, so my accuracy was a little rusty. I assumed she was going to go for my center, but instead, cuffed me across the face. Metallic taste indicated the blow split my bottom lip.

Next thing I knew, we were in a full out brawl, only to be broken up by a cop who had stopped in to get a coffee before his shift started. The boy onlookers scattered at some point, but the ratty-haired girl and I got hauled off to the juvenile detention center.

Humming from a near dead overhead florescent light threatened to trap me in the dark with the balding cop who came in to hear my side of the incident. It was not the first time I had been in the sallow cave they called the interview room. It was, however, the first time it was largely my fault.

It was a good run.

After I wrote out my version, with as much detail as possible, Officer Chet escorted me to a holding room a few doors over.

"You'll have to wait here until your social worker comes to get you," he said before shutting the door.

Tacky orange benches and gray walls were the only characteristics that defined the modern day hovel. Leaning on her knee, the ratty-haired girl sat with her foot flat on the bench.

"Are you serious?" I groaned at her sight. "Why would they put us in the same room together?"

She laughed. It made me want to hit her again.

"I guess they figured we'd be on our best behaviour while surrounded by cops," she said.

"I've never been that smart," I replied taking a seat on a bench across from her.

On one hand, I felt awful for wanting to slap her around some more, but on the other, she deserved it. Why would she come at me that way, saying such disgusting things about the most wonderful man on Earth?

"Yeah, right," she scoffed.

"What's your problem?"

"You."

She seemed unreasonably annoyed. Maybe it was because she had started to feel the pain of the black eye I gave her.

"I don't even know you," I replied.

"I told you, we go to school together."

"And?" I went to school with a lot of people, and the last time someone picked a fight with me for no reason, was in junior high.

She took a long breath and declared, "This isn't you."

"I assure you, it is. And, how would you know?"

"Look, I'm sorry I said that stuff about your foster parents. I know they must have loved you. Maybe I was trying to get a reaction. You haven't been the same at school lately."

"My foster parents died so—" I began in irritation.

"I know," she cut in gently. "It sucks. It feels like your insides are being ripped out. You feel hollow, and at the same time, you're filled with an unbearable pressure that makes you want to explode."

I nodded. That is all I could do.

"You're not like other kids, Sophia. You never have been. It's like . . ." She searched the ceiling for the right words. "You are yourself. And, you make other people want to be themselves. Except for now. You're too sad."

Her face crinkled as though she were trying to hold in her upset. It shocked me.

What's with this chick?

The door opened, and Chet poked his head through. "Bridget, your step-father's here to pick you up."

Bridget? That was the name of the girl who slashed Vera in a knife fight years ago. She picked a fight with me then, too. How is her face not ingrained in my memory? In my defense, she did have red hair back then, and she looks so old now. Like time has beaten her into a version that's five years older than reality.

"Greg!" she wheezed in a near panic. "No! Aren't you going to keep me at Twin Oaks? What about the three strikes thing?"

"It's time to go," Chet answered.

"Fine." Bridget switched off whatever anxiety she was feeling and sauntered to the door. "But, I'll be seeing you again soon Chet, and Sophia." She turned back to me. "I'll remember who you are even if you don't. But, don't hide for too long. That doesn't help anyone."

I had the feeling she wanted to say more, but did not. She slipped past Chet into the hallway, and he closed the door. Resting my head back on the concrete wall, I asked myself, *Did I just receive words of wisdom from a teenaged, try-hard-gangster?*

CHAPTER 9

As we mounted the entrance steps of Twin Oaks, I noticed a bronze Rolls Royce parked in the lot. Mr. Harold opened the door, and stepped aside to let me pass first.

Ms. Michaels, the director of Twin Oaks, was probably going to give me a lecture, and I was definitely going to get extra cafeteria duties as part of my punishment.

Whatever. I don't care.

Warm air rushed over from inside the lobby. Miss Michaels hurried to meet us.

"Sophia, you're back. I've got great news. We've found you a new home!"

"What? That's impossible!" I gasped and turned back to Mr. Harold who looked equally stunned.

"Sophia, please meet Jack Tripper."

She held her hand out to a giant of a man sitting on a wooden bench next to the reception window. I blinked, because he reminded me of an African version of the animated character who used to appear on green bean commercials.

"Jack Tripper?" I asked.

I was cautious of any man who would want to foster a teenage girl.

Is there a Mrs. Tripper? Or are they going to send me off with this strange man?

Thoughts scrambled trying to devise a way to put the California plan into action.

I need more time!

An Amazon of a woman rounded the corner to greet me. "This must be Sophia."

Acting like a long lost aunt, she cupped my hand with both of hers. My fingertips began to tingle. It should have weirded me out, but for some reason I found myself most curious.

"Hello," was all I could muster as I looked up at the gargantuan woman.

"My name is Janet Tripper. We're from Good River, a few towns over. We have been thinking of fostering for some time now, and when we read about Mr. and Mrs. Gordon in the newspaper, we . . ."

Jack took over. "We thought this was our time to step up and do what the good Lord put us here to do."

"Okay, great." I stared up at the towering giants. "Sounds . . . fabulous."

This will be fun, I joked to myself. *I'll spend the next year with enormous God folk. Well, it could be worse, I guess.*

"Sophia, we have most everything squared away here," Anne Michaels said. "I have taken the liberty of packing your belongings, so you're ready to go." She spoke with an abnormal cheeriness, almost looking dazed.

"Do check in with us from time to time," she continued. "Let us know how things are going, won't you?" Anne asked as she guided me to the door.

Again, I was speechless. It all seemed to be moving along rather quickly.

"We sure will, Ms. Michaels," Janet assured.

Jack shook Mr. Harold's hand before he pushed open the doors and made a sweeping motion to direct us to pass.

"Take care now." Anne waved.

We walked directly to the Rolls I noticed earlier. Jack held the door to the backseat open for me and shut it firmly after I sat down. The Trippers waved good-bye to Ms. Michaels, and we pulled away.

What on Earth can I expect from this unusual arrangement?

We travelled a few miles without a sound when a bead of sweat formed on Janet's brow. It trickled past the corner of her eye to a quivering jawbone.

"Are you feeling alright, Mrs. Tripper?" I asked.

A vein protruded from Jack's temple, and his face was turning an irregular shade of red.

Janet shot a nervous smile past her shoulder and replied, "Doing fine dear. Thank you."

In a foreign language, she whispered something to her husband. He answered back in the same unintelligible speech.

Ah, please don't start speaking in tongues, I groaned to myself. *Did Ms. Michaels send me away with cult members, or killers?*

There was another long silence. My anxiety increased.

"How are we going to explain her to the community?" Jack tensely asked Janet.

"We'll have to tell them everything. We can't hide her from them anyway," Janet replied. Rummaging through her purse, she pulled out a white handkerchief and patted her hairline.

"I don't know if this is a good idea, Phaidra," Jack said almost frightened.

We all jerked forward as he slammed on the breaks. It was just in time to prevent us from crashing into the back of a transit bus.

"Doing all right, dear?" Jack let out a jittery laugh.

I pressed my head against the back of the seat and grunted, trying to figure out what the heck was going on.

Why do they need to explain me to a community? Why did he call her Phaidra? Is it some sort of foreign pet name or something. Does this guy really have a license?

"I can't hold up this mask for much longer, Dio!" Janet whispered with desperation.

Darting his sight from his wife to the road, Jack tried to calm her. "The veil is ahead, dear. Try to hold off a little longer."

Why are they so anxious?

Groping for the door handle I shouted, "What mask . . . and who's Dio? What the heck is going on here?"

Janet whipped her head around in shock. Her features began to distort.

"You can understand us?" she gasped at me.

"Should she be able to understand us right now?" she asked Jack, who feverishly shook his head.

"Why wouldn't I be able to understand you? I'm sitting right here," I sent back sharply.

Amazon lady divided her angst-filled glances between Jack and me and squealed, "Look, she did it again! How can that be?"

He appeared just as mystified. Then, as if a mask made of wax, his face began to melt.

I could hear heart beats in my ears.

Are they actors in disguise? I wondered.

"Somebody better tell me what the hell is going on!" I demanded.

My mind took inventory of the contents of my purse. I needed something that could be used to inflict injury on an attacker. We were going too fast for me to jump out of a vehicle. Even if I did, we were in the center lane of a three-lane highway. Another driver would certainly hit me.

Eyes swept the road ahead for stoplights, or pockets of time where the car would have to slow down for one reason or another. An extraordinary pink cloud wall loomed a few hundred yards ahead. No other driver seemed to notice it.

"Dio, it's wearing off!" Janet warned.

The enormous woman vanished in a blink. Peering over the front seat, I saw a three-foot tall, elf-like creature had replaced Mrs. Tripper. Eyes widened as I shifted to Jack who sat, entirely overwrought.

In a panic, he yelled, "Take the wheel, Sophia!"

"What?" I yelled back.

Jack mutated into a male version of the odd, elf-creature who was screaming in terror beside him. His shrunken size made it impossible for him to maneuver the vehicle. I hopped into the front seat and squished beside the morphed Jack, slamming on the brakes as we passed through the pink cloud wall. Gripping the steering wheel, a trio of harmonized screams sounded in my ears—one of those screams was mine.

I closed my eyes and thought, *I'm going to die!*

CHAPTER 10

The car's front end banged roughly on the Earth before abruptly coming to a rest. My brain raced at warp speed, trying to make sense of the rapidly shifting of data.

First, I have a family. Now, I don't. These new foster parents were colossal, and now they are slightly larger version of the porcelain figures Elka used to decorate her flowerbeds. I was on a crowded urban freeway leaving Gettysburg, Ohio, and now I'm in a forest with no apparent sign of civilization.

It was a cold, slushy winter day, and now everything was dry and sunny. I had a death grip on a steering wheel, but now my butt was stationed on a dirt road, with the characters formerly known as Jack and Janet on either side of me.

Where did the car go? I looked around and shouted in my mind. *And where are my things!*

"What the hell is going on?" I cried, still holding the invisible steering wheel.

The woman-creature to my right placed a hand on mine, and kindly pressed my arm down.

"Sophia," she spoke softly. "We do wish to care for you. That much is true. Oh, where do we begin? We knew this wouldn't be easy."

"Don't care where you begin. Just talk—talk a lot, in fact—say something please."

Scared of what else might be realized if my view moved, I held my breath and faced forward.

The man creature stood. His head was level with mine.

"Diomedes Ballios is my name," he said. "Folks call me Dio."

He reached slowly toward me. I leaned away, still unable to look at him. After removing a tiny frog from my shoulder, he considerately took a pace back.

"I am Phaidra Ballios," the woman said. Still sitting, she leaned toward me. "We are gnomes. We have taken you through the veil to our town known as Desta, Calista, in Celsus. For simplicity, think of it as Magic realm."

"Why?" I asked.

Why . . . that was my question? Not how, or, am I insane?

Taking stock of the surroundings, eyes darted from side to side. The brown dirt road that my butt sat on, was wide enough for two small cars to squeak past each other. Considering we were in a bronze Rolls Royce, and it had mysteriously disappeared I wondered if they even had cars.

Visually, I swept the area, looking for evidence of the car. All that could be seen was a green space on either side of the road, bordered by a forest.

"Because, you needed us," Phaidra answered simply as she stood and adjusted the long white apron over her blue dress.

"I what now?" I asked.

How do I need them? Why am I even talking to them? Don't gnomes belong in gardens to scare away birds? Oh wait, that's scarecrows.

"Our home is a little ways up the path. There is someone waiting who can help explain the situation." The little man held his hand out to help me off the ground.

"I'm not going anywhere with you!" I jumped up and demanded, "Take me home."

Take me home? Why would I say such a stupid thing? I don't have a home.

While brushing his white beard the man nodded. "Okay. One of the queens will be here in a few days. We'll ask her to send you back, if you like. Until then, there's a nice cave up the road. It will keep you safe from the elements, and there are lots a berries and nuts to feed you."

"Don't bears live in caves?" I questioned meekly.

"Not all of them," Diomedes replied.

"Fine," I huffed. "I'll go with you."

We began walking. I was not sure if I was scared or ticked about the crazy situation.

"You see, Sophia, we've been watching you since you were a child," Phaidra began.

Diomedes shot his wife a warning glance.

She responded with a wrinkled irritation. "We saw you with those horrid Laroose people, and we couldn't bear to see you go through that again. So we made sure you got placed with the Gordons.

"We would check in on you from time to time to make sure you were doing okay. You were so happy, so we stayed at a safe distance and didn't interfere. We are not supposed to do that, you know."

She looked up at me and nodded. "Then, we got word of the accident."

Phaidra clasped her tiny hand to her chest. "Oh dear. What a terrible unforeseen tragedy."

"Why would you be watching . . . ?" The question started out strong, but once a tiny stone cottage came into view a few yards to the right of the road, thoughts trailed off.

A winding path of crimson pebbles led to a rounded-top, oak door on the cottage. Gloriously colored flowers, herbs, and low-lying bushes lined either side of the walkway.

"Yes, it is breathtaking, if I do say so myself." Diomedes boasted. "Figure if I'm going to look after everyone else's gardens, I should make sure mine is up to par."

A knee-high, rock waterfall stood poised in the garden streaming into a shimmering pond. Dazzling, multi-hued fish swam peacefully. Angelic figures charmed, while modest birdbaths and decorative mushrooms offered an honest simplicity.

I felt strangely at ease in the peculiar setting. The fragrance was more than flowers. It was fresh, like mint gum. It filled my lungs with an effortless intoxication.

Eyes drifted to the front door of the cottage. There stood a towering stone gargoyle. He was looking back at me! I gasped.

"I'm sorry. I didn't mean to . . ." The gargoyle was talking to me. Vibrations from his voice ran through my entire being.

"You look familiar," I answered back.

Taking a few paces forward, wonder came to me. *Why the heck would a talking rock man look familiar?*

The mammoth creature looked at me with regret. "I only wanted to give you the book."

He took one stride toward me, which would have equalled about five of mine.

"What book?" I strained to view him. He must have been ten feet tall.

"You were little, and were with a boy. I didn't want you to get into trouble for forgetting your book. In my excitement, I forgot you were human and would not react well to seeing an enchanted being. I'm sorry I scared you." He lowered his head and said, "But I fixed it for you before the human-hag could give you trouble."

Human-hag? His description amused me. I thought back to the time when Caleb and I would eat our lunch in the park.

He must mean Ms. Viden, from junior high. And he was the statue.

"You did look at me . . . How could I forget that? I came up with a billion different scenarios for what I saw, but who would have thought-- the real-life rock man was the truth."

Diomedes and Phaidra were beside me gauging my response.

"Is that why you were watching me?" I asked the little people.

The gnome man was quick to nod. The lady tilted her head, and raised a brow. One might consider I was getting conflicting answers, but I had just met these oddballs. There was no reason for them to lie.

"You felt guilty for breaking my book, so you continued to keep tabs on me?" I concluded.

"Well, 'we' didn't break it." The gnome man quietly corrected and shoved his hands in his pockets.

Phaidra put a hand on her husband's shoulder and spoke to me. "Right. That's why we did it."

"Okay. I guess, but you're gnomes. Clearly you're gnomes, and he," I pointed to the gargoyle, "is a talking, moving, stone statue. Where am I?" I held my hands out and regarded the space around me.

Reaching up, Phaidra set her hand on the small of my back. "Please come in for some tea, and we can explain further."

"Yes, tea would be nice." Diomedes agreed, and stepped onto the porch. "I am awfully tired after our exhausting transformation."

Tea? How about a shot of whiskey? I'm too young to drink, but isn't this the perfect time to take a swig of something stronger?

"Okay," I said. "Tea would be great. Let's have tea." A few guarded steps brought me next to the little man on the porch.

"I've got to get back to my post," the gargoyle said. "It was nice seeing you again, Sophia."

"Yeah, you too, uhhh . . ." I searched for his name, but, in all the confusion, did not think one was told.

"Gerard." He sent me a two-finger salute. "See you around."

Something rustled from his back as he took a step into the middle of the front yard. Enormous wings unfolded. They must have spanned sixteen feet. After a few wide flaps of his wings, he was up in the air, swooping through the sky.

Amazing, I thought.

Following the two gnome beings inside, I saw a child-sized wooden table with four chairs. To the left was a tiny kitchen. Hundreds of jars lined the far wall. I imagine they contained herbs and possibly eye of newt. To my right was a quaint living room with a moderate-sized sofa, rocking chair that faced a stone fireplace.

"Please sit, dear." Phaidra pulled out a tiny chair.

I carefully sat down feeling as though I were visiting a kindergarten classroom. Phaidra removed a gray kerchief from her head uncovering a smartly rolled bun of silvery auburn hair. As she tucked the kerchief into an apron pocket, three cups of tea, and a plate of cookies appeared on the table. I straightened in surprise and stared blankly at the items.

Tipping the plate towards me she asked, "Gingersnap?"

I pointed to the cookies and wobbled my head in no thank you. Only one audible note squeaked through.

Phaidra lowered my hand to the table. "It's not polite to point, dear."

"Huh?" I got out while wondering, *where did the cookies and tea come from? Should I ask?* I rubbed my temple.

Dio sat back in his chair and brought the teacup to his lips.

"Okay, drink your tea, dear, it's story time." After a thoughtful sip, he replaced the cup and began, "All of the magical creatures you have heard about in fairy tales are real. Sure, some details have been modified over the years, but humans got the gist of things right. You see, magical beings have always existed, and we used to live on the Earthly plane with all of the humans. You even have a few documents explaining as much."

Under normal circumstances, I think most people would have run away screaming, or just plain laughed at the lunacy of such a statement. After what I had witnessed, it seemed a little pointless to do either.

"We do?" I asked.

"Yes, of course. Look at Moses or Merlin," Diomedes explained as he added another spoonful of honey to his tea.

"I thought Moses lived, but Merlin . . . Merlin's real?" I asked.

"Yes, Merlin was a darn good man, too. Never met him myself. He died long before my time. I'm only two hundred and fifty nine years old, you know." The gnome man puffed his chest.

"I see." I rested my chin in the crook of my thumb.

Diomedes leaned forward and continued, "We lived side by side with the humans, even helped them out sometimes. No one ever talked about whether or not magic really existed. It was just generally accepted in the communities we lived in.

"Then something happened, and I'm not quite sure what. Humans and Magics, who were once friends, began to distrust each other. Magics were found dead in the woods. The fairies were the first to sense this wavering acceptance. Word got around to the elves, pixies, gnomes, and other Magics. Our tribes went underground, so to speak.

"Covens had the hardest time believing humans had turned on us. It's probably because, genetically, wizards and humans are most closely related. Anyway, most of us left Earth realm hundreds of years before the wizards."

"What finally made the wizards leave?" I questioned.

"Have you heard about the Salem witch trials of 1692?" The little man asked.

"Yes, I've read about it," I replied. "Housewives went crazy after eating moldy bread. It is somewhat suspect to me how it only affected women."

"Ergot poisoning," Phaidra explained. "It didn't affect only women. It was an elixir created by the malicious unseelie faeries and covertly sold to citizens as yeast for bread. Its purpose was to draw out magical beings by compelling them to use their abilities. Naturally, the public displays of enchantment caused havoc and jealousy in human communities. About seventy years earlier, the poison was released in France. It caught over thirty thousand wolves."

"What's so magical about wolves?" I took a sip of tea.

"I'd say humans transmuting into wolves are somewhat magical," Phaidra mused as she reached for a cookie.

Tea went down the wrong pipe. "Werewolf!" I gasped through coughs. "Werewolves are real?"

"Not on Earth . . . anymore," Phaidra simplified. "After the ergot fiasco, they were confined to their own realm a few levels down. They're extremely pushy and troublemakers, from what I hear. The faerie queens would never let them come up again."

"Well, that's good news," I said in an exaggerated understanding on the whole werewolf situation. "So, what's with the faerie queen?"

"Faerie queens," Phaidra clarified the plural. "There are twelve queens who rule over twelve districts. Each district is comprised of four towns. As Dio said, this is Desta, Calista. The other towns in our district are Larrant, Page, and Crandall. The district is affectionately referred to as Calista's Court."

"Faerie queens are appointed by the spirits of our realm," Dio added. "It's their job to keep order among all their citizens and to guard against danger."

"What kind of danger?" I was picturing a cartoon pixie armed with a machine gun and belts of artillery strapped around her tiny body.

"Nothing truly treacherous has happened in over a hundred years, so it's nothing for you to worry about," Dio explained. "Mostly they deal with realm-to-realm travel, settling civil complaints, and discipline accordingly. There are supposed to be twelve queens, but two posts are without. Ours is one of them."

Astonished, I took in the story, not as a fairy-tale, but current events. "If Desta is without a queen, who stops the werewolves from sneaking back here," I asked.

Diomedes patted my hand to sooth me. "The existing queens take rotating shifts to monitor empty posts. It's not really possible to sneak through. You have to be granted passage by a queen. That's how we were able to pass through to your world. We got an appointment with Gloria. She rules district nine. We told her of the situation, and made our case to retrieve you.

"She said she needed to confer with the other queens. We thought it would be a complete lost cause, since you're a human and all, but Gloria came to me a few days later. I was working in the garden at Lee Chariot's estate. Naturally, I was stunned out of my pants when I noticed her majesty standing behind me. Faerie queens don't normally make personal appearances, especially in public." He broadened his shoulders to display his honor. "Gloria said I was to retrieve you right away, and that she would leave a doorway open for five hours."

"Hence, the pink fluffy wall we drove through," I recalled while absentmindedly reaching for a gingersnap.

"Precisely!" Phaidra agreed excitedly. "She's getting it, Dio. This is fun. Much easier than expected."

"I am still not clear about why you brought me here. If humans are not allowed in this realm, it doesn't make much sense that I should be allowed just because Gerard startled me into breaking my science text book." I took another bite of the yummy cookie.

Dio and Phaidra looked blankly at one another.

"We're not supposed to interfere with humans," Phaidra said slowly. There was a question mark at the end of her statement.

"Why was Gerard in my realm in the first place?" I pressed on, imagining the lawyer presence of Edwin at my side.

"It's his job." Dios brightened. "He has a work pass. One of his duties is to oversee the remaining magics on your Earth plane."

"There are magic people on Earth?" I questioned, while a dish of cheesy broccoli, whole-wheat buns, and roasted peppers magically appeared on the before us. I struggled to keep focus on the conversation.

"Some decided to stay with their families in Human realm. Magics are also not supposed to show obvious displays of their power, or take advantage of the humans. There are unspoken laws regarding this. That's why gargoyles and other beings oversee the

Earth plane. They report back any inappropriate behavior." Dio went to a bottom cupboard to retrieve plates and cutlery. Placing them before us he said, "Let's take a short break to pray and have some dinner, shall we?"

"Of course," I bowed my head and folded hands while Dio prayed.

"Dear Lord, I'll keep it short for tonight. I think we are all tired from the activity of the day. I want to thank you for the food you have created for us and the protective home you have granted us to enjoy it in. Thank you also, dear Lord, for allowing Sophia to come and live with us. Please help us to learn and grow through each other and through you. Amen."

He looked up at us and said, "Can you pass the broccoli, I'm famished."

We passed the food around and began to eat quietly. I took note of the beautifully woven blanket resting on the back of the sofa and hand-painted portraits, perhaps of family members, hanging from the walls.

"I have two other questions." I rested a hand on the table.

"Yes, dear," Phaidra looked up from her plate.

"You pray. Who are you praying to? If there are all of these magical creatures with all sorts of powers and important jobs, who are you praying to?" I asked.

"We pray to the same God humans pray to, of course." Dio smiled. "There is only one God and He is the creator of all. It is He who has granted us our abilities. Even the most powerful of Magics are no comparison to the Divine. Most folks around here are Sorceian. It's a predominantly wizards religion, not that it really matters."

"What do you mean?" I asked.

"Here, most all Magics understand that no matter what temple they belong to, everything ultimately comes from the One God, no matter what you call him. The tiny differences in ritual and ceremony don't matter to us." Phaidra smiled.

After dinner, I helped Phaidra clear the table and wash the dishes. Dio struck a fire in the fireplace, and rested in the rocking chair that sat in front. Rummaging in a sack beside him, he pulled out a pipe and lit it.

It was getting quite dark outside and snow began to fall. That seemed strange. It was January, but when we got here, it could have been t-shirt and shorts weather.

"Yes, it's snow." There was aggravation in Phaidra's voice. "Weather here is a little different than in your realm. Normally, we have seasons that would compare to your spring, summer and a moderate fall, but things have gone a little haywire in the last decade or so. It can be hot and sunny one day and a blizzard the next. It happens in regions without queens. District Eight is having the same issue, but we manage. You'll get used to it." She handed me a platter so I could dry it. "You are looking tired, dear."

"I am getting quite tired. It's been a very lively day."

That had to be the biggest understatement of the year. I woke up in an orphanage, passed through a magical veil transporting me to the land run by fairies, and got taken in by a pair of gnomes. Oh yeah, and did I mention, I still believe I'm sane?

After we finished up in the kitchen I followed Phaidra to the entryway between the kitchen and living area. To the left, she explained, was her and Dio's bedroom. To the right was mine. A bathroom was located in the middle.

Phaidra handed me a lantern that nicely illuminated the room that was to be mine. The inviting chamber held a human-sized bed. For some reason, I think it was specifically made for me. A simple wardrobe and small, mirrored dresser sat against the wall across from the foot of the bed.

Placing the lantern on the night table, I sat down with a bounce, to test its jump worthiness.

"You'll find a nightgown in the wardrobe and there are some towels in the bathing room." The tiny woman stood at the doorway.

Not that it ever crossed my mind, but I never would have guessed that gnomes looked so human. They were just short, stocky humans. The Ballios did not have pointed ears, or weird features. By Earth standards, the lovely couple looked to be in their seventies. In actuality, they had been around since Beethoven.

"Okay, sounds good. Thanks, Phaidra."

She stepped into the hallway and was about to close the door when she said, "Earlier, you said you had two questions."

"Oh, yeah," I remembered. "Why did you disguise yourselves as giants?"

Phaidra laughed. "Sometimes it's fun to pretend you are something exactly the opposite of what you are, but all that magic has sure tired us out. It takes quite a bit of energy to keep up appearances on your side. Here, it's easier, due to the electrical fields, although it is somewhat frowned upon to use magic excessively."

"I'll remember that, not that it matters to me, being a human." I pulled a pillow from the bed and placed it on my lap, "But . . ."

"Yes dear?" She invited after seeing my face.

"Did you put a spell on Miss. Michael? She seemed dazed."

"Of course we did," she answered. "All of your Earth processes take way too long, and we didn't have time to dilly dally. She's been implanted with a sleeper spell and will take care of all of your loose ends."

"Good. That's helpful," I answered.

Perhaps I should have wondered what that entailed, but the truth was I did not care.

Good riddance to that crappy world.

"Alright, dear Sophia, I'll leave you for the night. Sleep well."

I nodded, and she closed the door behind her.

I retrieved a long, white night gown from the wardrobe, and dressed for the night. After slipping into the cushy bed, all the day's events began to run through my thoughts. It was curious to me, why I was so at ease in this crazy supernatural world.

"Magic is real," I whispered to myself before my exhausted brain fell off to sleep.

CHAPTER 11

Warm beams of sun shone through window sheers the next morning. Stretching comfortably, I rose and went to my suitcases. They were sitting inside my room next to the door. Dio must have gone back to get them. I did not remember any of us bringing them here.

I pulled out a pair of black cargo pants, a white t-shirt and a squishy set of garden shoes.

Am I really going to live here? Is this actually possible?

I figured what the Ballios explained about magic made sense, in theory. And there was the fact that I had seen some of it with my own eyes.

Barring the possibility that death had found me after the car crash, and this was a topsy-turvy purgatory, one would have to assume it was all real. Even if I had died, this would still be real, in a dead, bizarro sort of way.

Given the fact that I witnessed giants morphing into midgets before the alleged crash, it would stand to reason that the odd occurrences happened before any deadly crash.

There was no deadly crash. I resolved. *I'm not dead. This is really happening. I might as well go with it.*

I tidied up in the bathing room, brushed teeth, and loosely braided my hair. It was a relief that in a world as antiquated as it was, they still had indoor, flushable toilets and running water.

Not hearing anyone scuttle around the house, I peeked into the kitchen. A yellow bowl, a basket, and a pitcher of juice sat on the kitchen table next to a note. The note read, "Hope you slept well. Please eat. I'll be in the side garden. Phaidra."

Walnuts overflowed in a yellow bowl next to a basket of freshly picked blueberries. I grabbed a handful of each and washed them down with a glassful of the most uplifting green juice. Taste buds told me it was aloe and kiwi. After giving the living room a patrolling walk around, I joined Phaidra outside.

"Good morning, sunshine," the little woman greeted while she picked mint from the garden.

"Are you collecting that for tea?" I crouched down to watch her.

"Some of it will be dried. I also add it to lemonade." Phaidra set a handful of mint in the basket beside her. "How did you find your bed?"

"It was perfect." I plucked a piece of mint from the garden and popped it in my mouth. The leaf was warm from the sun but became cool and refreshing when chewed. "Could you use some help?"

Phaidra looked up at me and grinned. "Sure, if you're offering. I have enough mint, but these tiny weeds are a bother. They keep coming back."

She pointed to a thin, menacing green vine that had woven itself among the flowers.

"These weeds are much worse than they have ever been. Have to check on my babies every few days to make sure they're not being strangled to death by these dastardly critters."

"Yeah, I see it." I ripped one of the nasty vines from its roots. "Where's Dio?"

"He's off to work." Phaidra dug her fingers into the soil to get a better grip on the base of a weed.

"What does he do?" I followed her lead and poked my fingers in the soil around another root.

"He tends to the foliage around the town. We all do,—Gnomes, I mean—but I'm taking a little time off."

She pulled up a handful of weeds and placed them in a large bucket by her side.

"Because of me?" I asked.

"I couldn't leave you alone your first few days. This must be quite overwhelming for you," Phaidra said. "Do you like apples?"

"Sure, apples are good."

"Follow me." She hopped up and skipped to the back of the house.

Now that I had a better handle on my situation, more time could be spent checking out the yard. Varying shades of pink and purple hollyhocks grew along the side of the house. Hues of the flowers were made even more vibrant with the thick ivy backdrop blanketing the wall. The back of the house shared a similar floral décor.

Phaidra stopped and stood proudly under a giant tree with plump red apples. I was waiting for her to lift her hands and say, "Ta da!"

A smile started in my chest, followed through my lips, and concluded with my eyes.

This little woman's awesome.

"Do you want one?" she asked eagerly.

"I would love an apple." I came closer to receive her offering. "You've got some patch here, Phaidra."

The garden spanned about double the length and width of the house and was filled with every vegetable imaginable. The far end was enclosed by a fence of blueberry bushes. A row of cherry trees helped wall one side, and oranges lined the other. I strolled up and down the bountiful rows of avocado, kiwi and other mouth-watering fruits.

"How do you get all of this tropical fruit to grow here?"

"Invisible greenhouse," Phaidra answered like it was the most natural explanation in the world. "Anytime you're hungry, you can come out here and pick anything you want, Sophia. You'll never want for food again," she offered tenderly, but with a curious hint of regret.

How much does she know about my life?

"Last night's snow doesn't seem to have damaged your vegetables. Is that because of the magical greenhouse too?" I asked, restoring the conversation to the topic of vegetation rather than my childhood hunger. It was not something I cared to remember.

Phaidra leaned up against the trunk of a cherry tree and watched me admired her garden.

"Partly," she answered, "but, there's also an inclement weather spell on the garden. An entire crop was lost a few years ago. Thank goodness, we have such good neighbors. They helped us through that rough period. Finding all of the ingredients for the spell was a little tricky. I had to call my sister, all the way in Desta, Gloria, to send me orange lichen root."

"Is the spell on all the time?" I asked.

"This particular spell has a ten-year guarantee. I'll have to start the whole process over again in a three years," Phaidra said walking towards a wooden bench at the back of the house.

I came up behind her and sat down. "Can't you just wish something into existence, like you did last night for dinner?" I questioned.

"You can't create something from nothing. We had all that food here, it was just prepared differently. The only way Magics can manifest things is if it is possible from the elements surrounding them," Phaidra said.

"But, when your crops died, all of the elements were still around you even if they were damaged," I commented.

"Yes. We did produce food that way for a while, but it takes much more energy to pull together a meal from bits and pieces of scattered molecules. After working all day, we didn't have it in us to do it night after night." Phaidra looked tired just talking about it.

I took a bite of the apple.

"These are delicious."

Juice ran down my chin. I quickly wiped away the drip with the back of my hand.

"These would make a great pie."

"Do you bake?" Phaidra asked.

"I used to bake with Mrs. Gordon all the time." My mouth tasted the memory of the flaky, butter-crust over delicious spiced apples, and my lungs remembered the sweet warmth as I inhaled.

"Well, maybe you should make a pie," Phaidra suggested.

"Yeah, I'll do that." I nodded.

"Very good, you'll find everything you need in the kitchen or in the garden. I've got to get back to weeding."

The little woman patted my knee before disappearing to the front yard.

After finishing the apple a large wooden basket appeared at my feet.

"Thank you," I called out to Phaidra.

I dropped the core into a two-foot hole dug in the earth next to the bench. The little pit already had potato and banana skins in it. Figured it must be compost.

After plucking a few low-hanging apples, the cherries tree called to me. I fantasised that they cried, "Sophia, come and eat me, I'm yummy. Promise." The do-gooder in me went to them and put their pleading to rest.

Once satisfied with my heaping basket, I headed inside. Phaidra, back to weeding, winked at me as I passed by.

Rummaging through the kitchen cupboards made me feel a little intrusive, but I had permission. For whatever reason, these beings went out of their way to take me in. Despite my head urging me to keep shields up, intuition reassured they could be trusted.

Low-standing countertops took some getting used to, but in no time, enough apples for one pie had been cored and peeled. Assistance was needed when it came to actually baking the pie. Home economics class never taught me how to use an old fashioned, wood-burning oven.

When the crust turned golden brown, and the aroma of sweet apples and fresh cinnamon filled the cottage, I pulled it out. I placed my creation on a cooling rack on the kitchen table, and gave myself a pat on the back. It felt amazing, almost magical, to be creating in a quaint little gnome home. I decided to start on a second pie. This one would be peach.

Thoughts drifted off to a spectacular forest with soaring trees. I pictured myself strolling through sweet smelling grass, hearing the rush of water in the distance.

In my mind's eye, I followed an earthly hum until a great waterfall came into sight. It was cascading into a beautiful purple body of water. Standing in front of the water, I inhaled. Humid air filled my lungs. I sat atop a huge, smooth rock and just breathed deeply for a while.

Squawking from high in one of the majestic trees caught my attention. A bird resembling a parrot mixed with a peacock perched above. He nodded and beckoned me to follow, so I did.

In the middle of an open space was a grand tepee made of massive fronds. I was curious about what lay inside the tepee, so I stepped closer...

"Wow, someone has been busy today." Dio stood at the front door carrying a burlap sack over his shoulder. "I can see why I smelled baking all the way down at Tuckers Cove."

Snapping back to reality, I was speechless when I saw the room filled with ten more completely baked pies.

"Oh my, where did these all come from?" My bewildered eyes followed the trail of pies along the counter.

Dio chuckled. "You're the only one here, darling. Don't worry, I'll help you eat them. I've never met a pastry I didn't love." He patted his round tummy.

"How the heck did I?" My jaw dropped open.

Phaidra peered in through the hallway. "Good, you're home, Dio. I need to speak with you, right away."

"Yes, dear." Dio set his sack down and hobbled to the bedroom. I began to clean up after my mysterious baking frenzy.

Phaidra tried to speak quietly, I am sure, but I could still hear her in their bedroom. She whispered, "She quickly familiarized herself with the kitchen, so I assumed it would be fine to leave her. But, she wasn't alone for more than an hour."

"So what if she knows her way around a kitchen," Dio said. "And, if this is how she chooses to ease herself into our life, who am I to complain?"

"I'm not concerned about the pies, Dio. I'm excited, because it means she's getting more comfortable with us. Our little one's mystical side is beginning to appear."

Mystical side? What's that supposed to mean?

"Of course it is, darling," he replied gently. "I told you there was nothing to fear."

Moments later, Phaidra came out from the bedroom to help me clean. "You did a wonderful job on the pies, Sophia. You don't mind if we share with the neighbors, do you?" she asked, picking up a pie from the table and looking around for a place to move it.

"Please do," I said. "I'm so sorry, Phaidra. I must have gone on autopilot. I didn't realize."

"It's no problem. You will make us very popular with our friends," she reassured. "We'll get dinner going, and then we'll have one of your pies for dessert. Now, let's see. Where am I going to put all of these pies? Hmmm, ah yes." She pointed her tiny finger at the back of the sofa, and a long thin table suddenly appeared. "That'll do." She picked up a second pie and set in on top of the table.

"Did you manifest the table from the elements?" I asked.

"No, silly, it was in the attic. Now, help me make some room in here." She giggled.

CHAPTER 12

"How are you finding things here, Sophia?" Dio asked me while pouring a large spoon full of peas inside a hole he dug in his mashed potatoes.

Adding a few spears of asparagus to my plate, I answered, "Oddly, I am dealing better than could be expected. I think I'm missing the Gordons a lot today." I glanced to the long table of pies in the living room. "I used to make a pie with Elka every Sunday afternoon."

"That's understandable, Sophia. The Gordons were very good people, and you loved them. They loved you, too. Whatever you're feeling is okay, just don't hold it in. Bad things can happen when you hold on to hurt," Phaidra said, glossing over my split lip, which I had forgotten about.

Dio added, "Yes dear, and if you feel you need to talk about anything, anything at all, we are here."

"Thanks, I'll keep that in mind. What did you do at work today?" I asked, shoving a fork full of potatoes in my mouth.

"It was the usual kind of day. Started with the relocation for a colony of ants taking over the Harlo's lawn, and ended with weeding at the Chariots. Most of the day was spent trying to find the right formulation for an elixir. A new fungus keeps popping up around town."

He attempted to spear a baby tomato with his fork, but it kept sliding away.

"I hope you find a remedy soon," Phaidra said. "The disease is becoming quite bothersome and hard to manage. Just last week, I had to pull out the Holbrook's entire garden and incinerate the sick foliage. I'm even fearful to replant in case the soil itself is contaminated. Alary Holbrook and I decided we'd cover the barren grounds with rocks and fountains until we can get the infestation under control."

"An acceptable solution, under the circumstances," Dio agreed with a tsk-tsk in his tone.

I jumped when the sound of rapping came at the front door. My fork clanked loudly on the plate before dropping to the floor. I scolded myself, thinking it was an awfully extreme response, and bent to pick it up. Knocking at the door did not usually evoke such a spastic reaction in me. Perhaps, I feared some new and frightening being was waiting outside.

Dio went to the door.

"Good evening, Mrs. Chariot. What can we do for you this evening?" Dio greeted.

I was seated behind the open door, so the caller could not be seen, but it was a woman's voice.

"I came to offer you a basket of mushrooms," she said in a cool, articulate tone. "We got a shipment in today from Crandall, and I wanted to give you an extra thank you for the wonderful job you are doing at our home."

"We love mushrooms. Many thanks, Mrs. Chariot," Dio said. You could almost hear his mouth watering.

"What a great deal of pies you have there." The woman must have been referring to the long table behind the couch, as she would not be able to see the pies on the counter behind me. "Are you having a party?"

"Nope, no party." He chuckled. "I would love to give you one to take back to your family."

Dio offered and sidestepped to the pie table.

"I couldn't," the woman said as she took a step inside.

Unsure why, I took a deep breath when she entered. The slender woman wore a floor length sage colored dress, covered with a stylish sea foam cape. She pushed back a section of her dark, chocolate-colored hair. It was not a whimsical flip, rather a deliberate motion that restored her mane to its previous state of order.

Stopping, she tilted her head like a cat, picking up on a distant sound. Turning first with her head, and then with her body, she halted me with her gaze. The woman had a mature beauty and an air of someone who needed to do little more than snap her fingers to get what she wanted.

"How's it going," I asked, trying to hide my intimidation.

Should I stand to shake her hand or bow at her feet?

I ended up sitting there, frozen.

"I don't believe I have ever made your acquaintance," she said, poised and unmoving.

Phaidra got up from her chair and stood slightly ahead of me. Her movement was that of a lioness protecting her cub.

"Sophia has come to live with us." Momma lion then spoke to me, "This is Mrs. Eve Chariot. Her husband, Lee Chariot is the Alcade of Desta." She whispered so only I could hear, "Alcade is what you would call the mayor."

I stood and nodded slightly, wanting to show a level of respect without getting too close. It was as if she held an unseen barrier around her, one only the unwitting would dare to invade.

"Nice to meet you, Mrs. Chariot," I answered with a surprising calm.

"Where have you come from, Sophia? You're obviously not kin to the Ballios," Mrs. Chariot inquired.

"Umm . . . Earth?" I looked to Dio and Phaidra to see if that was the appropriate way to respond.

They stood silent, anticipating a reaction from the woman.

"And, what are you?" the woman asked.

What a funny question, I thought. Someone being asked that question back home would truly be offended. It could possibly even invite violence in some parts.

"I'm human."

The quiet room became even more still.

The Ballios, who were motionless, stood as if they were listening for the ticks before an explosion.

"Human?" the woman responded.

I had the feeling that if this lady actually had any emotion she would be screeching. Instead, she remained composed. That was even more unnerving.

"A human has never to been to Celsus. How is that even possible?" Mrs. Chariot asked.

"Her majesty from district nine granted her residence here in Desta." Phaidra took another pace in front of me.

I was getting nervous.

What exactly did she think the woman was going to do to me?

"I see." Mrs. Chariot flicked her eyes from Phaidra to me. "How old are you?"

"Seventeen, tomorrow actually." I had forgotten until now.

Ignoring Dio, she split her information between Phaidra and me.

"I'm on my way to Jane Aristotle's, the head mistress of Ambrose Academy. I will let her know you will be registering for school tomorrow. You were planning to enroll her, I trust," Mrs. Chariot said leaving no room for discussion.

"The thought had crossed my mind," Phaidra started. "But, since she is not a Magic, I wasn't sure how people would react—"

"But she is a child, and children must go to school," Mrs. Chariot interrupted. "Surely you were not trying to keep her hidden." A hint of accusation tinged her question.

"Of course we weren't," Phaidra protested. "It's just a delicate matter."

"Yes it is, but youth of our town come from well-bred and conscientious families. I have two children who attend there as well. I am sure they will act with the utmost of decorum." Mrs. Chariot raised her brows and rested her case.

Phaidra smiled through gritted teeth and said, "Of course you're right, Eve, and thank you for taking it upon yourself to notify Head Mistress Aristotle for us. We will have her there tomorrow morning."

"Very good. I will be on my—" Mrs. Chariot stopped mid-sentence.

Hunching her shoulders, she cocked and rolled her head with a prehistoric sweep. I had only just met this woman, but the way she moved seemed completely out of character. She began to speak in a deep, husky tone not of her own, "Nunc exsisto paro vox."

Stepping back, I gasped. Dio and Phaidra remained calm.

In an instant, she straightened her posture and reverted to her previous speaking voice, "Enjoy your mushrooms."

"We will enjoy them. Thank you, again, and don't forget your pie." Dio handed her a platter, politely waved, and closed the door.

"That was fun," the little man said sarcastically.

I am sure my face was deathly pale. "What was that?"

"It's nothing, dear," Dio answered simply. "Sometimes she gets messages from other places and they speak through her."

"She gets possessed?" I cried out.

"I suppose you could call it that," Phaidra said. "She's a conduit, so it comes part and parcel with her particular gift. Most of the time she doesn't even know what she has said."

Phaidra returned to her seat.

"And, sometimes she does," Dio said as he set the box of mushrooms on the counter behind me.

"What does that even mean? Nunc exsisto paro vox," I mimicked Mrs. Chariot's disturbing, possessed voice.

"It's Latin meaning, soon to be set right, and outstanding pronunciation, Sophia," Dio commended.

I sat down and asked, "Why didn't she just say that?"

"She didn't say anything," Phaidra corrected. "It was the spirit speaking through her. I don't think Eve even knows Latin."

"Ooo-kay." I changed the subject. "So, school tomorrow, that sounds terrifying."

"Oh, you'll be fine," Phaidra reassured, then turned nervously to her husband. "She will be fine, won't she, Dio?"

"Of course."

After cleaning up the dinner things, I relaxed with a hot soak in the Ballios's bathtub. The porcelain claw-foot tub was practically the size of a laundry basket, but they did have fabulous scented bath oils. Phaidra French braided my hair, and I went to bed.

Pangs of anxiety seemed to be worse the longer I stayed in one position. I decided flopping around might make me feel better. I could hear the Ballios murmuring in the living room. The only thing I could make out was Dio saying, "I'll take care of it, don't worry."

He seemed very adamant about something. In all probability, it was me. I chose to believe him and closed my eyes.

CHAPTER 13

Phaidra was sitting on the end of my bed when I woke the next morning.

"Good morning," she said as soon as she noticed the whites of my eyes.

"Morning. What have you got there?" She had a pile of folded material on her lap.

"Some garments for school. There's a bit of a dress code. I wasn't sure you'd have the proper pieces."

She set the clothes next to me and hopped down to the floor.

"You get dressed, and we'll have some breakfast before we leave."

Lifting the garment by the shoulders, I held it out to examine. "A dress," I questioned in a whisper while slipping it overhead.

It was a black, three-quarter length, dress that ended just above the knees. The flared bottom was trimmed with a slim band of periwinkle. A thick ribbon belt, of the same color, rested loosely at my waist.

Is she sure about these boots?

I laced up knee-high, black boots. They squeezed snug around my calf.

Already wrapped in their coats, the Ballios waited for me at the front door.

"I'm afraid I let you sleep in too long. I put some food in a basket for you to eat on the way."

She held up a small picnic basket in the same periwinkle color as my caped jacket.

"You'll have to put your hood up. It's a bit misty," Phaidra cautioned as Dio opened the door.

Wow, she was not kidding. It was more than mist. It was so foggy, I could barely see to the bird bath at the far end of the garden. I followed them as they headed down their crimson walkway and continued to the main road.

"We didn't have time to wrap it, but happy birthday, Sophia." Dio reached into his pocket and pulled out a chain.

He stopped and looked up at me.

"You didn't have to do that," I said, gazing at the silver-chained jade pendant.

Dio tapped his knee. The chain vanished from his hand and reappeared around my neck.

I giggled and cupped the stone in my hand. "That's a neat trick, Dio. I love it!"

"It looks lovely on you." Phaidra wiped the corner of her eye.

Fog thinned quickly to my surprise and Dio pointed to a mini-mountain, with a rose-colored, dungeon-shaped door. Pink horse troughs with oversized purple and yellow flowers sat on either side of the entrance.

"That's Tuckers Cove to your left. Nickel and Ada Tucker are good friends of ours. He made those boots special for you last night."

A shoemaker?

I did not know there was such a thing, although, I suppose, once upon a time, there had to be shoemakers. There were not always factories, and assembly lines to mass produce footwear. I was getting the feeling the entire town was about a hundred years behind times.

"Is he an elf?" I asked a little tongue-in-cheek. Elves are stereotypically shoemakers. At least that is what my Grimms Fairy Tale textbook says.

"No. He's a dwarf." Dio sent me a knowing grin. "We brought him two of your pies last night. Ada was plumb mad after he ate them down in ten minutes. We told them we would bring an apple over after dinner."

"I'm glad he enjoyed them." A hint of embarrassment about my prolific pie-making episode struck again.

"Shamus is an elf," Phaidra said. "He lives a little further up the road in the last house before we get into town."

I pulled the cape a little tighter around my body. A chill was getting to my bones. It was not raining, or especially cold. The air just felt wet. If not for the hood, I would have looked like a drowned kitten.

"Hello, Shamus," Dio called to a petite man sweeping his walkway. His house appeared as if someone literally carved a castle out of a grassy hillside.

"Good day to you all." He set his broom against a tree and stepped up to greet me. "You must be Sophia. Nice to make your acquaintance, love. Are you off to school?"

He warmly shook my hand with both of his.

"Yes I am."

Tipping his hat, he pulled out a metallic clover charm.

"For luck, dear Sophia," he said as he offered it to me. "That's a real four leaf clover, dipped in silver."

Shamus was not extraordinarily short. He had to be at least four feet. His gentle face appeared to be about thirty, but I imagined he had to be much older.

"That's very kind of you. Thank you." I smiled and examined the charm.

"You're most welcome." He nodded and pivoted to view Dio. "Where are you going to be in about an hour?"

"We'll be working the grounds at Ambrose Academy, all day." Dio scratched under his green cap.

"Good. I might have come up with the missing ingredient to your fungus concoction." Shamus stroked his neatly trimmed, red beard.

"Let's hope you have. We'll run some experiments," Dio replied.

"Alright. I'd better get off then. See you later." Shamus waved.

We continued a little ways until we came upon a pair of wrought iron gates that opened towards the town. Walking further brought us to the center of the village. Polished wooden walkways lined storefronts. Street merchants in portable carts began to set up for the day.

A horse-drawn carriage slowed beside us. When the woman inside called out, the Ballios went over to talk. Instead of waiting for them on the sidewalk, I wandered toward a large fountain in the center of the cobblestone road.

Water shot out from the hands of a woman sculpture in the fountain. Her arms gracefully reached for the heavens with thumb and ring finger touching. The spray created a shimmered mist that rained into a coin pool. I wondered how the sculptor was able to make something so breathtaking.

"Sophia, we must keep going." Phaidra came up beside me.

The town was already active with human-looking citizens. They were headed off to work, shopping, or do whatever it was they did in a mainly retail section of town.

After traveling through the business sector, we entered another residential area. Grand homes with wrap-around decks and porch swings decorated the streets and avenues. The gnomes were probably responsible for all of the stunning landscapes.

I could not be sure if the stone gargoyles that guarded the properties were real, like Gerard, or simply adornments. While some of the homes were fanciful, others exuded darkness.

If Desta were a square, and we entered the township at the bottom right hand corner, we would have journeyed diagonally, to the opposite side. We stood in front of another set of gates opening into Ambrose Academy.

I feel like I'm going puke.

CHAPTER 14

Perfectly trimmed, lush grass carpeted the school grounds and led to a castle-shaped structure. I half expected to see a drawbridge with a moat. Happily, all I found were stone steps leading to two oversized doors and teenagers dressed in the same basic garments I had on.

Score one for me!

We were stopped at the base of the steps when a girl's voice spoke from behind.

"You must be Sophia," she said.

Spinning around, I saw a pretty girl with long red hair secured by a wide, black headband. She was dressed in a dark blue, knee-length dress, black boots and a cape.

"Yes," I replied.

While the corners of her mouth rose softly, the rest of her face was unreadable.

"I'm Divina Holbrook. Head Mistress Aristotle asked me to show you around."

"Divina's parents are Alary and Abraham Holbrook," Phaidra explained with an approving gesture. "They're good friends of ours. I will leave you in Divina's care. We'll meet you at the school gates at dismissal."

"Okay," I said, and watched them as they tootled off to the back of the school.

"We should go," Divina said as she climbed the steps. "We have mostly the same classes, except the magic ones, of course. Mistress Aristotle has enrolled you in elementary Charms and Stones for the semester. It's the last class of the day."

Upon entering the grand school, you had the choice of going up the right or left staircase, or going straight, past the foyer, to another set of hallways. Divina took me up the right stairwell.

The upstairs hallway had a spooky, two-lane, single file, student-highway already in progress. Divina joined the silent line migrating north. I quickly fell into step behind her. I hoped my footsteps were not too loud, or that my breathing would not disrupt the eerie calm.

No one looked at me from the opposite line. Actually, nobody looked at anyone. I followed Divina into a classroom. We went to two empty seats in the first row. Other students filed in behind and took their seats.

Divina observed the piece of paper she was holding.

"This is your course schedule, Sophia. As you can see, we have poetry first." She pointed to the first block of the day.

Leaning towards her and brushing her arm with mine as I did, I looked to where she was pointing.

"Poematis. What's this? Latin?"

Handing me the sheet, she nodded and said, "Etiam is est. Latin est nostrum secundus ordo."

I paused for a moment while Divina took her seat.

"Okay, so it's poetry, Latin, art, lunch, and elementary charms. Got it."

Divina seemed stunned when she answered, "Good, you know Latin. That will make things easier."

Setting my cape on the back of the chair, I laughed. "I don't know Latin."

Seated in the desk behind me, a girl with milk chocolate colored hair flicked her eyes in my direction. She fixed her gaze. It appeared she was struggling to keep her appearance indifferent.

Is this a stare down?

She blew a puff of air from her nostrils before returning her attention to the book that lay open on her desk.

After setting her case on the floor, Divina expressed confusion. "But, I just spoke to you in Latin . . . and, you understood me?"

"It sounded like you said, 'Yes, it is. Latin is our second class.'"

I appreciated Divina's first attempt to make a joke.

Her forehead furrowed.

A delightful little woman skipped into the room. She wore a cream colored, cashmere sweater, under a baby blue coverall-dress. Joyously, she flipped a tam off her sunshine, shoulder-length hair and flung it atop the teacher's desk at the front of the room.

"Good morning, young people," her sweet voice chirped. "Has everyone welcomed our new student, Sophia?"

The elfin-lady danced towards me. "I am Miss Luna Updar, and it is a joy to have you with us."

"Thank you," I said.

"Class, say hello," Miss Updar sang out to her students.

A choir of monotone voices droned, "Good day, Sophia."

Rotating, I nodded in acceptance of their less than heartfelt greeting. No one met my glance. I returned to a forward-facing position.

"Okay class, we will begin today by reading a selection of poems."

Miss Updar took a stack of books and deposited them to the first person in each row.

"Take one and pass them back. Normally, we learn about poetry as it relates to spell writing. Today, we'll focus on the more poignant aspect of the craft. Turn to page twenty-three."

Once everyone found the page and she began to recite. She spoke of a rod and staff, and how it comforted. I listened carefully, sure I had heard them from somewhere before, although, not sure how. It must have been written about the magic world, referring to staffs and such. After the second selection, Miss Updar paused to gauge the class. When they appeared less than enthralled, she let out a glum sigh.

"Can anyone share a thought about what these two pieces might have in common?"

She posed her challenge with bright eyes. No one responded.

I peered over my shoulder. They were virtually mannequins. The sweet lady's face fell. I half raised a hand and spoke as soon as Miss Updar focused on me.

"They both talk about an overall protector who is with us in dangerous or sad times," I blurted.

Eyeballs shifted in my direction. I could practically hear them . . . or it could have been merely the dread filled notions of a self-conscious girl.

"Indeed they do, Sophia." She brightened. "Now, I have an assignment. I need you each to write a paragraph, or so, about where your strength comes from. Please begin, and finish up at home."

She clasped her hands together, then noticed the only thing I carried was a lunch basket. After springing to her desk, she retrieved a brown leather case from the bottom drawer.

"My father sends me a new case every year," she whispered as she set it on the floor beside me. "I have at least a hundred of them. Please keep this one."

"Thank you so much, Miss Updar."

I was grateful for her thoughtfulness, but felt I was turning into a charity case.

Maybe I could get a job here and make a little money.

Winking, she replied, "Think nothing of it. I have a feeling you are going to be of more help to me this semester."

A chime sounded. Looking around, I could not locate the source. There did not seem to be an intercom or speakers anywhere. In unison, the students closed their books and rose from their desks.

"Sarah," Miss Updar spoke to the chocolate-haired girl behind me. "I know your brother was supposed to be gone all week, but I saw your father in the office earlier. Did Saban come back with him?"

"Yes. Father decided to come back from the conference early. Since they traveled all night, father took Saban straight home to sleep. He will be returning tomorrow."

Sarah did not wait for a response from Miss Updar. After her last word, she inched past me to the door and left.

Divina slipped into the same hallway procession we were in before. I was able to find a spot after several boys. The parade of footsteps hit the floor in cadence, right-left, right-left, right-left.

Further up the line a boy stopped. All of the students behind him did so as well, except me. I ran into a redheaded boy. He stumbled into the guy before him. Like dominos, each person tumbled into the next until the wave hit Divina.

What have I done now?

CHAPTER 15

Thankfully, Divina was stable enough in her stance to stop the progression. Snapping her head back, she met my horrified eyes. Her expression went from shock, to a peculiar sense of relief.

"Oh, my gosh. I'm so sorry," I said to the red haired young man ahead of me. My cheeks felt hot.

The boy turned to me and smiled. "That's okay."

While bending to pick up his books, he said, "You caught me off guard. I'll be ready for you next time."

Humiliation lightened as he teased. This boy was unquestionably cast from different clay then the rest of the drones.

Is he allowed to make jokes? Wish I could ask him his name, but should probably zip it for a while.

The rest of the dominos refused to acknowledge the disruption even happened. They simply reorganized themselves and waited for their turn to proceed.

How odd they all are.

The catalyst for my clumsy demonstration waited for the opposing line to end. Once it did, he proceeded to the classroom on the other side of the hall. Sarah, Divina, and the kids ahead of me followed.

Must be Latin class.

A human-looking teacher met us at the door. "I have rearranged seating to accommodate our new student."

The thin, pale-haired man looked terribly inconvenienced.

"Please look for your name tag at your new desk," he said.

In a bit of an upheaval, students searched for their new location.

"Sophia, we're here," Divina called, slightly above a whisper from the last seat in the first row. She pointed ahead of her.

I promptly took a seat before I could cause any more havoc.

The teacher bobbed his head trying to control his annoyance.

"Alright class," he said. "Take your seats. If you haven't already heard, we have a new student named Sophia Templar. Sophia is not familiar with . . . anything. We will have to take things very slowly to allow her to catch up."

I sent him an indignant glare.

Who the hell is this jerk?

"I am Magi Brunaqua," he said as if he read my thought.

His tone left no doubt he knew there was no way I could catch up, and my presence was a complete nuisance.

"Open your texts to page seventy, and let's begin."

What an ass! Could he be any ruder? It's as though he scrambled the students on purpose to tick them off. I don't need any help getting them annoyed with me. I'm doing fine on my own, thank you, Magi Brown-Water.

Magi Brunaqua's jacket slipped off the coat rack in the corner and crumpled in a heap on the floor. He cocked his head at the occurrence. It was a might theatrical, if you ask me.

Ohhh, are you picking up on a sound only heard by awesome, windbag magicians? I mocked him to myself. *Did you feel a tremor with your super astute senses? What is it you are trying to convey?*

He stalked to the coat rack to return his jacket to its hook.

Stepping back to his stately position at the head of the class, he began a boring story. Dante walked on the bridge. Dante walked under the bridge. Dante walked to a dragon. Dante killed the dragon.

After each sentence the Magi spoke, students repeated in unison. I could not figure out what was so darn interesting about this Dante guy.

When, exactly, was he going to take things slow for the new student? I huffed to myself. *Wow, I better cool off. I wonder why he angered me so much. It's not like I've never been picked on before.*

I decided to think about something else for a while, so I scanned the classroom.

Vintage garments had a flashy, modern flare. All the girls wore dresses, and the boys wore exquisitely tailored jackets. Not everyone wore black. Although, the only bright colors appeared on the outer cloaks with inside clothes being various hues of navy blue, forest green, grey, black, and brown. It was apparent only faculty could get away with wearing lighter shades, evidenced by the off-white dress shirt and harsh copper-toned vest Magi sported.

"Sophia, are you listening? Or are we boring you?" Magi grumbled.

"Yes, Magi Brunaqua." I apologized. "I will pay better attention."

Under his breath he muttered, "Bardus humanus. Quare did they loco suus huic ordo? She'll nunquam utor Latin in suus vita."

Two girls beside me, one of them being Sarah, released a little giggle in response to the teachers rant. Swiftly collecting themselves, the girls covered their mouths, giving me the impression they were disturbed by their own lack of self-control.

After a short examination of the girl's unusual behaviors, I replied to the teacher, "To answer your question, Magi Brunaqua, I don't know why I was put in this class. And, you're correct in saying I'll never use Latin again in my life. I am also fairly certain it's not appropriate, in any realm, to call your student a stupid human."

A collective inhale swept the room.

Magi's jaw dropped.

The chimes sounded, informing us class was finished. Nobody moved.

"Class is over. Off you go," Magi finally snapped, before scuttling to his desk.

Divina stood beside me. She studied me for a long moment. I am not sure if she came to any conclusion, but she moved her head, indicating it was time to go to our next class.

CHAPTER 16

Massive mounds of clay waited to be molded on top of twenty small tables in the new classroom. A disembodied voice instructed each student to find a station that called to them.

I was the only one who scanned the room for the source of the voice. Once accepted that it must be a common experience for everyone else, I moved the only station left at the back of the room.

"Create," the voice boomed.

I stared at the mound hoping inspiration would strike. Other students had already dug their hands deep within their clay. They appeared well on their way to something promising.

"Feel the clay. Listen to what it tells you," the voice spoke at my ear.

Jumping slightly, I let out a nervous twitter, startling a few students ahead of me. They did not turn around, but I saw them twitch.

"Okay," I whispered in reply.

It must have come from a towering individual. That is, if he possessed a body, which I was not sure, he did.

Slapping my hands on the clay, I squeezed it between my fingers. The pliable texture was quite enjoyable. It smelled earthy and clean, unlike the modeling clay used in my other schools. I decided it must have been dug right out of a natural source, and it must be nearby.

My mind drifted to the walk into town earlier. The weather was gloomy, but I appreciated meeting the Ballios' friends. Though I never actually met Ada and Nickel Tucker, I saw where they lived. What an interesting home they had.

I imagined that at the back of the mini-mountain house, a pink push-mower would be found. And, there would be a pink shovel inside a pink tool shed. No wait . . . a purple tool shed. Perhaps they even had a wheelbarrow with flowers painted on it.

It would be very embarrassing for a dwarf man, or any man for that matter, to haul rocks and dirt around in a girly wheelbarrow.

The resonant bass voice chuckled beside me. It broke me from my daydream. "That's a remarkable likeness of him, Sophia."

"Of who," I asked.

"Nickel Tucker," the voice said.

Looking down at my clay mound, I saw the bust of a man who was not known to me. Heavy brows rested on top of generous, friendly eyes, and a beautiful open-mouth smile.

"Might you allow me to offer your project as a gift to Nickel? He would love it. It was he who donated the clay for the assignment. Dug it right from a pit in his backyard."

"Sure." I stood blankly.

I don't even remember molding it. Wow, it's good! Didn't think I was even capable of drawing myself out of a burlap sack.

"Good. If you're done, I'll take it to the kiln," the voice said.

"Yep, I'm done. Take it away," I joked, trying my best to sound casual.

The table I was working at lifted off the ground, floated to the front of the class, and out the front door.

Is this ever going to feel normal? And how was I able to make a sculpture of a man I had never met? Maybe Mr. Tucker was looking out his window this morning when we walked by, and my sub-conscience noticed him . . . but then, there weren't any windows on the front of the rocky home. Oh well.

I observed the class to see what everyone else was working on. Sarah was etching symbols into the sides of a bowl. It would not have shocked me if they were black magic, coming from a sour puss like her. Although, there were almost certainly rules about dark practices. Since she was ashamed to show emotion in public, she would definitely not be breaking greater laws.

Divina was molding a horse, or maybe it was a unicorn.

I'll have to remember to ask if unicorns are real.

Next to me, I saw a beautiful mocha-skinned guy with brilliant blue eyes. For some reason, the sculpture he was working on felt familiar. But why? It was a lovely young girl sitting with her legs curled to the side, and palms held open like she were waiting for a butterfly to land.

"That's fantastic," I complimented him and inched closer to get a better look.

The boy seemed uneasy with my closeness. In consideration for him, I matched his step in the opposite direction.

"Sorry," I said. "I don't mean to be nuisance. You're statue is amazing."

I thought for a moment. "That's it! Your project reminds me of the fountain in town square, or Main Street, or whatever you guys call it."

Narrowing his eyes, he sloped his head in what could be contemplation. After a short spell he spoke.

"The fountain in the Squares Centre was made by my great-grandfather, Asher Darius Griffiths. He made it to honor our queen."

"The faerie queen? I thought this district was without one." I questioned, remembering the stories Dio and Phaidra had told me.

With no expression, he stared at me. I hoped he was not thinking about blowing me up with his eyeballs or anything.

"He made it when she came into power, ninety-three years ago," he responded.

"Wow, he must have loved her," I commented.

He softly blew a puff of air from his nostril, while his mouth turned upward. In the land of humans, it could be construed as a chuckle.

"He was in love with her from what I understand."

"Really? Did she love him back?" My interest was piqued. "And, is this her?"

I hoped the boy was not getting irritated with all my questions. It seemed so intriguing. I was getting first-hand information about a fairytale, literally.

"No, it's just a girl, and I don't know if the queen loved him back. You would have to ask her. Unfortunately, you can't. She died long before her time."

The boy bowed his head. It was not the hard dip of someone waiting to get their head cut off, but a reverent acknowledgement of a beloved leader. Since he was either not born, or a toddler when the queen died, his genuine sorrow must have stemmed from stories retold by trusted sources.

Hmmm, they certainly seem to love their queen. She must have been a great gal.

"Long before her time?" I asked. "How long do faeries live?"

"The oldest known faerie is over three-hundred-years old. It's Queen Zarya from district six."

He reconsidered his statement.

"It's true, she is a faerie, but she is also part fish."

"She's a mermaid?" I gasped at the never-ending bombshells that continued to blow me away.

"We refer to them as water faeries. District Six is mostly underwater."

He wiped his hands on a cloth.

"I see. Do you know how old Calista was?" I asked.

"Great grandfather and Queen Calista were the same age. He tells me he was twenty when he made the fountain."

I did the math in my head. "So if she were still alive, they would both be around one hundred and thirteen years old. Did you say he told you? He's still alive?" I asked.

"He is King Darius of District Four," the boy replied.

"You're a faerie?" I asked happily. I am not sure why it excited me so.

"King Darius sort of assumed responsibility of my grandfather," the boy said open-ended.

Does that mean he was adopted or an illegitimate son? I could not ask, but really wanted to.

A ring sounded from what I could only imagine was an enormous brass bell.

"What's that for?" I felt a bit worried.

"It's the bell for lunch." The boy picked up his case from the floor.

"I'm sorry I didn't introduce myself. I'm Sophia Templar."

"I know." He took a partial step away before turning back to me. "I'm Asher Griffiths, the third."

CHAPTER 17

Ambrose Academy schooled over three hundred youths. Despite that count, only a soft murmur could be heard in the commissary. It was incredibly different from any cafeteria from my realm.

In the interest of symmetry, eight rows of nine tables were spaced evenly apart. Divina and I were the only occupants at our table. Others were mostly full. Embarrassed-to-laugh-Sarah and her nasty sidekick sat at a nearby table. The funny red-haired boy, whom I ran into in the hallway, and the great-grandson of a king, Asher Griffiths accompanied them.

Miss "sidekick" looked agitated. She reminded me of a bird the way she turned her head one way, before pausing to observe through her peripheral. She repeated this action on the other side before taking a bite of her bread.

Divina inspected me through hooded eyes. She definitely had something to say. I thought about asking what it was, but decided we were not well acquainted enough to press.

After lunch Divina walked me to my last class. For some reason it was exceptionally long—taking up two periods. It was located across the courtyard in a smaller building.

"I probably won't see you until tomorrow," Divina said after a long silence. "I can meet you at the front steps."

"That would be cool. Thanks Divina."

"Good bye for now."

"See-yah." I waved.

Upon entering the building, I came into a coatroom. Hooks ran the length of the wall. The coats were small in comparison to mine. Maybe the class was full of gnomes or elves.

I hung my wrap on the only remaining hook, and continued around the corner.

"Good afternoon, Sophia. Please take a seat." A three-foot-tall elf woman, with moderately pointed ears, greeted. With an open hand she directed me to the back row of four pew-like benches.

I was surprised when the students turned to me and smiled. The course was actually full of elementary-age wizard. I took a place between two little girls who appeared to be fraternal twins.

"You will make the perfect barrier for Tracy and Lacy." The Elven woman grinned through a clenched jaw. "We have had repeated discussions on how not to make poor choices, but they continue to press my buttons."

"Happy to be of service." I eyed the two innocent enough looking seven-year-olds.

Leaning toward the girl on my right, I teased, "You're not hiding a monster inside you, are you?"

"Oh, I hope not," she said with wide eyes.

"That's very good to hear. I once sat next to a girl with a monster inside. When she got too grumpy, the monster would reach out of her mouth, and tickle her nose with a feather until she laughed her grumpy away."

I lowered my voice to a whisper as if ready to divulge a great secret. The little girl, along with our teacher, and the rest of the class, drew nearer to hear.

"This doesn't sound so scary," I said. "But, it really interfered when she wanted to eat her favorite dessert . . . ice cream with strawberry syrup on top."

"What's ice cream?" asked a boy ahead of us.

"You've never had ice cream?" I questioned.

The children shook their heads.

How would I explain ice-cream to children?

"Let's say it sweet, silky snowball-clouds." I was not sure what point of reference I had to work with. "I'll have to make it for you sometime. That is, if you have cows. Or, goats I guess."

"We do!" Another boy twisted in his seat to hang over the back of his bench. "My uncle does. He's the Alcade, and I'm sure he would love to give us a cow for your ice cream."

I giggled. "I actually only need the milk, rather than the whole cow."

"I'll ask him next time I see him," the boy exclaimed.

"Okay Charles and children. As wonderful as ice cream sounds, we have to begin our lesson on stones." Mrs. Carita said, "Eyes front, please."

She uncovered a silver tray on her desk, which held a display of colored stones. While holding up a yellow and black stone she asked, "What is this one?"

Caught up in the energy of the room, my hand shot up. With all the enthusiasm of a seven-year-old I said, "I have that one in my lunch kit. I found it under an apple. Mrs. Ballios must have put it there."

"That's tiger eye, Sophia," Lacy explained to me from my side. "It's used for protection. It also strengthens the convictions and confidence of the bearer."

This kid sure knows her stuff.

"Awesome." I nodded in approval.

Lacy's eyes twinkled. Her brown ringlets and rosy cheeks reminded me of a porcelain doll that Elka kept on her dresser.

"I like you," she said.

"I like you, too."

I resisted the impulse to pick her up and cradle her in my arms. The girl was adorable. All of the children were.

The rest of the class was spent running through all of the stones and their uses. Mrs. Carita sent me home with a study guide, and advised there would be a test the next day.

Tracy and Lacy walked me most of the way to the front gates after school. They continued on with their mother who refused to look at me.

As promised, Dio and Phaidra waited for me. I was happy to see them, and to get back home. It had been a very long day.

CHAPTER 18

Phaidra sent me to my room when we got back to the cottage. Handing me a bowl of berries, she instructed me to begin studying at once.

"Elementary Charms and Stones—won't they be surprised," she muttered under her breath on her way out of my room.

"Pardon." I laughed a little over her apparent irritation with the school.

"Uh, well, we asked Shamus over tonight to give you a little tutoring."

It sounded as though she feared I would consider it an intrusion. In actuality, I was quite flattered they would want to help.

"That sounds great. Thanks," I replied.

Her face brightened. "You're welcome. Now get to work while I get dinner going."

Lazily, I lay back across my bed and began skimming the ten page study guide, starting with amethyst.

It read, *Greek meaning, without drunkenness. Protection against witchcraft and power to focus energy. Rub it across your forehead to ease headaches.*

"Huh. Interesting."

Engrossed with reading, awareness faltered. Two hours had passed. Dio knocked on the door to let me know supper was ready. I leapt from the bed and joined them in the kitchen.

"Hello again, lovely," Shamus greeted from the dinner table. "How was your first day at school?"

I sat next to him and explained everything. The story started with the creepy hallways, and subsequent demolition, then ended with Mr. Cranky Latin guy, and is co-worker, invisible man. You would have thought I was a standup comedian with the way they burst into hysterics over my awkward day.

After adding a mushroom skewer to my plate, I passed the platter to Phaidra.

"What's his name, anyways?" I was referring to the invisible art teacher.

"Dr. Sekou Akin. He transferred here about twenty-five years ago from Nakato-Lumina. District one," Shamus informed.

"Was he invisible back then?"

Pulling a mushroom off the skewer, I bit it in half. It was so juicy the liquid ran down my chin. I quickly wiped the drip and hoped nobody would mistake me for a savage. After scanning the table, it seemed they were all having the same issue.

"Yes," Shamus answered, as he rubbed mushroom juice from his chin.

"Has anyone ever seen him?" I asked. "Or, was he just born that way?"

"Lumina, the faerie queen of that district has seen him. She vouched for his integrity," Shamus explained. "He comes from a lineage of witch doctors. Although I'm sure he knows the trade, his field of study veers more towards science. In your world, he would be more of a PhD type. Other than that, he keeps his past private."

"If he's a genius science guy, then why does he teach art?" I asked.

"Maybe you should ask him," Phaidra suggested, while refreshing the ale in the men's mugs.

Shamus nodded to Phaidra in appreciation of his replenished mug, then grinned in my direction. "How did you find the youngsters of the school?"

"The little kids in my charms class seem normal, but the teenagers are . . . I don't know." I searched for the best way to describe them. "Repressed robots."

Shamus laughed. "You're right on the money, sweetheart."

"What's the deal?" I asked. "Are they all under a spell or something?"

Phaidra replied, "Ever since witches left the human world they have tried to phase out human emotion. They feel it makes them weak."

"But you guys don't act that way," I pointed out. "Even Magi Brunaqua displays more passion than they do."

"Yes, but remember, wizards stayed in the Earth realm longer than we did," Phaidra explained. "The wounds run much deeper for them. As for Magi Brunaqua, he has family in your world, and has spent some time there. From what I hear, they don't care for him much either." She sounded a touch gossipy.

"Oh dear, that was very uncharitable," Phaidra scolded herself. "I shouldn't say such things."

Shamus chuckled. "In Desta, wizard people teach their children to refrain from anything other than fact and logic. Order and uniformity are foremost in their minds."

"That's why most of us wee folk live outside the gates," Dio grumbled. "Order is great, but being bullheaded is quite another."

"Okay Dio." Phaidra stood to clear the dishes. "Now that dinner is over, we'll leave Shamus and Sophia to their studies."

"Sounds good." Shamus winked. "Maybe after, you can fill me in a bit more about your Miss. Luna."

"You have a thing for Miss. Updar?" I smiled.

Shamus chuckled as he took his empty plate to the sink. He made no attempt to hide his interest in the woman.

"She is a very attractive lady."

"Yes she is." I giggled.

A knock came on the door. Dio rose to receive it.

"Good evening, please come in," he said welcoming the visitors on the other side.

It was the man from my sculpture. A lovely little woman stood by his side.

"You must be Nickel and Ada Tucker." I rose to shake their hands, knowing they would not be offended by my contact the way witches were. "Very nice to meet you."

The couple chuckled.

"It is good to meet you, too, Sophia," Ada said. "We were already on our way to deliver a few outfits Phaidra ordered when Dr. Akin called to drop off a present."

"Good timing, I must say." Nickel's grin practically lit up the room. "Now, we get to thank you for the pies and the sculpture."

"You're very welcome, and thank you for the incredible outfits. You guys are super talented. You should be designing for the runways of New York," I replied.

I inspected the three new dresses, cloaks, and footwear that Ada handed me. A closer look would have to come later. However, I knew they would be elegant, and acceptable within the constraints of the school. A hint of rebellious sass to set them apart from the rest of the student outfits was also certain.

Phaidra pulled a small sack from her apron pocket and offered it to Ada.

"That's not necessary, Phaidra." Nickel held up his hand. "Let's consider it a birthday present for our new friend."

Phaidra thanked them, and replied, "It's so generous of you both. Won't you join us in the living room for some ale, or tea?" She motioned for them to have a seat on the sofa.

"I'd love a mug of ale." Nickel rested his hand on his midsection.

"I'll take some tea," Ada said.

"What's this about a sculpture?" Dio asked Nickel as they took a seat in the living room. Ada followed Phaidra to the kitchen to help her with refreshments. Shamus and I remained at the kitchen table to get to work on Charms. In a short while, the pleasant chatter from the living room was blocked out by my elf friend's informative studies.

After I developed a good handle on charms and stones, Nickel joined our conversation. His specialty was metals and minerals. With their combined knowledge, more facts than could be found in any text book filled my information banks. They both delighted in sharing.

Time passed quickly. It was getting late into the evening. With a yawn, I excused myself from the crowd and put myself to bed.

CHAPTER 19

Towering trees encircled me. Branches seemed to salute in the gentle breeze. They were letting me know they were armed to be my sentry. At first glance all forests could appear the same, although, I had been here before. It was evident immediately by the way it made me feel. I was protected.

Thoughts brought me to the same forest I had been to days before, when making pies. I figured it was another day dream, or nighttime brain wander. It happened from time to time. I had grown to consider them a normal escape that everyone experienced.

Hearing a particular song hummed in the distance confirmed it. I recalled it from my childhood. Not knowing where the tune originated, I used to imagine my mother sang it to me as a baby. A more probable reality was that it came from an old commercial.

As a child, I called it the "cry song." It was not necessarily sad, but the rise and fall of melody drew out emotions I was trying to hide. It haunted me. It forced me to feel.

I held the special song close to my heart.

The song drew me along a well-worn path. It opened to the purple body of water that I came across in previous dreams. A fair-haired girl, maybe a bit younger than me, danced to her own hum.

As a kid, Mrs. Tifton was the neighbourhood shrink. On our duplex steps, I often ran into ladies who were on the way in for a chatty coffee-and-Danish consultation. If this scenario was run past her, I bet she would have said the singing girl was a projection of me.

Only the back of the dancer could be seen as she gracefully swayed her arms, so I could not be sure. The way she leapt about however, felt familiar . . . just the way I would move.

Quietly, I tiptoed behind and joined her in step. What could be more fun than dancing with yourself?

After a few symbiotic skips and dips, my voice merged with hers. A few bars carolled out before the girl whirled around in alarm.

With a scowl, she zeroed in on me, raising a pointed arm. An unseen force hit me in the chest and hurled me backwards. I became winded as my back slammed into a tree. Rough bark from a trunk scraped my right arm.

Even through her twisted expression, the girl was beautiful. And definitely not me.

"What are you doing here? No one is allowed access to this forest." She lifted and hovered across the ground to meet me.

Looming above, her slender arm poised, ready to administer another mystical blow.

"Does it matter?" I felt for my arm, inspecting it to see what damage had been done. "It's my dream. I can go where I want."

Argh, I groaned, *another scrape. I'm getting tired of this.*

"What?" she replied. "You think you're dreaming!"

"Uh, yeah." Sliding with caution, I held my hands up in surrender and got to my feet. "I'm still in my night gown, and the last thing I remember was going to bed. Plus I've been here before. It's my special imaginary place."

"Your place?" She chuckled and dropped her hand to the side. "Okay, so, I am imaginary too?"

"You must be," I answered. "At first, I thought you might be a reflection of me. But I would never toss myself into a tree, so clearly you represent something else in my mind."

She laughed. "Are you often aware you are dreaming, when you're dreaming?"

"Yeah, it happens sometimes, more so, since I've gotten to Celsus."

"What do you mean 'gotten to Celsus?' Where were you before?"

"Earth. Dio and Phaidra Ballios took me in."

"Are you human?"

I nodded.

"What's that mark on your arm?" She signaled with her head to my scar.

"I don't know. It's been there for as long as I can remember."

"Why did you think I was you, in your so-called dream?" she asked.

"The song you were singing. It's been in my head my entire life."

"I see." Her feet lowered to the ground. Probably so she could get a better look at me. "How long have you been with the Ballios in Desta's Court?"

"Not long," I replied. "But, we don't live in Desta Court? It's the town of Desta, in Calista Court."

"What?" the girl gasped. "Calista doesn't rule this land."

"Not anymore. She died nearly two decades ago."

"How did she die?"

The news must have been devastating. Her face went white.

"I'm not sure anyone knows, but people still seem to miss her terribly. She must have been a great leader."

The girl stumbled back, absently replying, "I always liked her."

"Hey, are you okay?" I clutched her arm.

"Sure, it's just not every day you hear about your own--" she broke from thought to examine me again. "Why do you live with the Ballios? Where are your parents?"

"I've never known them. I've been in foster care for . . . forever, it seems."

"You've never known your mother?"

She grabbed my hand in hers.

I stared at them, pondering her unusual gesture.

Minutes before, she flung me across the forest. Now, she wished to bring me comfort. Perhaps, it should not have shocked me. Dreams rarely followed natural rules of conduct.

"It's no big deal. You can't miss what you never knew," I said.

I felt a twinge of emotion. It made me feel vulnerable, so I pulled away to observe some flowers.

"I bet you look like your mother," the young girl offered, moving up behind me. "Maybe you even got some features from your father."

She swept the scar on my arm with her fingertips. It made my skin warm and tingly.

"Maybe," I replied.

"What's your name?"

"I am Sophia."

She expressed amusement. It sounded like a gentle hum.

"I've always been partial to that name. I have a dear friend named Fi Fi. I like to tease her about stealing her name and giving it to my first born."

Oh yeah, Fi Fi could be a shortened nickname for Sophia.

"That wouldn't work out very well if you had a boy." I turned to her.

She giggled. "That's true. Although, years from now, when that time comes, I think I'll be having a girl."

"How can you be so sure?"

"Sometimes things are revealed to you," she said. "It can be confusing. You don't always have to know why or how. You just need to allow yourself to believe." She gazed upon me. "I also know that you will do remarkable things, Sophia. It's ordained."

"Ordained?" I asked, and then thought better of it. "Okay, we'll go with that."

"I know who you are, Sophia."

"Wonderful, cause it's my dream, and I still have no idea who you are." My reply could have been considered a touch flippant.

Her laugh chimed harmoniously. It sounded a bit unreal, yet pleased my ears.

"My sister is going to be back soon," she said. "You should go before she sees you. She's more of a gust-first-and-interrogate-later kind of faerie."

"Gust?" I laughed. "Is that what you just did? Okay, whatever. I don't know how I got here, but maybe if I just wander along I'll find a way home."

"Yes you will." She smiled. "I look forward to meeting you again. Sophia."

"You too," I gave her the gun fingers sign as I backed up towards the path.

CHAPTER 20

"Goodness me, Sophia. We slept in!" Phaidra squealed at my door.

I shot up like a gun fighter in the Wild West. Phaidra had already closed the door. Hurried footsteps scampered across the kitchen floor.

Bounding out of bed, I grabbed the first outfit seen from the wardrobe and threw it on.

Very cool, I thought when paused in front of the mirror. It was a straight cut, chocolate brown dress with matching mid-calf boots from the Tuckers.

Dio called from the door as I headed for the bathing room. "We have to go, dear. Can you make it on your own?"

"Yeah, absolutely," I called back through a partially opened door.

"Your lunch is on the table," Phaidra instructed before they rushed out the door. "Grab some nuts and juice on your way."

Brush teeth. Wash face. That is all I had time to do. I wrapped myself in a green velvet cloak, grabbed my leather satchel, lunch basket, and jumped for the door handle.

A violent gust blew against the door. It forced me into the side of the house. Pain stuck my right side as I slammed into the stone wall. I shook it off and heaved the door closed.

Hesitant to attempt the weird hallways without my new comrade, Divina, I stopped outside the school. Mid-way up the limestone steps, I leaned against the banister to review my study guide.

My flailing cloak had other ideas. As I started to read, it began to lift overhead. I caught it around my neck.

Asher and the red-haired boy approached the school. They were accompanied by the most gorgeous guy ever created. With an alluring air of confidence, he seemed to guide the boys, even though they walked beside him. I surely would have noticed that stunning creature yesterday with his adorable wavy ash blond hair.

Hello stranger.

He looked up at me as if he heard what I was thinking. Of course, that was impossible. I think. Realizing I was gawking, I dropped my view to the study guide.

Quartz was the only word read before the wind blew up again. Its mission was to snatch the paper from my grasp. Whirling my hand around, I trapped the paper against my midsection, and prayed the nearing boys had not witnessed the circus act.

Before composure resumed, my cloak caught a mischievous current and took flight. Stretching arms, I attempted to reclaim it but was too late. The cape danced above as if to tease me. It continued its journey across the path. I huffed in frustration. The red-haired boy caught the action and tried to grab my cloak. It faintly exceeded his reach.

With a calm ease, the middle guy raised his arm. I thought for a second he might be mocking me, but then a blue streak of lightning shot from his hand and connected with the taunting cloak. My wrap instantly drew down to his waiting grasp. He strode to within a few paces of me and offered my cloak.

I nonchalantly perused his slim, sturdy build before meeting deep green eyes, which surely could coax me into sinful acts.

"Thank you," finally rolled out.

Clearly unaffected by me, Mr. Gorgeous barely replied, "You're welcome." Then, he stepped past with his friends.

I sighed inside.

Asher and the red-haired boy turned back to silently greet me.

I felt a tap on my shoulder and turned. It was the strangest sight. Divina was beaming. This was a completely different girl than I met yesterday.

"I have so much to ask you," Divina said.

"Ask away," I offered.

"For starters, what are you?"

She asked with all of the anticipation of a child waiting to open their presents at Christmas.

I cleared my throat. "I'm human. What are you?"

Committed in her goal, she reacted with acceptance.

"You don't want to talk about it now, fine," she said. "But answer me this. How do you know Latin? I don't know a lot about Earth realm, but I know Latin is not readily taught, at least not to a simpleton youth."

Divina appeared unaware that calling me a simpleton was actually insulting. I let it go.

"I don't know what you're talking about. I have no idea how to speak Latin. Never heard it before in my life," I answered.

Divina exhaled. "Sophia, please, I don't understand. Is this what humans call a joke?"

Her optimistic demeanor faded. "Latin was spoken to the entire class, and Magi Brunaqua insulted you. All I could make out was 'stupid human,' but you had to have known what he said in order to reply to him the way you did. You sent him into such a tizzy. No one's ever been able to ruffle him the way you did."

I got the impression she was congratulating me. I decided to play along for a bit. It seemed to mean so much to her.

"Did I speak back in Latin?"

"No, you answered in English."

The bell sounded, alerting us to get to class.

"Maybe we should talk about it later," I suggested.

Divina consented and I followed her to our first class of the morning. Poetry.

I took the same seat as the day before. It was in front of Laughing Sarah. The gorgeous lightning bolt guy sat three seats back, in the next row. The seat was vacant the prior day.

This guy must be Saban, Laughing Sarah's brother. No wonder he was so cold to me. She probably already told him all about my blunder-filled first day.

"Good to have you back with us, Mr. Chariot. I trust you had a good trip," Miss Updar asked Saban.

In a detached eloquence, Saban Chariot replied, "It was quite productive. Thank you, Miss Updar."

I see! The pieces of the puzzle started to come together. Chariot was his name. *He must be Eve Chariot's son. Eve didn't take much of a shine to me. Guess I can forget about being friends with either of these guys.*

"Okay youngsters, let us begin. Yesterday, I asked you to write me a bit about where you think your strength comes from. Who would like to start? Sophia?" Miss Updar stood eagerly in front of my desk.

"Umm . . ." I stumbled, and motioned with my head for her to come closer. The little teacher's lips curled up at the corners, and she tilted an ear in my direction. I whispered, "I'm sorry, I mean no disrespect. The Ballios arranged for Mr. Shamus to tutor me for my Charms and Stones class. Before I knew it, the night was gone. Could I have more time please?"

"Mr. Shamus, you say." Her expression brightened at the mention of his name. "Of course, dear. Things must be overwhelming for you right now."

Miss Updar posed the question again to the class. Sarah's sidekick, who was seated in the row closest to the door, put up her hand.

"Yes, Shea. Please share with us."

Shea, the dark haired bird girl, opened a leather folder and read her paragraph. "I get strength from the knowledge that my family's lineage is wizard. In recent days, I have also come to appreciate my supremacy in being a magic. Some beings give the illusion of being the same due to similar genetic proportions. In reality they are weak, pathetic facsimiles who have not yet evolved past something comparable to a clumsy howler monkey."

Ouch! Is that meant for me?

"Oh, I see." Miss Updar searched for words. "I am not accustomed to you expressing such extreme sentiment, Shea. Uhhh . . . good work," she said in an alarmed approval. "Does anyone else have a feeling about what Miss Harlo has shared?"

A boy in the row next to Shea raised his hand.

"Yes, Thaddeus," Miss Updar said.

"Wa . . . wa . . . well, I th . . . think the only ill . . . illusion is in the false sense of strengths. If one has not yet reached their pa . . . potential, then they are still able to adapt. This makes them somewhat more suh . . . superior."

If I did not know better, I would think the stuttering boy was defending me.

"Is tha . . . tha . . . that so, Thaddeus?" Shea venomously mocked.

A chorus of shocked inhalations could be heard.

Saban twisted in Shea's direction and sent her a cautioning glare.

Realizing her outburst was unacceptable, she shifted her head toward her paper.

What a strange exchange. True, she was terribly rude, but to be silently chastised by another student for an action that would be commonplace in my old school?

Miss Updar had high hopes for her assignment, but things had veered off course.

"Alright then, I think we are going to take a tiny step back to poem writing, as it relates to spells. We can revisit this section at a later date. Please open to chapter four entitled, Rhyming Words, and if Harris could begin reading," she directed to the redheaded boy.

CHAPTER 21

Sitting across from Divina at the oak lunch table, I enjoyed a perfect view of Saban who had joined the group including Asher, Sarah, Shea and Harris. I considered myself ridiculous for still admiring the guy after the way he dismissed me earlier, but I could not help it.

He appeared to be lecturing Shea. Perhaps about her conduct concerning that Thaddeus kid. After Saban was done with his speech, he lowered his head to study the contents of his lunch.

Shea took the opportunity to shoot him proverbial daggers. Sarah, who sat next to Shea, witnessed the exchange. I could see the wheels spinning. In what direction, I was not sure. Did it bother Sarah to see a friend give her brother dirty looks?

"Hey, what's the deal with that group over there?" I asked Divina.

Popping a blackberry into her mouth, she turned to see what I was viewing.

"They are Harris and Shea Harlo, children of Herb and Fiona Harlo who own the apothecary. Saban and Sarah Chariot are children of Eve and Lee Chariot. Lee is Alcade of Desta. And, finally we have Asher Griffith's. He is the son of Cinder Anne Griffiths who is an RBI." Divina's monotone made a comeback.

I was not particularly concerned in what the parents did, but now that she mentioned it, I was intrigued.

"Apotha-what, and what's an RBI?"

I tossed some almonds in my mouth.

"Apothecaries are similar to your pharmacists, and RBI stands for Realm Bureau of Investigation," Divina replied before returning her attention to her lunch basket.

"Interesting," I returned my view to the tables in the commissary. Again, I noted the groupings of students. Everyone seemed to have a cluster of five or more, except ours.

Where would Divina be if she wasn't babysitting me? Does she have a gang of friends to hang around with? Is she a loner? Could I find a way to ask without calling attention to it?

Can't imagine why she wouldn't have friends. Divina seems great. She's a pretty girl, smart, friendly. Hmmm . . . friendly. A smile does seem to come easier to her than the other up-tight individuals. Maybe it's just because of her nearness to me. Maybe I rub some human off on her. What a funny thought . . . I'm contagious!

I laughed.

Maybe Miss Holbrook was already predisposed to smile easily, but she certainly tried to hide it. Is Divina a reformed radical? Is she trying to mask her happy outlook in order to fit in? It looks to be too late, because the students have already cast her out for her merry ways.

"What do your parents do?" I hoped the question was not too personal.

"My dad is a doctor and my mom paints." She took a sip of tea from a canning jar.

That's an neat reusable cup.

"Really, what does she paint? Houses?" I asked.

Divina looked at me strangely, almost like she was trying to figure out if I was insulting her. "No," she answered. "Pictures."

"That sounds great. Does she paint landscapes or people?"

With a different strange look Divina replied, "Both."

"I would love to see her work. Bet she's wonderful."

Her expression elevated.

"Maybe you could stop by my house on your way home today. The Ballios are working there, so you can meet up with them."

"Sounds like a plan." I smiled back. "Hey, do you want to walk outside a bit before we have to go to our next class?"

Divina thought for a moment. "You know, I would."

Earth-colored flat stones paved an area at the back of the school. Divina called it the courtyard. Unusual trees and statues dotted the grounds, while a magnificent gazebo resided in the far corner.

The courtyard nestled inside emerald grassland that extended to a forest marked by old, deep-rooted trees. Many students strolled in and out of the courtyard, or sat contentedly on its many benches and picnic tables.

"Amazing!" I remarked.

"Yes, it is lovely. I used to come out here a lot, but now I mostly read in the commissary until afternoon classes," Divina commented.

This was my chance to find out a bit more about Divina.

"So, how long have you spent your afternoons indoors . . . alone?" I asked as we wandered.

"Since the beginning of the school year," Divina answered.

"What happened before that?"

"I moved here in the middle of last year. No one even acknowledged my existence for the first few weeks. Then, I met Daphne and Wisteria. They're over there."

Following her gaze, I saw two girls sitting at a picnic table near the gazebo. A blonde and a brunette sat primly with their backs against the table, one foot tucked behind the other. Their haircuts were identical. Long and straight with bangs cut flat across their foreheads about half an inch above thin, manicured eyebrows.

"I started spending all of my time with them, in school and out. We spent a lot of afternoons at Daphne's house. Her mother was gone a lot. That left the spell rooms open to us whenever we wanted."

Divina turned to me like she had just decided I could be trusted with her secrets.

"We found an ancient spell-book, and figured we'd try our hands at a few of them. It was fun. We sat at the fountain in town's center and would manifest rodents on the shoulders of anyone who passed by."

She stifled a giggle.

"We rearranged a few ornaments on Daphne's neighbor's lawn and watched them scramble. At first, they wondered where their items had gone. When they realized their neighbors had their possessions, they began to bicker. Voices got raised, fists got raised, and then they began to use magic on each other."

She fiddled with her fingertips for a moment as if trying to decide how much to tell me.

"Things had definitely gone too far. I pleaded with the girls to come and explain what we had done, but all they did was laugh. I had no other option. I ran into the middle of the feud and screamed, 'It's me. I did it!' Mr. Jasper had already hurled a tree stump through Mr. Beatty's front window, but they stopped when I admitted my crime."

I could feel her discomfort and reluctance to admit her role.

"The men marched me home to my mortified parents. I ended up telling them everything and was grounded from ever seeing the girls outside of school. The grounding was irrelevant. They had already ex-communicated me."

"Did those girls ever get in trouble for what they did?" I asked.

"No, and I am not about to tell on them either. They're scary."

I could see the fear in Divina eyes.

"Do you think they're still playing dangerous pranks on people?" I asked.

"They can try, but they're not strong enough right now to do too much damage. The only reason we were able to pull off the other spells was because there is a certain power in numbers."

"What do you mean they're not strong enough yet?" I asked.

"Magical beings aren't just born with a full range of powers. We develop them as we mature. Most wizards our age are able to perform minor illusion spells, more brain trickery. For instance, I can make you think that this necklace is a serpent."

Cupping the chain around her neck, it morphed into a yellow snake.

Jumping back, I gulped, "I hate snakes!"

Divina let a friendly giggle slip through her lips. She made no attempt to hide it.

"It's okay, Sophia. It's just an illusion. That's what I mean. We're not old enough to actually make a snake appear. A good number of wizards never even evolve past illusion."

The snake disappeared. Distress eased.

"So, you can do illusion . . . and move stuff with your mind?"

"Moving objects is pretty advanced, but some wizards have a natural affinity in certain areas," Divina explained.

"But, Saban shot a lightning bolt from his hand, and willed my cloak into his grasp." I protested, remembering the morning.

"What a show off," she said. "He seems to be one of those exceptions to the rule. For whatever reason, Saban is a little stronger than the rest of us. And, he knows it."

A loud whoop-whoop sound came from above. We looked to the sky and saw a giant creature coming straight for us. Students gasped.

CHAPTER 22

Gerard set down softly and nodded to the two of us.

"Hello there, Sophia and friend."

"Hey, Gerard. What do you have there?" I pointed to the basketball under his arm. "Did you bring it back from Earth realm?"

"No, but somebody else must have. I found it in the sanitation grounds and thought it might bring you joy. I washed it in Calista's river."

Gerard held the ball out to me.

"That's very considerate. Thanks, Gerard."

I accepted the ball and pressed it between my hip and forearm. Divina leaned away like it was a bucket of acid.

"How did you know where to find me?" I asked.

"Friends told me they heard Eve Chariot muttering about a human child joining Ambrose." Gerard's answer implied there was more to that story, but he was not going to tell. "How are you finding school?"

"It's different."

I did not want to say too much and risk hurting the person standing next to me.

"Ask me again at the end of the week." I laughed.

"Will do," Gerard said. "I hate to drop and run, but I'm headed back on assignment. I just wanted to give that to you. I'll check in with you later."

"Okay, good to see you," I said as he launched back into the air as quickly as he had landed.

"No problem." Gerard two-finger saluted from above.

"That's something you don't see every day," Divina said.

"The gargoyle or the basketball?" I chuckled. I would think in magic realm, seeing a gargoyle coming in for a visit would be routine.

"Both. What is that?" She pointed to the ball.

"It's a basketball. You can play games with it," I explained.

She looked at me blankly.

"Basketball is team sport, in which two teams of five players, try to score points by throwing a ball through the top of a basketball hoop."

Divina remained unmoved.

"Here, let me show you." I spotted two trees that had crossing branches, leaving a space in the middle to act as a hoop. I showed Divina how the ball bounced off the ground.

"This is called dribbling."

"Dribbling?" She appeared disturbed.

After explaining the general rules, I decided a demonstration would be the best course of action. I dribbled to the hoop made of interwoven branches, stopped short, and, with a flip of my wrist, tossed the ball through the opening.

"Can I try?" Divina asked, still hesitant.

"Of course." I was not sure if she was ready to catch a ball, so I walked over to where she was and handed it to her.

Divina bounced the ball once and grabbed it. "Hmmm," she said studiously and began to bounce it again.

"Very good," I cheered. "See if you can walk while dribbling."

Divina frowned at the word dribbling but took a step, and then another, until she was in front of the hoop.

"Good. Now, raise your arms and flick your wrist." I mimed the motion.

Divina did as I told her, but the ball was not even close. "Ah darn," she grumbled.

"It's okay. Try again." I collected the ball and handed it back. Standing next to her, I pretended to bounce an imaginary ball, and then rose up to shoot it.

"Do it with me."

She bounced the ball as I had.

I followed along with my pretend motions.

While keeping me in her peripheral, she rose up and the ball swept neatly through the branches.

"Alright, Divina! Great job."

"I did it!" She beamed.

When recovering the ball, I became aware of the commotion we were making. In my old schools, play was ordinary, but here it could be considered disturbing. Almost everyone stopped what he or she were doing and stared in our direction.

I held a hand up and motioned, "Sorry."

The majority of students went back to what they were doing before the basketball exhibition, but a few came in for a closer look. I figured it was either out of curiosity or to get a better feel for how to shut us up.

"Okay, so I'm going to pass you the ball. Are you ready?" I asked Divina.

"Yes," she answered eagerly.

I tossed the ball gently, but I guess she had no idea what to expect. She doubled over making a loud "ooof" sound as the ball hit her in the stomach and bounced away to the feet of one of our onlookers.

Stopping the ball with a size ten, penny-loafer, a hefty girl towered over me. I gulped.

Size ten bent down to pick up the ball. Time could not have moved slower. Once she raised, hazel eyes bore into me. I was definitely going to die.

With a great force, she threw the ball back. I caught it before it slammed me in the chest. That would have hurt.

"Hey great pass, that's right," I commended.

"Can I try?" Size-ten asked in a soft, deep tone.

Divina and I swapped baffled glances.

"Absolutely," I answered, pretending there was never any fear.

Grabbing a coin from my lunch basket, I placed it on the ground where a reasonable free throw line would be. "How about you try free-throwing first? Stand here." I directed her to the coin.

The girl trudged to the marker and tossed the ball as I had shown Divina. She missed. A grunt sounded from her chest.

"No problem, it takes some practice. Try again."

"Can I try too?" A boy called from a growing group.

"Yeah," I replied. "Why don't you come line up behind . . . umm?" I did not catch her name.

"Misty," the large girl answered.

"Line up behind Misty," I called out.

There must have been two dozen students crowded around.

"Does anyone else want to try?" I posed to the crowd.

Six inquisitive students raised their hands. I was truly shocked. Judging by Divina's reaction, she was too.

"Alright," I said. "Why don't you all line up and give it a whirl."

Two girls and six boys formed line and took turns shooting. Divina and I acted as ball gophers and cheerleaders. Tiny cracks of pleasure crept through a couple faces.

Scanning the rest of the grounds, I saw that everyone who was not playing had stopped in their tracks. Some had expressions of muddle on their faces. Others wore smidgens of grief. Most observed, as if they were studying something they had never seen before. I suppose that was the reality of the situation.

Bells chimed, alerting us to afternoon classes and a collective moan was heard among the players.

"Could you bring the ball again tomorrow?" Misty asked.

"Yeah, definitely," I replied.

"What do you make of that?" Divina asked as we watched the kids return to school.

"That was crazy."

Divina looked at me confused. I imagine she did not understand my use of the word crazy.

"It was odd, but fun." I tried again.

"It was fun." Divina beamed. "Okay, I'll meet you at the gate after school, and we can go to my house."

"I'll be there. Can't wait to meet your mom."

Divina waved then dispersed with the rest of the crowd. I tucked the basketball under some bushes, and happily went off to class. I loved being with the little kids, although, I did have a test coming up.

Hope my studying has paid off.

CHAPTER 23

After placing my belongings on a long bench in the coatroom, I rounded the corner to join my classmates.

"Sophia!" Children cheered at my arrival.

"Hello, beautiful ladies and gents. How are we all today?" I took a seat between Tracy and Lacy.

Obviously, the question was too broad. Every student huddled close and began to churn out all the toils of their day.

"Alright, children." Mrs. Carita entered the room. "We'll have to talk about it later. Right now you have a test."

A resounding "ahhh" sounded from the children, and they returned to their seats. I watched and copied the children as they unlatched an airplane-seat-style workstation from the back of the seat in front of them.

Mrs. Carita sat at her desk. Glancing to the wall clock beside her, she said, "Okay students, you have one hour to complete your test. When you're done, I want you to bring the tests to my desk. Then you can read silently until everyone else is finished."

The test was as easy as making pie. I completed it in twenty minutes. After placing my test on Mrs. Carita desk, I started back for the bench.

"Sophia, one moment," Mrs. Carita whispered. Reaching into her desk, she pulled out a second test, and handed it to me. "Why don't you try this one also?"

"Okay." I took the test and returned to my workstation.

While skimming the fifty-question exam, I became excited. A closer look told me that, thanks to my private tutoring session with Shamus and Nickel, all the answers resided in my noggin.

What great luck!

After completing the second exam at the same time as the last student finished his first, I followed him to the teacher's desk to deposit it.

"Well done, Sophia." Mrs. Carita was drawing a red circle around a capital A on my first test.

"You marked it already?" My stomach did a little dance. I was relieved to know I had at least the knowledge of a first grader.

"Yes." She received my second exam. "Would you do me a favor and entertain the children for the last bit of class. I'd like to get the rest of these marked."

"Absolutely. Can I take them outside and play some games?" I asked.

They were wizard children, so I was not sure if they were allowed to play games.

"Sounds perfect," the teacher replied.

I led the children outdoors. We found a nice spot to play just beyond the entrance. The children's schoolhouse rested a fair distance from the main school. This allowed a side view of the courtyard.

Divina and her classmates followed behind their teacher. They were examining various flora that surrounded the school. Divina waved merrily when she saw me, and I waved back. Saban witnessed our interchange. I shook my head at his disapproving expression.

That guy is such a bore. I can see I'm going to have to spend all of my time with children, if I am to have any fun here.

Attention returned to the children huddled around me.

"Has anyone ever played duck-duck-goose?"

Everyone got a turn picking the goose before the end-of-the-day bell rang. Mrs. Carita came outside as the children hopped up to go inside.

"You haven't been here long, but I am sure going to miss you." The teacher spoke from my side.

"Why? Where am I going?" I peered down at her.

"Your test tells me you are far too advanced for elementary. The second test suggests you can skip past the next few levels." She patted the small of my back. "You'll have to go to see Head Mistress Aristotle tomorrow morning for your new schedule. Good luck, dear."

"Thank you, Mrs. Carita." I could not help but feel a little sad. *This was the most normal class here.*

Mrs. Carita went to help the children with their coats as Divina approached.

"I thought we were meeting at the gate?" I asked her.

"I know," Divina bubbled over. "I couldn't wait to tell you what I overheard."

"Hang on I'll be right back," I said and ran inside to grab my stuff. After saying a few good byes to the remaining students, I returned outside to Divina. She looked like she was going to explode at any moment, if she did not reveal her story immediately.

"What's the scoop?" I asked.

Her jiggling stopped. "The scoop?"

I smiled. "What did you overhear?"

Enthusiasm returned. "When we were studying the herbs and plants, Saban looked over at you. He said, 'she's such a disruption"

Divina flipped her eyes upward, putting her hands on her hips as she voiced Saban's words. I'm sure she was only adding in her own interpretation of his attitude. Even with the little knowledge I had of Saban, it was clear he would never make such a gesture.

"Ouch. That's what you couldn't wait to tell me? I could have survived not knowing that Mr. Chariot thinks I'm a disruption."

Divina giggled, "Yeah, I know, but then Asher said, 'I don't know, I find her pleasant to converse with.' Then Harris got into it, too, saying, 'I find her pleasant to look at."

After pausing for breath she continued. "Saban glared at them, and asked 'what's wrong with you two? You're completely different since she got here.'"

Divina comically provided each speaker with a different voice.

"It was almost gallant the way Asher stepped in to defend your honor. I think he feels passion towards you."

"Passion? Toward me? I think you are using that word incorrectly, my friend," I mused as we walked towards the gates.

"Then, Shea shoved Harris on the back of his shoulder." Divina progressed with the story. "Oh Sophia, you should have seen Saban's face. I've never seen him look so mad. He whipped around and said, 'You two have been acting like . . . like humans!"

"What's with that guy?" I snarled. "Why does he hate me so much?"

"Forget about him. He's a troll. And, so is his sister," Divina snapped.

My jaw dropped. Giggling was odd enough for a witch in this bottled-up town, but a heated outburst? It was enough to make me feel almost . . . well . . . relaxed.

"Where did that come from, Divina?"

"Sorry. I've just been holding it in for so long. Guess I feel safe with you, which is a little scary. The last people I let myself slip with turned out to be psychotic little imps."

"My goodness, you're letting it all out, aren't you?" I laughed.

"I am. Please, forgive me," she pleaded. "You have no idea what it's like to be so subdued. It wasn't like this where I used to live."

"Where were you before?"

We veered to the right when we got outside the school gates.

"We lived in Elle-Gloria, District Nine," she answered.

"And, people there were happy? They could laugh and cry freely?" I asked.

"There are more faeries and elves than wizards," she answered. "It's partially the ratio that makes things so uptight here."

"It's the wizards who have a problem with feelings, huh?" I asked.

"Not all of them. Although, it's certainly the case in Calista's Court," Divina answered. "Eve Chariot has a lot to do with it. She is the Alcade's wife, and has a lot of influence over the citizens."

After passing a couple houses, we stopped in front of a white picket fence. It surrounded a blue and white colonial home with a horrid, dirt-only yard. Rolling a boulder bigger than her, a familiar face entered the front yard from the back.

"Phaidra, what are you doing?" I called.

CHAPTER 24

"Can't you use your magic for this?" I rushed to her side and began pushing. "You're going to break your back."

"It is getting tiring." Phaidra panted. "Unfortunately, powers are on the fritz. I have to do it all by hand."

Divina put a hand on the little woman's shoulder. "You should stop until your powers return, Mrs. Ballios. This is too much."

"Maybe you're right, dear. I'm going to go tell Dio that we need to call it a day," Phaidra agreed. "I'll come around in a moment to inform your mother."

"Okay. Sophia and I will be inside." Divina smiled naturally.

Phaidra did a double take before returning to the backyard. Divina's more upbeat persona probably shocked her as well.

We stepped onto a white, wraparound porch. A rush of warmth welcomed us as we entered a nice-sized foyer. Flames dancing in a large hearth from the graceful living room provided the comfort.

High windows were draped in heavy, emerald curtains. A mint settee sat against the opposite wall, while two fauteuil chairs of the same style rested on either side.

"Mother, I'm home," Divina called out. "I brought a friend with me."

"Back here, button," a sweet voice announced.

"Come with me," Divina invited.

In a room past the fireplace, sat a woman in front of an easel. She was painting a picture of Divina holding a round, orange object. Stepping closer, I realized it was Divina playing basketball. She even illustrated the hoop improvised from the interlaced branches.

"Hey, that's pretty good," I said. "I didn't see you there today, Mrs. Holbrook. You should have come to say hello."

Although the woman shifted towards my voice, she did not look into my eyes. It quickly became evident that Mrs. Holbrook was blind.

Divina's mother smiled. "I lost my vision years ago, but that doesn't stop me from seeing. Come sit with me, Sophia."

She motioned to the padded window bench across from her. I did as she asked and Divina sat next to me.

"When I was young," Mrs. Holbrook began. "I was able to touch an object or hold a person's hand and see elements of their past. This gift left me when I lost my eye sight."

"That must have made you angry," I commented.

"Yes, it did. I think, however, that the gift left me due to my anger. When I came to terms with the loss, it came back, even stronger. Sometimes, I'm able to see things as they happen," Mrs. Holbrook explained.

"You paint them as if you were there." I glanced to the easel.

She nodded. "I had no idea I was even able to paint before my sight left. It came about more by accident. I can see things with my mind, but am able to feel the emotion when it's transferred to canvas."

"You get to see things from an outside point of view?" I surmised. "It's like you're there, but nobody knows it. A fly on the wall."

Mrs. Holbrook hummed in acknowledgement.

"It's really amazing," I said, "that you're able to see Divina as she looks today."

Mrs. Holbrook smiled. "I count my blessings every day."

"Mother, I'd like to show Sophia more of your paintings. May I?" Divina asked gently.

"Of course, button. Don't be too long though. I'm going to put a pot of tea on."

Her mother held her hand out towards the sound of her daughter's voice. Divina bent down to embrace her.

"Come on, Sophia," Divina said.

I rose and set my hand on Mrs. Holbrook's shoulder as I came near. I imagine it must be unnerving to not know how close people were when they passed by. Mrs. Holbrook placed her hand over mine and took in a large breath before she said, "I'm glad you and Divina found each other."

"Me too." I gave her shoulder a little squeeze.

Divina waited for me at the base of the stairs. A grey, almost blue, cat with fur like rich suede trotted down to see her.

"I missed you, Elvis." Divina scooped up the cat and cuddled him.

"Did you miss me?" she questioned the cat in a falsetto as if it were a baby.

I half-laughed. "You named your cat, Elvis?"

"No, I didn't name him. That's his name," Divina answered.

What? Did the cat name himself?

"He's actually mother's cat. She has had him for over thirty years."

"What?" I gasped.

That's one old cat. I once knew a cat that lived to be around twenty, but he was falling apart at the seams.

"How long do cats live here?" I asked cautiously.

"Fifty, sixty years."

Divina took me upstairs to a hallway full of beautiful paintings. They were of important events in their lives. One picture showed Divina blowing out sixteen candles on a cake. Another was a fun family scene of a picnic in a garden.

The picture of a cow carelessly chewing on grass made me laugh aloud. It was mostly funny because of the man lying in the mud puddle, beside the cow.

"That's my dad," Divina giggled. "One of our cows loved to graze on a particular thistle in the field, only it gave her terrible stomach pains. She would moan all night in agony until mother discovered the reason. Dad thought he cleared the fields of the nasty weed, but one day when he was checking on the cattle, he discovered one of the cows snacking in a large patch that was missed.

"He grabbed a leather strap from the barn, hooked it around the cow's neck, and pulled with all his might. Miranda was very stubborn. He pulled a little harder, and lost his grip, sending him straight into the mud. You should have seen him when he walked into the house."

I looked back at the painting and we erupted in laughter.

Mrs. Holbrook called up the stairs, "You know how your father feels about the cow picture, Divina."

Stifling her amusement, she proceeded with her tour of the picture hallway. I found the last one particularly compelling. It depicted a younger Mrs. Holbrook, hugging her small daughter, and staring off into the distance. It must have been just after she lost her sight. There was a crowd of people in the background. One was a beautiful woman who looked fraught with remorse.

"Who that?" I asked her.

"Gloria, the faerie queen of District Nine. Mother used to work in her gardens before she lost her sight."

"Do you know why Queen Gloria looks so sad?"

"I imagine because it's her fault my mother is blind," Divina growled her answer.

"What?"

"Mother was in the royal garden collecting medicinal herbs. Queen Gloria was there, too. Gloria had just heard the news from her messenger that Queen Calista died. She was so distraught she fell to her knees in agony, causing a massive supernatural energy wave. It caught my mother in the crossfire and she was knocked unconscious. When mother awoke she was blind. Gloria tried everything to reverse the condition but couldn't find a way."

"That's terrible."

Mrs. Holbrook called up again, "Tea's ready."

The formal dining room was located directly under the stairs. You could get to it by first entering the kitchen, then rounding to a little nook. Dio and Phaidra were already seated, propped up on cushions at the far side of the table. Alary Holbrook sat at the head, closest to the door. Divina and I took places across from the Ballios.

"What do you have there, Dio?" I questioned the towel-covered basket on the table next to him.

"Mrs. Chariot gave me another basket of mushrooms. Only she and Lee eat them, and he's away again. She didn't want them to go to waste," Dio explained.

"That's nice of her. She must be lonely up there in that big house," Alary commented, while brushing her daughter's hand.

Divina took it as her cue to pour the tea.

"She has her children to keep her company," Dio responded.

"When they're home," Phaidra replied. "Young Sarah has been spending a lot of time with that girl. What's her name?" She snapped her fingers trying to stimulate her memory.

"Shea," Divina grumbled as she began passing cups of tea to everyone.

Phaidra stared mindfully at the corner of the room and crumpled her face.

"Yes, but there's another one," she said. "Iris's daughter. What's her name?"

While reaching for her cup, Divina bumped it, questioning, "Daphne?"

Tea spilled all over the bright white tablecloth. She nervously righted her cup before grabbing a napkin to clean up the mess.

Wow, these girls did a number on Divina. She seems super scared.

Mrs. Holbrook placed a soothing hand on her daughter's arm and shook her head. "It'll clean up just fine, button. Don't worry about it."

Alary returned to the topic. "Saban also spends many weekends away with his father when he goes on business trips. I imagine he's being groomed to follow in his father's footsteps."

"He is getting to that age." Phaidra nodded.

I must have made a face in response to Saban's name, because Phaidra chuckled and asked, "What is it Sophia?"

"Nothing, he just hates me."

I glanced to the ceiling and took a sip of tea.

Mrs. Holbrook tapped her hand on the table in front of me saying, "I can't believe that, Sophia."

"It's true, mother," Divina said. "You should have heard what he said about her today."

Divina relayed the earlier conversation between Saban and his friends.

After hearing the evidence, Alary turned to Phaidra and said, "That behavior is nothing short of pulling a girl's hair."

The older women began to laugh. I did not understand what was so funny. I knew Saban did not care for me, but could never see him pulling my hair.

"Divina," Alary broke from her laughter. "Would you get our guests some coffee cake? It's in the bread box next to the sink."

Dio jolted to attention. I knew what he was thinking. He never met a dessert he did not love.

Divina rose from the table and started for the door.

"Hey, why is it in the bread box?" Divina asked. "I got you a lovely, covered cake-holder for Christmas, so you could display your yummy goodies on the table."

Alary smiled. "Because your father loves coffee cake. If he saw how yummy it looked, there wouldn't be any left for our guests."

Divina nodded. It seemed to be a reasonable explanation. The same would be true of Dio at our house. I got up to help my friend in the kitchen.

When we returned the adults were in a heavy conversation concerning horticulture. Divina and I took our seats, and silently devoured the sweet spiced cake.

After some time, Phaidra took her last sip of tea, and set it next to her empty dessert plate.

"We'd better be getting off now," Phaidra said. "Thank you ever so much for the refreshments, Alary."

She hopped down from the cushioned chair as I looked around and wondered where the time had gone.

"You're so welcome. It has been delightful."

"Before we go, let's quickly try the spell for the front of the house," Dio suggested. "If we have another windstorm the dirt lawn will make a mess of the house."

I pictured their lovely white home soiled by a shadow of dark black dirt.

That would be a mess.

Alary replied, "Yes, Dio. I do hope you get your full powers back soon. In the meantime, I'm sure the four of us can pull together a spell to contain the bare ground."

Alary carefully rose from the table and Divina led us all to the front porch. I stood back while the four magics joined hands in a circle and lowered their heads in a unified hum.

Dio began to chant, "We ask for help to find a temporary solution to save my behind. Please cover this yard because it's getting too hard to fix this land without our powers at hand."

Divina opened one of her eyes. She must have been thinking the same thing I was.

That's a funny spell.

One of my text books said, the power in magic comes more from the chanters intent, than their words. Under normal circumstances, Dio would not even need a spell. He and Phaidra were already powerful.

The four took a breath, and deepened their hum. I found myself expelling air through my nostrils in rhythm with their drone. A vein protruded from Dios head. Phaidra began to shake. All at once they opened their eyes and searched the lawn.

"Aw, nothing," Phaidra complained. "Let us give it another try."

Again they hummed, and Phaidra recited the chant.

"We ask for help to find a temporary solution to save our behind--" Phaidra uncovered an eye. Probably wanting to see if anyone was giving her a weird look.

I withheld a laugh.

"Please cover this yard because it's getting too hard, to fix this land without our powers at hand."

The bulging vein returned to Dios head, accompanied by a bead of sweat that rolled down his cheek. I moved near Phaidra, resting my hand behind her neck as she began shake. They were frightening me. The Ballios were being completely drained of what little energy they had.

What can I do? I need to do something.

The humming stopped.

"It worked!" Divina exclaimed. "But, what is it?"

We stepped down to see what had been conjured.

"It's patio carpet?" I answered.

"What's patio carpet?" Divina asked.

CHAPTER 25

Phaidra stepped off the porch. Bewilderment washed over her weary expression. Dio followed. They bent down to feel the carpet's texture, touching it gingerly like it was a meteor from outer space.

Dio finally spoke. "I suppose it'll keep the dirt from blowing around . . . for now."

"That's all that matters." Alary seemed pleased with the result, even if it was tacky patio carpet.

I presumed the Ballios were not happy that their marvelous landscape techniques had been downgraded to synthetic plastic.

That must be why they seem so stunned.

"It is real, isn't it? Not an illusion." I turned to Divina who had previously schooled me in the difference between real manifestations versus illusions. She nodded.

"Oh, it's real." Dio's eyes widened as he stared at the strange lawn.

Phaidra sighed. "I don't know about all of you, but I am incredibly tired."

"Yes, we must be getting along. I'll be by in a day or two," Dio said.

"Wonderful. Good work everyone." Alary waved.

Phaidra and Dio were so beat. I worried they would not be able to make it home. I recalled the events of my day kept them awake, ending with Divina's strange accusation about me speaking Latin. This made their ears pop up, but they were too exhausted to say anything.

My strange dream popped into mind. Even though it was a mix of my own jumbled thoughts, I still had to ask, "Where is Desta Court? Does it exist?"

"This is Desta's Court," Phaidra replied. "At least it used to be before Queen Calista took over. As we said before, the court is named after its queen."

"Queen Calista," Dio added, "changed the name of this town to honor the former ruler."

Interesting, I wonder where my subconscious picked up that bit of information.

At long last, we made it back to the cottage. I offered to make the Ballios something for dinner. They declined, saying they were too tired, and were going to go to bed. I could not blame them. I was feeling a bit weary myself.

CHAPTER 26

After scarfing down a bowl of Phaidra's delicious guacamole and corn chips, I did some homework. When that got boring, I went for a walk. My eyes were tired, but it was too early to go to bed.

Town square was busy, even more so than in the morning.

Three men argued in front of the apothecary. It was over the last sack of frankincense. Judging by the heated, yet refined, conversation, I surmised they were a farmer, a holy man, and a barkeep. Smiling to myself, I took a seat at the fountain. The situation had all the makings of a typical joke.

"I need this frankincense to ward off mosquitoes," said the farmer. "My cattle are so irritated, they've stopped giving milk."

Somehow I doubted that would happen, unless cows were more temperamental in this realm. The other men were not buying his story either.

"Please, Angus," said the barkeep. "All you need to do is talk to Dio Ballios. He has many remedies for mosquitoes. I need the resin for my Avalon liquor. Mr. Chariot bought out my last case today."

Mr. Chariot? I thought Alcade Chariot went out of town again.

"Desta, Calista does not need another batch of Avalon liquor, Mr. Daniels," the holy man interrupted. "What it does need is for its young ones to be anointed properly. I need the frankincense to infuse my oil."

Wow! Who knew there were so many uses for frankincense? I thought it was just something wise men gave away as gifts.

Enjoying the show, I crossed my legs to get more comfy. That's when I noticed Saban, Asher and Harris headed down the walkway in my direction.

Harris was telling a story to the other boys. He had one hand in his pocket while the other one waved to define his thoughts. With Saban in the middle, Harris walked along the outside edge. They were taking up too much room on the sidewalk. With their compulsion for etiquette, I was surprised they were not already well aware of that.

A woman pushing a baby carriage came towards them. Harris hopped out of the way, onto the street to let her pass.

Saban stopped mid-stride and blinked. He was astounded at the manner in which his friend bound out of the way. I was sure he thought it was much too animated a movement. He shook his head.

Harris laughed. So did Asher.

I scooted around to the other side of the fountain. Half a second later, I reprimanded myself for being such a silly girl.

What are you scared of? I asked myself. *Does it really matter if that boring Saban sees you? Sure, he'll give you a nasty look, as he did to Harris, but what else is new?*

"Come on, Saban," Asher teased as they sat down in the same spot I just vacated.

I hid behind the middle of the fountain and prayed they would not notice me.

"You have been so distracted lately," Asher continued. "What's the matter?"

"Nothing's the matter," Saban returned with an edge. "Why do you keep asking me that?"

"Because," Asher replied, "on a good day, I'd refer to your temperament as aloof, but today you've been down-right cantankerous. Could it have anything to do with our new student?"

I suppose he's talking about me.

"Don't be ridiculous," Saban said. "That girl's eccentric behavior has no effect on me."

"I don't find her that odd," Harris interjected. "She is quite similar to the wee folk, and I am sure her conduct fits in perfectly in her own realm."

He's comparing me to elves and gnomes?

"She is not on Earth," Saban retorted. "She is in Desta, Calista. She should carry herself as we do. Your fascination," he addressed Harris, "with other philosophies has clouded your judgment. Refraining from senseless prattle has many benefits. One of which, it allows adequate time to observe without becoming confused by the falsity others try to convey.

"Studies indicate, humans are always wondering why they never know another person. How could they when they are more concerned with making a spectacle of themselves. They're insecure about imagined flaws, or in a race against themselves to acquire obscene amounts of worthless possessions in hopes of filling the massive hole they created inside one another."

They boys paused to take in the unacceptably broad and potentially damning statement.

Not all humans are like that. . . Okay, a lot of them are. But come on. I'm being judged by an outside view of humanity, which he read about in a book. That's not fair.

"True, I haven't studied humans as you have, but those flaws exist here too," Asher pointed out.

Harris added, "And if your theory is correct, Saban, that quiet observation allows improved knowledge, then you must know a tremendous amount about our human classmate."

Yeah Saban. No one's forcing you to look at me, you jerk. Wait . . . did he say a tremendous amount?

Saban shook his head in frustration. I saw it while glancing past my shoulder. His elaborate diatribe fell on ears that could not care less. Or perhaps they did not believe Saban's argument matched his true feelings, whatever they were.

"What has gotten you so troubled, Saban?" Asher asked. "Do you think she'll confuse your soldiers, and they'll start to follow her?"

What does that mean?

Still keeping hidden, I swiveled around to get a better look. Their words were only half the story and the increasing volume of the frankincense squabble was making it hard to hear.

Harris stood above the boys, splitting his attention between the two seated on the stone bench.

"I don't ask anyone to follow me," Saban spoke deliberately.

Asher did an admirable job of hiding his anger vocally, but it came through his smooth mocha skin with a flush of cheeks.

"That's what makes it so infuriating," he said. "You don't even have to try. Whenever anything happens, even moderately shocking, all eyes turn to you. 'How is Saban going to react?' And, everyone mindlessly follows suit. It's pretty sickening actually."

That's a mighty bold statement for this place.

"You think my life is so easy, do you?" Saban asked. "I assure you, if I could give it away, I would."

Babies began to cry from several corners of the square. It added a level of agitation to the city's atmosphere.

"Fellows, really?" Harris tried to calm the discussion. "I don't know why this is such a problem all of a sudden. Things have been this way since we were kids. Nothing has changed."

"Something has changed," Asher snapped. "Saban is jealous that he has some competition."

"She is no competition," Saban replied.

Is this me again?

"Admit it! You're jealous of her." Asher's lip twitched.

"No," Saban's tone pulled back in a way that was unexpected, especially considering the direction their dispute was going. "I am not jealous of her."

Asher's hostility tempered. His shoulders relaxed.

Assessing Saban's posture, Harris replied, "Then I have to say, I find your opposition towards the lovely lady puzzling. It can't be because she's human. I have never known you to be prejudiced."

"I find," Saban swatted a mosquito from his arm, "your persistent defense of her puzzling."

"It shouldn't be." Harris laughed while he waved his hand in front of his face. Several bugs had flown at him. "I have made no secret that I am fond of Sophia."

Sweetie.

"Right," Saban scoffed. "How could I forget? You never feel the need to hide what you're thinking. I always hoped you'd grow out of that."

"Not to worry," Harris replied, "I conceal plenty."

Asher's voice became tight when responding to his jovial friend. "Does that mean you wish to court her?"

Court? What does that mean? And why does Asher sound so irritated?

Saban searched Asher's face. He was wondering the same thing.

"No." Harris grinned. He appeared to be getting an impish pleasure out of the conversation. "She is beautiful, but my feelings are more . . . fraternal."

"You put her in the same category as your wretched little sister, Shea?" Asher gasped. "How is that possible?"

"Strange, I know," Harris replied. "I'm sure neither of you will hold it against me."

Saban and Asher glanced at Harris, and then turned the examination back to one another. Both looked as though they had discovered something about each other, and themselves, at the same time. What was it? Harris seemed to know.

"Will you please stop?" Saban demanded out of nowhere.

Huh?

Harris and Asher exchanged baffled glances.

What's he upset about now?

CHAPTER 27

Saban stood and marched over to a slight of a man, lurking around the corner of the apothecary store. He seized him by the arm.

"Your use of enchantment is inappropriate, sir," Saban advised. "Desist now."

"I see," Asher said. "The man must be an amplifier. I noticed there was an unusual amount of calamity going on here."

"But, I need that sack of frankincense," the man pleaded. "My wife's joints have swollen up. She's in agony and can't even get out of bed."

Harris sat next to Asher and took in the exhibition as if it were a Broadway play.

"An amplifier?" Harris said. "That's a rare ability in these parts. He must have wanted to ramp up the argument between the men so they would be distracted, and he could snatch up the frankincense."

A hand-pump well in the small yard between the apothecary and cologne shop exploded from its platform. After shooting a few feet into the air, the heavy iron contraption crashed back to the grass. Water blasted out of the hole.

Witnesses slapped their hands to the chest in fright. Babies howled, and mosquitoes swarmed everyone on the sidewalk. Those who were not swatting away the pests were covering their ears, or jumping out of the way of the spewing waterfall.

"Calm down," Saban told the man.

The man quivered. It was distress over his wife that caused the pump to explode, yet I did not think he meant it to happen. Saban was cross with him for abusing his powers, but even he knew it was an accident.

Holding an outstretched hand toward the geyser, Saban pressed down. In a whisper, he repeated the phrase, "Return to form. Return to form."

Water receded and citizens calmed. By the time the gusher disappeared into the hole, all eyes had turned to Saban in heartfelt gratitude. Some of the ladies even cracked a smile.

With a broad, graceful sweep of Saban's arm, the mosquitoes flew away. Babies settled, and their mothers exhaled in relief.

Asher took in the display with pleasure, until he noticed admiration on the faces of the town's people. Then he rolled his eyes.

I covered my mouth to prevent a giggle from escaping.

What an fascinating relationship they all had. The jealousy was apparent, but so was their loyalty. They were very much like true brothers. It comforted me. It made them more real, less mechanical.

Saban visually scanned the square to make sure the disorder had eased. He paid little consideration to their appreciation. Once he shifted his focus back to the amplifier, everyone reverted to their previous state of silent order.

"White willow will help your wife's inflammation," Saban advised, as he pulled a bill from his wallet. Handing it to the man he said, "You can get a pouch in the apothecary."

The amplifier eyed the bill. He stared at it like it was a foreign object.

Rubbing a hand over his mouth he said, "I don't know how to thank you. Mr. Chariot, is it?"

"You can thank me," Saban replied, "by not behaving irresponsibly."

I chanted a classic hero anthem in my head and smiled.

It's Decorum-man to the rescue. He's fending off rudeness one commoner at a time.

The man took the money and nodded before slipping into the store.

Saban proceeded to the pump. After heaving the large iron contraption back in place, he searched the ground for fly-away bolts. He found one next to the platform and began to screw it in by hand. Giving the area another glance, he turned to his friends.

Asher acknowledged the unspoken message by getting up to help in the hunt.

Harris motioned, "one moment" with a raised finger. He had to tie his shoe.

I was so intrigued with their interchange that I did not realize immediately I had been found out. Turning my attention from the pump reconstruction, I noticed Harris smiling at me.

Oh no, he's seen me. He's going to tell Saban.

He released a chuckle and winked.

I let out the breath I was holding.

Don't be silly, I told myself. *Harris already said he likes you.*

He got up and jogged over to his friends. Saban was rather busy searching for bolts, otherwise, I am sure he would have made some comment about Harris traveling too fast in a municipal area.

"Hello Sophia," a tiny voice greeted.

Tracy and Lacy were standing in front me. They looked ever so adorable with pigtail ringlets.

"Good evening, lovely ladies. What brings you out at this hour?" I asked.

"Our nanny had a meeting at Ravines Mount," Tracy said.

I had already been informed that Ravines Mount was a spot where ladies met on certain times of the month, depending on the phase of the moon. My imagination told me they danced around an ancient tree, chanting to evoke some primeval spirit. In a town full of witches, I probably was not far off.

"Mother doesn't go anymore," Lacy continued. "Esther, our nanny, told the chimney sweep man it was because the other ladies believed her to be pompous. What does that mean, Sophia?"

"Oh," I tried to think of the best light to shine on the disparaging remark. "It means she holds herself in very high regard."

"Yes," Tracy agreed. "I find that to be true. Anyway, mother is at the bookstore. Esther told her she needed to get better acquainted with invocations before she decided to reapply to the coven."

"Mother told her," Lacy added, "that she had more enchantment in her foot than the rest of the coven combined."

"Esther said she understood why mother would feel that way," Tracy concluded, "considering the size of her feet."

These kids sure do disclose a lot. I hope when I have children they aren't so free with my information. But it is rather funny.

"You should consider yourselves fortunate to spend some quality time with your mother," I said. "I bet she misses you when you're at school."

"She does," Lacy said. "That's why she has to invite Harold, the piano tuner, in to visit every day. She asked us not to tell father, because he would complain she is wasting money on frivolous things. We need that piano in top notch condition for our lessons."

"He comes every day?" I nodded slowly. "I see."

The piano is not the only thing getting tuned.

"Do you want to come with us to the traveling toy maker?" Tracy asked. "He's right over there."

She pointed to a man a short distance away with snow-colored hair, rosy cheeks, and a round tummy. He stood behind a portable cart and was handing a doll to a little girl with her father. She vibrated with excitement.

"We have never seen a toymaker before," Tracy said. "That man has a lively spirit. He's like Ms. Carita . . . and you, for that matter, Sophia."

I nodded in appreciation of the compliment.

"I would love to see the toy maker," I said.

Each girl took one of my hands. Hopping up next to them, I heard a high pitch gasp from across the square. Everyone else in the shopping area turned to see what the fuss was about.

With her hand at her chest, a woman, wearing a long black dress and peaked hat, dropped her jaw. Her brows knit as she stalked towards us.

"That's mother," Lacy exclaimed.

I could have guessed. It was the same woman who gave me a dirty look my first day at school. I felt as though a ginormous spotlight shone on me.

"What are you doing with my children?" screeched the mother.

She did not give me a chance to reply before speaking again.

"Isn't it bad enough they let you into our realm, but now they let you wander around unaccompanied. Where are your wardens?"

Although unsure of what would come out, I again opened my mouth to speak, but was cut off by the incensed woman.

My cheeks blazed from mortification. I could not believe she was making such a scene, especially since my goal the whole time was to stay hidden. I might as well have been a flea infested rat scurrying through the street. That is what it felt like.

"Stay away from my children, human." The mother snatched Tracy and Lacy from my hands and spun around.

"Sorry," both of the girls mouthed as their mother dragged them away.

With slumped shoulders, I turned. Sure enough, everyone had stopped what they were doing to witness the incident, including Saban and the boys.

I sighed.

The prior amplifier event surely was more noteworthy to me. I was not used to seeing magical displays, but being degraded by a townsperson would no doubt leave a more lasting impression for everyone else.

I could barely make eye contact with the boys, even though they silently observed me. Shivering, I pulled the hood up on my cape and willed myself to keep my head high as I exited the square.

Disgust on the woman's face tormented me. She hated me. And the boys-- they must have thought I was such a loser.

Shrouded in embarrassment, my ego was trashed. That is probably why the first few squawks overhead did not register.

Just past Shamus's house, a high-pitched caw finally caught my attention. Turning my head skyward, black talons loomed, already poised to imbed themselves in my face.

CHAPTER 28

Why is it after me! Does it matter? It's a wild animal, possibly filled with diseases. Run!

I ran. It was my only defense, but I knew it would be futile. Birds were much faster than humans.

Run into the forest, I told myself. *Trees will slow it down.*

The inky raven was so close. I could feel blasts of air from its flapping wings. Changing course gave me a small advantage. The fowl swooped in for the kill, missing me by an inch.

Glancing over my shoulder as I entered the trees, I could see the bird assessing me. It seemed to be re-evaluating. That made it more frightening. Its mannerism seemed more human than animal.

Branches grazed my arms as I fought through the trees. Uneven ground and diminished light hindered my escape. Hopefully, these added obstacles would slow my predator more.

I checked behind as I sprinted further. The bird swooped towards me. Ducking to my right, I wrapped my hand around a tree trunk, and shifted course, once more.

It came at me again. Smacked me in the face with its wings. Talons scraped my cheeks. When I swatted it, the bird crashed onto the forest floor.

Stumbling, I changed direction. After only a few strides, my foot pressed into something soft. Dirt gave way, and I fell into a man-sized opening in the ground.

With no chance to grab on to anything, I crashed on the bottom of an old, barren well. I feared my teeth had shattered. Running my tongue around inside my mouth, I checked to see that they were all still intact.

My tormentor perched at the lip of the hole. It was not there to further its attack. Rather, she wanted to gloat.

"Caw," she sang out, eyeing me with a smug victory.

"Screw you," I called back.

It flew away. I knew it would not be returning.

My thigh throbbed. It was hard to see. The sky was getting dark, and I was pretty far down. The drop must have been twenty, maybe thirty, feet.

Trembling, I touched my thigh. It had bashed into something on the way down. Pain shot up my spine. I pulled my hand away, trying to catch my breath. Gasps echoed in the small, stone space.

Carefully I moved my hand closer to the point of injury. Fingertips encountered something sticky. It must have been blood. I realized a stick or branch impaled me.

My first instinct was to pull it out, but high school health class stopped me. They told us it could cause massive bleeding.

I'll leave it in for now.

"Hello," I called up to anyone. "I'm trapped down here. Hellooo!"

I called a few more times, even though I knew no one could hear me.

Who am I kidding?

I leaned back, harder than I meant it too and one of the stones behind me moved. At first, it scared me, and then I thought maybe?

It took a great deal of effort to shift my body. Once I did, I found the stone that had moved, and pushed it. It slipped out of place and dropped to the ground on the other side. My heart leapt.

The stone beside it was a bit harder to budge, but it also moved. Piece after piece fell to the other side giving me hope. I pressed at all the stones I could, but my reach was not far, because it was too agonizing too stand.

Soon I had made a hole large enough to squeeze my body through, minus the protruding object in my leg. How was I going to get that through?

I poked my head in the hole. It was a tunnel which appeared to be at least a few feet long. The stones I pushed out lay inside.

What was on the other side? I could not see, but had to believe it was closer to civilization then this trap.

I have to get the stick out.

I felt for my leg. When my hand hit the obstruction, it was like lightning bolts surging throughout my body.

That can't be good. Don't touch it.

I had to get it out. There was no way to crawl through the narrow opening with a branch in my leg. It would tear my flesh to bits.

I grasped the bough and ripped it out. Blood gushed.

CHAPTER 29

Warm liquid spilled over my leg. It terrified me. I did not know how much blood someone could lose before it became fatal. If I was going to escape, it had to be fast.

Hoisting myself into the hole to who-knows-where, I elbowed my body through. Small spaces sucked. I always disliked them. It was not a phobia, but I certainly was not fond of them.

Whatever, I encouraged myself. *Not much you can do about it. Sometimes you have no other alternative, but to face fear . . . whether you like it or not.*

Inching along the tunnel, I tumbled into a cave, landing hard on gravel-covered ground. In front of me, a pond shimmered in brilliant emerald. It illuminated the cavern even though there was no light source to be found.

After shuffling to the pond, I dipped my hand into the water to wash my thigh. I prayed it was mineral-filled instead of parasite infested.

That's all I need, to get a flesh-eating disease in a foreign realm, lose my leg, and become even more of a freak.

The water soothed instantly. On some level, I knew I had made the right choice.

"Sophia, is that you?" a masculine voice called out.

I turned to the sound. It was Nickel Tucker standing on the other end of the pond with a shovel in hand.

My eyes filled with tears. "Thank goodness," I cried.

"What happened?" He ran around to my side.

"An evil bird chased me and I fell," I answered. "Thought for sure I would die down here."

"Oh," he soothed with confident reassurance. "You're safe now. Let's get you back up to the surface. My Ada can tend to your wounds."

He glanced to my blood soaked leg.

As we traveled, Nickel explained that he was mining for earzo jewels in the cavern pond when he found me. They only revealed themselves once a month, and it had to be at night. The month prior, he missed his opportunity to attend Ada's uncle's fifth wedding. Before that, he had a broken his ankle and was laid up in bed.

I could tell he was dying to get his hands on the precious earzo jewels, but was touched he would forgo another month to bring me to safety.

Nickel's home was a short distance through the forest. Ada was waiting with hot chocolate and whiskey when we arrived. Of course, she was only expecting Nickel, so I got the first batch of delicious warmth and he had to wait for the second.

"I know I should not feed you spirits, young lady," Ada said. "I am only doing it because we're out of white willow, and you'll need something to ease you when I stitch the wound."

"I won't tell Phaidra. Promise," I assured after the first sip.

Since I had never had alcohol, I had no knowledge of how much it would shield me from hurt. To my dismay, it did very little. I felt every poke and jab of the needle. Every tug of the string made my stomach turn.

Nickel tried to distract me with silly jokes. They were man jokes though. The same kind I would hear on Earth. Those did not amuse me either. But I appreciated his effort. He was very kind.

At long last Ada was done stitching. She knotted the string, placed a bandage over, and kissed the top.

"You will be better in no time, my lovely," she assured.

I had to believe her. She seemed so sure. On the walk home, Nickel told me about the cave water's healing properties.

"You have no idea of the power of natural minerals, Sophia. Why do you think I make a living at this? Your leg will be healed sooner than you think."

"I'm so grateful you found me, Nickel. I can't imagine why the bird came after me. I don't know how I can thank you and Ada."

"Why don't you thank me by coming to work for me? Have a feeling you've got a knack for finding precious stones." He laughed. "I bet you would find them when you're not even looking. Maybe even in your sleep."

"In my sleep, really?" I questioned as he walked me to my doorstep.

"Look, Sophia." He placed a hand on my arm. "I know what you think about yourself, and you couldn't be more wrong. You would be doing me a favor, working for me. Talk to your guardians, and think about it, okay."

"Yes, I will talk to them." I thanked him for the offer and said goodnight.

Slipping into the house, I quietly closed and latched the door.

Dio was snoring loudly. That brought me peace. I knew they felt awful all night, and I did not wish to burden them with another one of my famous catastrophes.

Before going to bed I slipped into the bath, hoping a few drops of Phaidra's lavender oils would make me feel better. Leaning back, I replayed the day.

Besides that awful mother, being chased by a carnivorous bird, and then being impaled by a stick, the whole Latin thing really kept nagging at me.

Is it possible what Divina said is true?

To be fair, nothing about this world was within the norms for me. Maybe I got knocked in the head with a branch of a magical Latin tree. Or perhaps, I had been bitten by a multilingual firefly.

Divina seemed to be an honest person, and she truly believed what she was saying. I concluded I should just accept this strange happening as a "Welcome to Desta" gift and move on.

With that irritating quandary solved, I drained the tub, grabbed a peach and went to bed.

CHAPTER 30

My body felt like a boulder imbedded into the mattress.

No kidding, Sophia. What do you expect when you fall to the bottom of well.

I searched my thigh. Ada's stiches had come out. Normally, that would have been a problem, but my wound had already healed. All that remained was a red line to remind me where I had been stabbed.

"Wow," I said aloud, "That earzo mineral water really is healing."

I tiptoed through the hushed home. Morning brain fog refused to fade away.

While searching through cupboards for something fresh and substantial, my stomach decided cooked quinoa with blueberries and maple syrup would hit the spot.

Amazing, I thought as the first spoonful of sweet cereal traveled down my throat.

I peeked into the Ballios bedroom. They were still sleeping. Grabbing a few items for lunch, I quietly crept out the front door.

A few yards from Nickel Tucker's home a peddler stood with a cart. His hooded russet robe had become tangled in the cart's wheel. He pulled at it to no avail.

Feeling a sudden sting in my right shoulder, I gasped.

Where did that come from? Ah, who cares? Brush it off. Probably just the sting from last night's fall. And it looks as though this guy is in trouble.

"Can I help you, sir?" I asked.

He twisted. A blackened-tooth sneer startled me. Blood oozed from a stitched gash across his cheek. I blinked.

"What's the matter," he questioned.

I searched the ground out of embarrassment.

My expression must have given me away. I've insulted this poor man, and now he knows that his appearance has freaked me out.

"I'm sorry. I--" As I returned my view to him, my words came to an abrupt halt.

Although pitted, probably by bad acne as a teen, his skin now looked normal. No gash. No blood. He even had perfectly aligned white teeth.

"I think my mind is playing tricks on me."

Feeling ashamed for my rude thoughts about the man, I went to his side. Bending at his knee, I easily unwound the robe from the wheel. I wondered why he was having such a hard time with it. As the sting in my shoulder persisted, I began to sense the man staring at the back of my head.

"There you go." I jumped back from him.

"Thank you. You must let me give you a gift for your kindness."

He flipped up the wooden lid on his cart and began digging inside.

"That's not necessary," I said. "I have to be going."

"How about a nice pair of earrings?" He pulled out a dangly pair with orange stones.

"No, thank you." I backed away.

"I understand. You're not a jewelry girl."

He carelessly dropped the earrings into a holding cell before plunging in for a second look.

I was getting a bit annoyed with his persistence. To be honest, he was kind of creeping me out. Instead of letting him address me again, I started to walk away.

"Perhaps, you're more into books," he said. "How about a story of a gal that gets kidnapped by a dragon, and is forced to live in a room full of little girls whose spirits are imprisoned in dolls?"

Disturbing.

I waved behind me and continued down the path.

The thud of a book being dropped sounded, followed by hurried bangs of merchandise being tossed against the inside of his cart.

What's with this guy? Why won't he leave me alone?

"How about this one?" He was getting a touch screechy, as if he felt he was running out of time.

"It's called Anguni," he said. "As a legend, they were merely time travelers. Modern rumors assert they are real, and if not stopped in their tracks--"

He must have been reading the dust jacket. "Nah, scratch that. I'm not really a non-fiction guy."

I heard another book tossed aside.

"Ah," he sang in victory. "This is the one I was really looking for. It's a story about an orphan girl who is taken from her bedroom by a smarmy bastard in the middle of the night."

I stopped. The memory of being attacked by Max as child rushed back. I wanted to keep walking, but my legs refused to move.

"In the end," he slithered up behind me. His words whistled in my ear. "Cops busted in, but not before the greasy fiend defiled her . . . made a woman out of her."

CHAPTER 31

Terror paralyzed me, but I pushed out through gritted teeth, "That never happened."

"It's only a story," he taunted, and brought his face to mine.

Cringing, I turned away. I did it not only from fear, but to withdraw from the scent of rot that emanated from him.

"Why are you doing this?" I said. "Who are you?"

Winding his neck, he forced me to face him again.

"What do you see when you look at me?"

"Just a man," I answered, keeping my eyes to the ground.

"No, you don't. You saw my true form. You are what they say, aren't you?" He sounded giddy.

"I don't know what you mean. Leave me alone."

Tears began to fall. Unable to help myself, I glimpsed him and shuddered.

Black pupils enclosed by sickly yellow gaped back at me. The oozing gash, accompanied by several more, became visible again.

Wind raged, blowing off his hood. It revealed a glossy, scarlet handprint on top of his bald head. An instant later, I realized that by some ungodly mechanism, a layer of skin had been removed.

"There it is, again!" He became excited. "You can see me now, can't you? But, you didn't see me the whole time. Why . . . why are you so weak, Sophia?"

Weak? What does that have to do with anything? And, how does he know my name?

Something heavy crashed behind me, sending tremors through the ground.

"Get away from her," a cavernous voice demanded.

It was Gerard. In one motion, he took a step and swept me behind him. It was the strangest feeling. One might imagine that being relocated by a boulder-like force would be jarring. He was strangely quite gentle.

"Greetings, rock-head," the peddler scorned. "I was chatting with the little gal."

"Chat's over, demon. Get out of my realm."

Gerard's voice seemed to rumble the ground.

Demon? I was talking to a demon? Why would he come to harass me?

"Your realm?" The demon laughed. "Aren't we territorial? Am I this rude when you come to my realm?"

"Earth is not your realm, psycho. Neither is this. Leave now, before I crush you."

"Fine," he said with a ho-hum quality to his reply. "This get-up is giving me a rash anyways. I'll catch'ya later, Sophia."

He pulled at his robe, and with a snap of his fingers, he was gone.

"Holy crap, Gerard. Thank goodness you showed up when you did. How did he get here? I thought there were rules about realm-to-realm travel?"

"There are," he growled. "Someone must have allowed him passage."

"Do you mean a queen? Who would do that?" I gasped.

"Listen Sophia, this is nothing for you to concern yourself with. He didn't hurt you, did he?"

"No. I think he was more interested in making up disgusting lies, than physically harming me."

"What did he say?" The great stone creature became defensive.

"Nothing I care to repeat, but he kept asking me if I could see his true form?"

Gerard nodded. "Celsus is not his realm, so it's harder for him to stay disguised under veils."

"Is that all? He made it sound like a big deal that I was able to see his mangled appearance. What with the hand print on his head?"

"It's the mark of his maker. The greater demon does it when he takes them."

"What do you mean? Takes them where?"

"All minor demons were human at one time. At some point in their lives, they determined their ultimate path. Just before death takes them, their chosen greater demon comes to visit. They ask the human if they are sure of their decision. If the human still wishes that path, the greater demon brands them, and takes them back to hell."

"Why would anyone choose that life . . . or death?"

"Some fear death," Gerard replied. "In their minds, life is sustained when they join a clan. Other humans are just evil."

"Are you saying minor demons are the dead that never die?"

"For a while," Gerard answered, "if they behave. Minor demons can be killed by even insignificant means. It depends on the strength of their maker, and how much power was used to transmute them. Nobody tells these bozo's that when they sign up."

"Was that guy strong?"

"Not especially, but whoever sent him must be."

"Why is he bugging me?" I cried.

"Sophia," Gerard cupped his giant stone hands over my shoulders. "I don't want you to worry about it. You concentrate on being a kid. You were probably in the wrong place at the wrong time. I'm sorry he upset you."

"He wasn't so tough." I tried to hide my actual fear.

Gerard smiled. "That a girl. How about I take you to school?"

Given that I was still totally freaked out, I accepted right away. He scooped me up and tucked me into the crook of his elbow. Minutes later, after massive amounts of wind, he set me down in front of the school.

"Thanks again, Gerard." I waved to him as he returned into the sky.

He sent me a two-finger salute and vanished.

By the time Divina arrived at the school gates, my mind was made up. I was going to keep the demon incident under my hat. Not only did I not want to worry her, but I knew she would have a million questions. Being reminded of that jerk's awful fabrications was also not something I wanted to do.

I asked Divina to show me to the office. A new course schedule was my first priority.

Divina took me straight past the foyer. We bypassed hallways leading to the junior's classrooms, to an office at the end of the corridor.

"I have to get to class," Divina said when we got there. "Don't worry. You won't get in trouble for being late. Mrs. Updar already knows you're here to see Head Mistress."

It was an average looking school office, but was constructed with a much higher quality of building materials. Hardwood lined the floors and walls. One undersized and one human sized, granite-topped counter marked the division between the secretary's work space and the waiting area.

No staff members could be seen, so I took a seat in the waiting area. As luck would have it, the guy who hated me was already seated.

Saban. Oh no, I groaned to myself the instant I sat down. *He smells good. Why does he have to smell so good?*

Unknowingly, I drew nearer.

"What are you doing?" he questioned in a smooth even tone.

CHAPTER 32

"Sorry." I pulled away. "I didn't mean to creep you out. It's just been so gloomy here, weather-wise, and your cologne reminds me of . . ." I took a slow breath to pinpoint the origin of each scent. "A spring-time picnic by the ocean. I can almost feel the sunshine and gentle breeze blowing saltwater mist through my hair."

While I drifted off, his expression softened from irritation to analytical.

"What's it called?" I asked.

His eyes narrowed, but it was not anger I saw. I think it was confusion.

What? Don't people talk in this town? Maybe I should have asked him what his mother adds to the cauldron when she makes soup. Or how many black cats he has wandering around his house. What does one talk about with a witch?

"It's called Rascal," he answered finally.

"Oh," I replied before I dismissed him to observe the plaques on the walls.

The door inside the secretary's office area opened. A regally garbed woman with a silver bun stepped out. Saban shot up at her arrival. I followed his lead.

"Good, you're both here," the woman's crisp English accent brought decisiveness to her words. "I'm off to a meeting shortly, so I'll take you both now. Please come in."

Saban held the swinging half-door between the counters open for me.

If he hates me, at least he's polite about it.

I passed through and followed Mistress Aristotle into her office.

"Have a seat." The woman motioned to the two-nail-head leather chairs in front of her desk. Returning to her own seat, she glossed over some papers in front of her. She must have been reviewing them before we came in.

"Sophia, Miss Updar has requested you stay in her class for the remainder of the year, so that won't change for either of you. Magi Brunaqua, however, feels you do not require *Latin,* as your comprehension exceeds his current class level."

Saban turned to me with a look of utter disbelief. I shrugged as if to say "I don't get it either."

"You will join Saban's Contraption class with Professor Wingbat," Head Mistress continued.

I could not help but giggle at the name, Wingbat.

Saban sent me a disapproving eye glint.

Head Mistress raised her head and asked, "What the matter?"

"Nothing, ma'am. I apologize."

I composed myself, pressing my lips together so as to not allow another outburst. Head Mistress went back to her papers and turned her sights to Saban. He raised his head to acknowledge her.

"Mr. Chariot, you are moving on to elite math and science with Dr. Holbrook. Sophia, you will be taking Saban's place in intermediate math. Now Sophia, for the afternoon you will be taking Junior Herb, Bark and Fungi. Hmmm." She paused thoughtfully before continuing.

"You *are* a ward of the Ballios, but we'll put you in it . . . for now. Come and see me Monday morning. We may need to change things around again. Saban you will remain in advanced magic, but your father has requested we add a dance course to your schedule."

Although his posture shifted only marginally, I had the feeling he wanted to leap out of his chair to express his dissatisfaction at the news.

"Dance? Whatever for?" he asked.

Was he objecting to the class itself, I wondered? Or because his father wanted him in it?

Head Mistress ignored his outburst except for a dart of her eyes advising him to mind his attitude. Picking up her papers, she tapped them on the table to realign the edges. It reminded me of the way a judge would bang their gavel to demand order in the court.

"He feels it will be beneficial to your future goals," she answered.

Showing no sign of disrespect, but also no trace of resign, he softened his demeanor, pressing his shoulders back.

"I suppose he knows what's best," Saban said.

"Sophia, you will be joining Saban in this course."

Saban inhaled deeply. I am sure he had no intention of letting a reaction slip, but he did. A micro twitch along his jaw line told me he was annoyed at not having more control.

Head Mistress appeared mildly amused. Turning to me she said, "It has been discussed that you would be best able to assist Saban in this area, and you are currently lacking a physical activity in your course schedule. Although, I've noticed that it hasn't hampered you from finding your own ways of incorporating activity into your day."

I assume she was talking about basketball the other day. She did not seem bothered by my disruption in the courtyard, but I figured I better double check.

"Is that alright?" I asked.

I could feel Saban ready to jump up and say no.

"It's fine. Physical activity helps the mind," she replied.

I wanted desperately to turn to that egotistical Saban and yell, "Ha! In your face, sucker!" Instead, I politely nodded to Head Mistress and deliberately avoided eye contact with the hater beside me. I feared, if I saw the look of shock on his disapproving mug, I would not be able to stop myself from laughing. Too bad it was such a beautiful mug. I sighed inside.

"Could you tell me why Miss Templar is so qualified to assist me in this dance course?" He asked while tapping his thumb on chair arm.

Guess Mistress Aristotle's acceptance of basketball is more disorder than he can accept in one day.

From the look on her face, I wondered if Head Mistress was deciding whether to send him to the corner, or take him over her knee.

Personally, I was getting annoyed by his insults. I lifted my arm up onto the back of my chair, opening myself in his direction. I sent him a blank, all be it, intent glare to the side view of his face.

Mistress Aristotle's eyes sailed between Saban and me. She crinkled her nose as if withholding a smirk.

Saban followed her gaze to me. His brows twitched when he observed my posture. Distain left his expression and was replaced with a look of "Uh-oh."

Lifting papers from her desk, Mistress lowered her face to them. Her shoulders jiggled a few times. I was sure she was laughing.

Saban did not notice. He was too focused on my reaction.

When Saban first questioned her, Head Mistress seemed taken aback--ready to give him a thorough tongue-lashing concerning his superior attitude. Now, for whatever reason, she seemed content, even pleased with the situation.

"It's customary on Earth realm for people to dance regularly," she explained. "Humans dance, not only at formal functions designated for the activity, but periodically throughout the day."

"We do?" I questioned.

"Yes," she continued. "We have observed that humans dance when they get happy news, or when they are cooking or cleaning. Mothers who hold their babies are apt to sway about. Even those in motorized vehicles are found to rhythmically move in time with any given musical selection."

Who knew one would ever be commended for these things. I've done all of these things, except dance with my baby, but I've danced with other peoples babies. I like babies.

"Yeah, you're right," I said.

"They dance in some districts on our realm, too," she continued. "But, it's not widely taught in ours. You see, Saban, dancing is more than simply learning the proper steps. It's about feeling the music."

"Feeling the music? Very well." I sensed he was holding back an eye roll as he rapped his knuckles lightly on the chair.

"That's all for now. You both can set off to class."

Mistress dismissed with a noticeable irritancy over Saban's conduct. Bet she could not wait to get us out of her office. She began to gather items into a leather case as Saban opened the door, once again, letting me pass first.

A dwarf man stood on the opposite side of the undersized granite counter.

"Možete li pustiti Naslov uz ime udane žene Aristotel znati njoj auto je čekivanje vanjština uzeti njoj Larrant?" the man asked.

"Yeah, absolutely," I told him, and spun around, almost running head first into Saban.

He opened his mouth to say something.

I sidestepped him and returned to Head Mistress's office.

"Excuse me, Head Mistress. Your driver is here. He says your car is outside, ready to take you to Larrant."

Regarding me sideways, she spoke several words singularly.

"You . . . talked . . . to my driver?"

She must have meant the question to be rhetorical.

Why wouldn't I talk to the driver? He talked to me.

I eyed her strangely. For a moment, we had a bit of a strange stare-standoff.

"Thank you, Miss Templar," she responded finally.

"No problem, ma'am."

Saban was leaning against one of the two desks in the secretary space.

Why is he waiting for me? Does he think I'll get lost and cause more havoc in his school?

"Where is the secretary?" I asked.

For some reason, he too, looked at me oddly.

"My mother's filling in for the usual secretary," he replied, "but she's feeling ill today. Do they teach Croatian in schools on Earth?"

He seemed disturbed.

"Sure, in Croatia." I walked past him. "See-yah." I nodded to the driver.

The man grinned and tip his hat.

Pulling the door open, I stepped into the hallway. On Earth I would have easily opened the door for a male and let him pass. However, I did not think they were that evolved here. Saban would probably take offense.

Diligently, he pulled the door closed behind him and hurried to catch up with me.

"Are you from Croatia?" he asked.

I laughed.

Guess they don't teach Earth geography here either.

"No, I'm from Gettysburg, Ohio. It's on the other side of the planet from Croatia."

He trailed behind.

"I don't speak it, but I recognized his accent," he started. "The driver was Croatian."

He reached for my shoulder in an attempt to gently halt me. Taking a quarter-step back, I hoped he would not feel inclined to remove his warm hand.

Although I did not mind him touching me, it seemed out of character for the ultra-dignified Saban to make any form of physical contact, and certainly not to a human.

When he realized his improper act he quickly brought his hand to the side. I felt a mischievous warmth radiate from inside me at his discomfort.

"Okay, so he's Croatian," I replied.

He squinted and clarified. "He was speaking Croatian."

"How do you know? I thought you didn't speak it?"

I was actually shocked at Saban's revelation, but chalked it up to that whole multi-speaking, bug-bite, tree-slapping hypothesis I had already come up with. I was also quite enjoying the floundering show, starring Saban Chariot.

"Humans don't speak many different languages," he insisted.

"Of course, they do." I pretended to be offended and continued to the foyer.

I have never been one of those people, but there has got to be thousands of them. Why is he questioning me about this? Does he think I'm a spy or something? Who cares if I understand Latin and Croatian for no apparent reason? It IS kind of cool, though.

"Not that fluently, at seventeen," he protested.

It would have been funny if he stomped his foot. Of course, he did not.

"That is unusual, I suppose, but not impossible," I acknowledged as he followed me up the stairs.

Saban seemed mildly redeemed at being able to prove that one point. I glanced behind in time to see him make a gesture as if a bulb lit up in his head.

"What is it that French faerie woman said to me?" he asked. "Voulez-vous coucher avec moi, ce soir?"

Unable to control myself, I fell against the wall and burst out laughing.

Saban seemed unnerved by my movement. He flinched and readied himself to catch my fall. But I was not going to fall. I was just being dramatic to express how silly he was. Guess from his point of view, it might have looked like stumbling.

"Why did you say that?" I finally got out.

Saban furrowed his brow. I could tell he was in the middle of assessing and reassessing the situation.

He finally said, "I wanted to prove you knew what that meant, too."

"Everyone knows what that means," I said.

I started back up the stairs. This seemed to relieve him. He would no longer be responsible for saving me from a laughter-induced tumble down the stairs.

"Well, I don't," he innocently replied.

I walked backwards down the hall to our class while he came toward me. I did not want to miss one single unintentional facial movement or flustered gesture. This was way too funny.

"You mean your French faerie didn't enlighten you?"

He scrunched his face and looked away like a child who was pondering which day of the week was his favorite.

"She took me aside and was going to tell me, but my father found me and told me it was time to leave the Gala. I asked him if he knew what it meant, and he told me he would explain it later. Then, he kept avoiding the question. I asked around, and Shea was the only one that knew what it meant. She told me it would be easier if she showed me."

"Oh really?" My laughter broke off. "Well, did she show you?"

A hint of jealously slipped through. Thankfully, Saban was impervious to such inflections of tone.

"I don't think so."

We paused in front of Miss Updar's classroom.

"So, what does it mean?" he asked with a childlike naiveté.

"You know," I said. "This vulnerability looks good on you."

I purposely brushed his shoulder expecting the inappropriate physical contact would set him into a tailspin. As predicted, I saw a combination of confusion, irritation, and what I hoped was arousal. He stared at me, speechless.

"This has been great fun," I was able to include before Miss Updar opened the door for us.

"Good, you're here." Miss Updar welcomed us as if she were waiting by the door for our arrival.

"I am sorry for our tardiness," I began.

"Not to worry." She opened the door further so we could pass by. "Come in, and take a seat."

Sarah made a sour face in response to her brother's ruffled demeanor. She then shifted her glare to me.

At the end of class, Saban retreated to his manner of superiority, which made me giddy. I had gotten under his skin.

CHAPTER 33

My mind was on other things when Mistress Aristotle had told me about Contraptions class. I never thought to wonder what the heck it was. After I passed into the room which Saban entered, I stopped in my tracks. Not believing my eyes. It was a good old-fashioned computer lab.

When I say old fashioned, I mean high tech, relatively speaking. Long tables with twenty modern computers encircled the room.

I took a seat between the window at the far wall, and my basketball buddy, Misty.

"Good morning, class," the teacher spoke. "For the next week, we will be learning about computers. They are very popular in the Earth realm. However, they haven't quite caught on here yet. We thought we would see how it panned out for the humans before we subjected our people to the plague of rampaging technology," the teacher jested.

I kind of giggled. Even though the joke was at human's expense, I did not think he meant anything by it. The rest of the students gave him nada.

"Moving on," he continued. "We will be exploring the ways in which computers can be used. At the end of this chapter, we'll do an essay, giving our evaluations of the technology. You'll answer questions such as, is it helpful or harmful? Could it benefit our society, or are humans continuing to dig themselves into a deeper hole?"

The teacher zeroed in on me and said in all sincerity, "No offence, Sophia-the-new-student."

"None taken, sir," I answered.

Professor Wingbat was of average height . . . well, average relative to a human. He wore brown cords with a bright green dress shirt that he left un-tucked. His wavy hair parted in the middle and draped over the side of his face to his jaw. Kind of like a geeky hippy.

"Do you have any thoughts on the subject, new student?"

Professor Wingbat pushed up his wire rim glasses with his middle finger, before resting his hands backwards on his waist.

"Not at this time, professor."

I pressed my lips tightly together, revealing only the faintest of smirks.

Professor Wingbat used me as his assistant for the remainder of class. The goal of the day was to get everyone to turn on the computer and to locate the game Solitaire. It lent itself to the uses-portion of study, and familiarized the learner with mouse handling. Not the most stimulating of classes, but at least I was able to be useful by helping my fellow classmates.

It was amazing to me that they had always been able to use technology but simply choose not to. I wondered where Earth would be if we were not as advanced as we were. Would we be happier?

Saban appeared as I gathered my belongings after class.

"Your new math class is across the hall," he offered unexpectedly.

"Thank you." I looked up at him, searching his face for signs of continued irritation. He revealed nothing, only nodding before exiting the class with Harris and Asher at his side.

As expected, math class sucked. I was bad at math at home, so I would certainly be out of my league here. With no telephones, TVs, DVDs, or other computerized devices, these people had nothing better to do than be smart. Mr. Gerder noticed immediately that I was struggling. He asked the class if anyone would be able to tutor me for a few weeks.

"I'll tutor her."

The sickeningly sweet voice of some girl crawled up my spine. I twisted in my seat to face Sarah who was at the back of the classroom.

There's gotta be an ulterior motive involved.

"Yes, thank you, Sarah," Mr. Gerder said. "You are an exceptional math student. I am sure you can bring Sophia up to speed in no time."

Painfully, I nodded my thanks to Sarah. She accepted in kind before dipping an ear to hear Shea's murmurs.

The lunch bell sounded none too soon for me. Sarah appeared at my desk.

"If you want," she said, "you can come to my house after school and we can begin our studies."

She gave her best impersonation of sincerity.

"Sure, that's sounds great," I said.

"Meet me at the gates after school," Sarah said.

I agreed and went to lunch.

~

"What were you and Saban talking about?" Divina asked eagerly, even before she sat down to join me at the lunch table. "We could hear him out in the hall."

"It started with Saban questioning me about this Croatian driver we ran into." I paused to take a bite of bread.

"What was he questioning you about?" Divina asked impatiently.

"Apparently the driver was speaking in a different language, and I understood him."

"I knew it!" Divina shot up pointing at me. "How do you do that?"

My eyes darted around the room to see if she had called any undue attention to our table. Several students flinch, but no one looked over.

"Don't know. I have a theory though." I leaned into the table and whispered, hoping it would invite Divina to be a little more discreet. "I was avoiding Saban's questions to annoy him, and he ended up trying to test my skills. He recited a phase he heard from a certain French faerie, only he had no idea what it meant."

Divina matched my posture. "But, I bet you did." Excitement bubbled through her whispered tone.

Her eyes widened, alerting me to stop talking. Someone must have come up behind. I sat back in my chair and took a sip of iced tea. It was Saban and Harris. I waited until they passed by before continuing.

"Yeah, but it's a popular phase where I come from. They even made a song about it. The song was in a movie and there was dancing . . . very memorable," I rambled.

"Whatever. I'm sure you would have known what it meant anyways." Divina dismissed my explanation with a wave of her hand.

"What do you think's up with the whole understanding Latin thing?" I asked. "I honestly never noticed it before. It's kinda freaking me out. I don't even know when I'm doing it. It just sounds like everyone is speaking English."

"I don't know, but it does come in handy. Maybe you work for the RBI or something." Divina giggled.

RBI? Hmmm? I did wish to be a cop at one time. Would they even hire me? I'm kind of an immigrant here--an immigrant without papers. Was I even going to stay here after I turned eighteen, or would I go back to Earth? I'd probably have to take another term of Earth school, if I did. I doubt credits could be transferred.

"Maybe," I said.

"So, what did he say in French to test you?" Divina asked.

Leaning in to the table, I smirked.

"The translation is 'Will you sleep with me tonight?'"

I sat back and waited for Divina's response. My newly liberated friend erupted with the most genuine laughter. It was fabulous to see.

The entire commissary turned to witness her amusement. Some did not enjoy the commotion. Saban and the ladies at his table scowled in distaste. Asher and Harris looked on as if they wished to come nearer, so they could be apprised of what gave Divina such joy.

"Come on, let's get some air." I grinned.

CHAPTER 34

Junior Herb, Bark and Fungi, written in old English letters, displayed on a sign outside the door of my new class. I detected an attitude of supremacy from the students who were a few years younger than me. It must have pleased them to no end to know more than the older, dumb, new student.

"Miss Templar, we meet again," a disembodied voice spoke beside me.

"Dr. Akin?" I looked towards the voice.

With a rich welcoming laugh he said, "It is I."

A booklet floated into the air. It came to rest on my desk.

"Here is a test to assess your knowledge level. It will give us a better idea of what we need to work on."

"Sounds good, Dr. Akin."

Luckily, I have always had a fondness for flora in general. Maybe it started when I lived with the Laroose family. A ravenous Caleb and I would sneak out of the duplex in the middle of the night to scavenge through the neighbor's garden for food.

Fresh carrots pulled right from the ground tasted the best. We would fill our mouths and pockets with as many sweet peas as possible before the backyard motion light alerted our presence.

Elka also adored spending time in her garden, and I loved helping her. The patch at the side of the house was designated for teas such as chamomile, peppermint, Echinacea, and ginger. There was an entirely different section in the far corner for herbs. Marinara sauces and stews were made even more mouthwatering due to her fresh basil, oregano, dill, and sage.

Gardening took on a whole new level when Elka told me that people have been using herbs, barks, and other plant life to heal aliments for centuries. I started researching their uses after that. It would have been helpful to know earlier that garlic oil could be used to treat ear infections. Poor Caleb used to get them all the time.

"Wonderful, you're done," the disembodied voice spoke from my side.

So odd, I thought, *I never even heard footsteps.*

"We have about ten minutes left in class," he said. " I'll take your test, and you can spend the remainder of class reviewing this text."

The paper I was working on floated away and a thick brown book took its place.

"You can leave it on the desk at the end of class," he said.

Since I could not be sure if Dr. Akin was still standing over me, I quickly opened the dusty book, entitled Poisonous Plants of Celsus, to a random page and began reading.

"Druaudidon. Dru-odd-ah-don," I mouthed the syllables and read the passage in my mind.

It read, "Beautiful fuchsia blub with black, cape-like leaves give this plant a seductive appeal. Magics were known to use the insidious plant's leaves as compresses for swollen eyes. It is now outlawed in most districts due to the toxic effect it has on magics. Tasteless pollen can be added to any substance, and if ingested, the individual would be stripped of their powers. Repetitive poisoning often results in death. Minor side effects include dry eyes, lethargy, headache, nauseous, and nervousness in some individuals.

Ha! Sounds like the back of any bottle of pills back home, prescription or otherwise. Good to know they can't get it straight here either.

The change-of-class bell chimed.

"Thank goodness." I slammed the book closed.

"Your test looks good, Sophia," Dr. Akins commended as I approached the door to leave. "Say Hello to the Ballios for me."

"I will, sir." Words were spoken upwards, hoping they were not being directed to his mid-section. Judging by the location of his voice, I estimated he was about seven feet tall.

Once in the hallway, I realized I had no idea where the next class was. There was no room number listed on my schedule. I thought about checking in with the office, but remembered the secretary was gone, and Mistress Aristotle was away. My only option was to ask one of the students.

"Excuse me." I tapped the boy ahead of me in the equally creepy and eerily quiet junior hallway procession.

Twisting around, he rutted his brows saying, "Quiet!"

Withholding any assistance he returned to form.

*Okay then. Obviously, junior kids are as snooty as the senior one*s.

I wandered in the same line until everyone else was gone. Eventually, I found a door labeled, Physical Education.

Finally! I found it. I'll bet I get a critical frown from Saban for being late.

The room was the same size as most other classrooms. Only, it appeared larger, because there were not any desks or chairs. Correction, there was a teacher's desk against the far wall and a single long bench.

The room was also very bright. Sunshine coming in from the windows reflected off mirrors that lined the rest of the walls. I was relieved to see a friendly face sitting at the desk.

"Good afternoon, Miss Updar." I set my case on bench. "Are you teaching this class?"

"Hello, Sophia. Yes I am, but I'm afraid Saban has been called away." She rose from her desk and met me where I stood.

"Not here?" I grumbled. "Didn't they create this class for him?"

"Yes, I'm sure he will be here on Monday," she reassured. "We *were* going to work on the box step today. I know that's far below your skill level. If you would wait a few moments, I can run up and retrieve my dance book, so we can explore more sophisticated steps."

It was ever so cute that she was teaching from a book. I had to give her an A for effort.

"I'll be quick as a wink." She bounced out.

What did she mean by my skill level? Is that more of the humans-are-natural-dancers talk? Or do they know, that since being with the Gordons, I had the opportunity to dabble in a few different dance styles? I was no prima ballerina, nor was I going to take my limited knowledge to dance backup for famous rock stars, if that is what they expected. My last four years of lessons simply gave me a better range of steps to bop to when jumping on my bed and singing into my hairbrush.

After taking off my boots, I began to stretch in the middle of the room. I did not realize until that moment how tense I'd been. Muscles felt all balled up. That was another great thing learned in dance--how to really stretch muscles. After every possible part of my body elongated, I rested on the floor in child's pose and yawned.

Elka and I often went to the recreation center to do yoga. Child's pose was always my favorite, because it marked the end of class. It is not that the class was not enjoyable. Yoga simply relaxed me so much I always wanted to go home to bed.

Sleep would be good right now.

"Oh, Sophia, can you ever forgive me? I got locked in the classroom. Sophia!"

Miss Updar's natural soprano voice went up an octave as she said my name.

I shot up to my knees.

"Are you hurt?" the little teacher asked as she rushed to my side.

I blinked to focus on her. She seemed so alarmed.

Pushing out a sleepy chuckle, I said, "I'm not hurt. I fell asleep. How long have you been gone?"

"All class. Didn't you hear the bell ring?" She did not wait for my answer. "Would you believe I was locked in the classroom this whole time? It's the strangest thing. None of my usual spells would open the door. I would be up there still if it weren't for Miss Octibode. She forced the door open with her shoulder. She's much stronger than she looks."

I nodded.

"Can you forgive me, Sophia?"

"It's no problem." Feeling a bit lightheaded, I took a seat on the bench to strap up my boots.

"Thank goodness it's home time." Miss Updar plunked down next to me. "This had to be the longest week ever. I can't wait to get home and curl up on the couch with a great book."

"That sounds like plan," I agreed and gathered my belongings. "See you Monday, Miss Updar."

CHAPTER 35

Sarah waited for me at the school gates as she said she would. With her head resting against the gate, she appeared to be lost in her own world. Shea stood with her, admiring the arch of her brow in a compact.

Neither girl noticed me until I was a few yards away. Sarah acknowledged with her expression, which must have alerted Shea to my approach.

Shea-bird whirled around and spoke before I had the chance to say hello.

"How was your dance class?" It was more of a probe than a congenial inquiry.

Although taken aback by Shea's abruptness, I chose to brush it off.

"There wasn't one. Guess Saban got called away, and Miss Updar got locked in her classroom."

Shea's shoulders relax after advised I had been nowhere near Saban.

"Saban wasn't there?" Sarah sounded genuinely uninformed. "I suppose father took him on another business trip," she concluded with an indication of ice.

Geez, don't these people talk to each other?

Pursing her lips, Shea huffed at her friend.

Wonder what that meant?

As we turned in the opposite direction of Divina's home, the silence became palpable. It was like a weight that made me want to hunch my shoulders, searching the sky for falling debris. I fell into step next to Sarah, while Shea walked on her other side.

"What do people do for fun around here?" I tried my best to sound pleasant.

As though I had insulted her, Shea leaned past Sarah and snorted, "Fun?"

Sarah, who was focused on the sidewalk, flipped her eyes upwards. Her view was so far past anything worth looking at, it surely meant irritation. For some reason, I think the look was intended for Shea.

"When the weather's nice," Sarah finally answered, "we often go to the park and study. Sometimes we go to the library."

Shea set her glare on the white picket fence running the length of the neighbor's property. Had we been cartoon characters, steam would have been blowing from her ears.

Okay . . . obvious tension with these gals. Wonder what they're spatting over? Could it be a guy?

I forced a smile. "Right on. Is that more of a solitary activity or do you guys go out in groups?"

"Both," Sarah replied. "What did you do for fun where you come from?"

"The same, I guess. Sometimes I would go shopping with my friends, but I spent a lot of time with my foster mother at the rec center. We liked to take yoga and Pilates class together."

I laughed. "One time, she talked me into a belly dancing class. I told her I had a bad feeling, but she insisted.

"Halfway through class, she pulled an oblique muscle, doing one of those hip thrusts. She was in so much pain, she couldn't even straighten." I animated the story. "So here she was, stuck in this partially curled position, just mortified, and she wouldn't let anyone touch her but me.

"Luckily for us, the room had not been cleared from the first-aid class that used the space before us. I spotted a stretcher, tossed the resuscitation dummy aside, and wheeled it over to Elka. While I'm racing her out of the room she whispers, 'Sophia, we're never, ever coming back here.' I just laughed."

Shea stared at me. I think she was glad my story was over.

"Your foster mother liked to spend time with you?" Sarah asked with a faint twinge of sentiment.

I half-laughed, feeling a stab of irony as I answered, "Yeah, that one did. The other ones, not so much."

That was an understatement. I considered myself lucky when they forgot I was alive.

"What do you mean 'the other ones'? How many mothers did you have?"

Sarah's unexpected inquisitiveness forced me to look at her more closely. Her brown eyes became softer. I noticed warmer shades of chocolate in her hair.

"I don't know. Lost count . . . maybe seven." My reply was offhanded.

Shea snickered, drawing our attention. "So, it took you seven mothers to finally find one that liked you?"

I know I flinched. Pressure built up behind my eyes, but I pushed it back.

Shea's glower bore into me. She did not want to miss any trace of hurt she had inflicted. Had to give the girl credit. I had no idea she was clever enough to find exactly the right words to wound me.

"We're here," Sarah announced. "See you later, Shea."

The girls locked eyes briefly before Shea shifted her attention to me. "Good-bye then. Sophia."

I said nothing, and that suited her fine. Smirking, she whirled around and continued down the sidewalk.

Dagger-tipped, iron fence posts created an immediate sense of foreboding. Through an ivy-covered arch, I followed Sarah up a paved path. I forced myself to take note of the beautiful yard. The Ballios were no doubt responsible for the plush lawn, finely decorated shrubs, and perfectly placed statues.

Stone griffins protected either side of the home's entrance, while a lion-head knocker posed centrally on the grand door. It had to be the biggest home in Desta, certainly fit for a king. Although, I suppose with Lee Chariot being the Alcade, that was not far off.

"Have a seat." Sarah pointed to a sling bench as we stepped into the marble-floored foyer. "I'll be right back."

She disappeared up a stairwell.

While seated, I examined particulars of the elaborate decor. An out of place, and overbearing gold chandelier loomed above. I cringed, but it drew my attention to the lovely, white embossed ceiling.

White walls, white floor, white stairs . . . could there be any more white?

The home had stunning physical qualities. Unfortunately, I felt blinded by the sterility of it all. It was painfully controlled, much like the front yard, and lacking personality.

I found myself getting tired again.

How long had Sarah been gone?

With my back rested against the wall, my eyes started to droop until I heard movement from upstairs.

A figure stepped out of the hallway, stopping at the top of the stairs. It was Saban. He carried a tray, and, if he was startled by my presence in his foyer, he did not show it.

"Sophia, what are you doing here?" He questioned without showing any of the annoyance I expected.

CHAPTER 36

I stood as he made his way down the curved stairwell.

"Your sister offered to tutor me in math," I replied. "She asked me to wait here for her."

"Sarah left some time ago," Saban informed. "I watched her meet up with Shea in the backyard, and then they disappeared off the grounds."

Can I feel comfort in the fact that I saw it coming a mile away? Nah, not really.

"She set me up," I expressed with dark amusement.

"It appears so," Saban said as he reached the bottom of the stairs.

An ironed dishtowel slung over his right shoulder, and he held a tray of barely-touched food. In a home as grand as this one, I would have assumed they had servants to take care of these things.

My naturally inquisitive nature begged to find out what was going here, however I knew I had no business asking.

"I'll be going then."

I reached for the door and heard a crash at my feet. The sound reverberated off the walls. I whirled around to see what happened.

Saban peered down at the mess. Food, silverware and an upside down bowl scattered at his feet.

"Foxglove and myrrh," he grumbled crossly as he stooped to clean the mess.

Without thinking, I reached for the towel on his shoulder and knelt down to begin mopping spilled soup and juice from the gleaming marble floor. I felt Saban's momentary hesitation, before acceptance of my help.

"I apologize for my profanities," he said.

What profanities?

"My mother isn't feeling well," he divulged. "She sleeps all the time and isn't eating. The doctor has been to see her, but he doesn't know what's wrong. He says to let her rest and the illness will run its course."

I carefully picked up large broken bits of glass and set them on the tray beside him.

"Doctor Holbrook?" I asked.

"No. Magi Brunaqua is our doctor," he answered reluctantly.

"You don't care for him?" I deduced.

"He's an academically accredited doctor with decades of experience," he said, perhaps trying to convince himself of the doctor's competency.

"Alright." I acknowledged his statement.

Saban uneasily shifted his glance from me to the broken items on the tray. He lifted. I rose as well, still holding the sopping towel.

"Do you have another cloth?" I asked.

"Yes, but don't worry about it. I'll take care of things," Saban replied with an appearance of fluster.

Taking the towel from me, he set it on top of the tray.

"Thank you for your assistance," he said in a dismissive manner.

Oh, that again, I huffed. *This guy has more mood swings than a Schizophrenic with PMS.*

"Fine. You're welcome. Hope your mother feels better soon." My palm smacked against the door knob.

"I could tutor you," he blurted as though his offer stunned him more than it did me.

"Seriously?" I turned slowly. "You're not going to just lure me to a secret room and lock the door?"

"Why would one do such a thing?" He appeared genuinely puzzled.

"I'm only kidding. It was more of a comment towards your sister's little prank."

"Yes. I don't know why she would offer to help in math. She's probably worse than you."

Does he know he insulted me? Or, is that just an unfortunate side effect of him talking?

"Really? The teacher said she is an excellent student?" I recalled.

"She cheats," Saban answered as he turned and started down the hallway.

He disappeared through a door that I assume led to the kitchen. I pondered his statement for a moment. My first impression was that Saban kept all of the students in line with a single glance. Now, he carelessly tells me his sister cheats.

"I know what you're thinking," he said, reentering the foyer.

"Do you?"

"You're thinking, how could I possibly let my sister cheat."

An arch of my brow indicated he was on the right track.

"I get tired of watching everyone all the time," he replied. "I can't control everything."

"What! You . . . tired? Isn't that a human aliment?" I teased.

A faint smile broke through. He tilted his head to the staircase, inviting me to follow.

"I have an old text book in my room. I made many notations on the pages. You might find them helpful."

He wrote in a book? I might have to alert the authorities.

I had a feeling Saban would have no idea that inviting a girl into his bedroom could be considered inappropriate. I followed with full knowledge that his request held absolutely zero chance of a proposition.

He looks pretty good from behind, I thought while looking up at him.

The upper level was a half circled hallway with many closed doors. He opened the second door at the top of the stairs.

Wow, his room is bigger than the Ballios entire cottage!

The room was as tidy as it was elegant. A royal blue, velvet comforter spread across a large bed. Thick curtains of matching luxurious fabric dressed the tall windows.

An item on top of his grand dresser caught my attention. While Saban searched his shelves for the book, I stepped closer to get a better look.

It was a child's toy train, about three inches long. It was not one of those cheapo toys you would get from a dollar store, or even the ones you might get from a regular toy store. It was elaborately detailed, handcrafted of wood and steel. I had an overwhelming urge to pick it up, but did not dare, in case it was a priceless item worth more than my head.

"Here it is," Saban declared and turned in my direction.

He saw my interest in the toy. "You can pick it up if you wish."

Without taking my gaze from the train, I jumped at his invitation.

Running my finger along the tiny details I said, "This is cool. Where did you get it?"

"I was about four or five," he spoke behind me. "Mother had taken me to a store. She had me trapped in one of those buggies."

When I rotated to face him, he gestured to where a belt would sit across his mid-section keeping him secured. Remembrance of his annoyance to the event showed on his beautiful face.

"I don't know why my mother would have me in one of those blasted contraptions at that age. I was very upset, howling for her to let me out. Out of nowhere, this little girl walks up to me.

"She had this long, wavy hair. I'll never forget her eyes, because they seemed to look right through me."

He paused, and I wondered if he was waiting for me to laugh at him. I did not.

"I know it seems odd for a child to take notice of such characteristics," he continued. "It also seems silly to attribute such qualities to another child. Maybe, it's just the way I remember it now."

A blissful air of peace swept over him.

Wish he looked that way when he thought of me.

"Anyway, I forgot about how angry I was with my mother."

"How did you get the train?" I probed, anxious to hear a happy ending to the tale of toddler-love-at-first-sight.

"Her mother called to her and she left, but not before she handed me this silver train."

"And, you never saw your gift-giving angel again?" I asked.

"No. I don't know if I had seen her before that either."

He looked past me, as though he was considering, only now, why that was the only time he saw the little girl.

"Maybe she was traveling through town," he said finally.

"That's a super cute story, Saban." I smiled then handed the train back to him. My pinky brushed his hand.

Breath sounded as he inhaled. Gently, he grasped my hand and I allowed it to relax in his palm. Meeting his incredible green eyes, all I could hear was the beat of my heart. He stared back at me with an expression not quite blank, but perhaps foreign even to him. His lips parted, and I felt self-conscious--almost naked, but could not look away.

Why doesn't he look away? Why isn't he saying something insulting, or flippant to break me from this spell?

Lips tingled. They wanted to be next to his. Drawing closer to him was beyond my control. He felt like a magnet.

CHAPTER 37

"Saban," a woman's voice sounded from the doorway. It was Eve Chariot. Although withered from sickness, she still exuded an nostril flaring bull vibe, and I was the matadors cape.

"Mrs. Ballios is here for Sophia." She took a step in.

"Darn, I never got to tell her Sarah was going to tutor me." I moved anxiously towards the door.

"Sarah was going to tutor you?" Mrs. Chariot's question impeded my escape and trapped me between them. I was about to speak, but Saban did first.

"Yes." A few strides brought him next to me. "Sarah told Sophia she would help her, invited her to the house, and slipped out through the back to meet Shea."

"That is inexcusable." Mrs. Chariot frowned. "I don't know what has gotten into that girl lately."

"So, I am going to assist Sophia with her math," Saban announced as he handed me the text. I awkwardly took it, not daring to look in his eyes again.

"You are going to tutor her?" Mrs. Chariot's inflection raised in pitch. Her shoulders pressed back, creating a posture that looked unnaturally rigid.

He turned to her as if it were the first time he had experienced that reaction from her. "Yes, I trust there isn't a problem with that."

Mrs. Chariot did her best to conceal a gasp, before replying, "That's good of you, Saban. I suppose you are an excellent candidate to help Sophia."

"And Sophia is going to assist me in dance," he continued.

Like a shield, I clutched the text to my chest. It appeared that he was filling her in, little by little, just to torture her. Did he have any idea his mother's poised exterior was about to blow?

Mrs. Chariot's chin quivered. Nostrils began to flare. Saban remained unmoved by his mother's increasing anxiety.

Speaking slowly, she asked, "Why would you need Sophia's assistance?"

Carelessly, Saban picked a piece of lint from the sleeve.

"Apparently, it was all father's doing. I'll explain later." He coolly fixed his sights on her and said, "Sophia's mother is here. Let us not hold her up any longer."

My mother? Why would he say that? Everyone knows Phaidra is not my mother.

Eve also caught her son's slip of speech. She sent him the most peculiar look. I wished I could find out what it was all about, but Phaidra had been waiting long enough.

"Nice to see you again, Mrs. Chariot," I lied cordially and raced from the room.

Phaidra occupied the bench I had already spent much time on.

"I'm so sorry, Phaidra. I must have had you worried."

She smiled up at me. "I was worried at first when you didn't come home. Then, Gerard's friend passed a message that you were here."

"Gerard's friend," I asked, closing the front door behind us.

"Yes, I'm Sam." The stone griffin guarding the entryway turned from its post to greet.

"And, I'm Able." Another griffin on the opposite side saluted.

"My goodness. Well, I'm . . . I'm pleased to meet you," I said, becoming aware again that this was a magic land, full of unusual sights.

"Pleased to meet you, my lady." They bowed in unison.

Matching their civility I replied, "Thank you for passing the message of my whereabouts. I'm afraid I have lost all sense of courtesy in the last day or so."

"No need to be so hard on yourself," Phaidra reassured. "It's not that grave a mistake. I actually just wanted to get out for a walk, and thought I would come get you at the same time."

"Are you feeling better?" I asked.

"We are. Our powers are still on the fritz, but after spending most of the day sleeping, we're doing better," Phaidra said. "I even made some nice cream of mushroom soup and fresh sourdough bread for dinner."

"And, lemon-glazed, honey cakes for dessert?" I gleamed.

Phaidra nodded with a chuckle and we set off for home.

~

In his favorite winged-back chair, Dio smoked his pipe after supper. Phaidra French-braided my hair and I filled them in on the events of the day. Phaidra got a kick out of the Mrs. Chariot story. Not the part about her feeling so ill, just the story about Saban messing with her.

"That boy does seem to know more than he lets on." Phaidra laughed. Then, her tone shifted to concern. "Eve did look in a very bad way, didn't she?"

"She really did," I agreed. "With her eyes all dark and sunken in."

Dio raised his glasses that hung from a chain around his neck.

"So, the boy plays with toy trains, does he?"

Phaidra waved her hand and giggled almost nervously.

"I'm super tired. I'm going to get to bed." I yawned.

"We'll not be far behind. Good night, Sophia," Phaidra said.

"Yes, good night, dear." Dio squeezed my hand as I passed by. Warmth from his strong clasp brought about an unexpected twinge to my nose.

Where did that come from?

I brushed it off and carried on to bed.

CHAPTER 38

Sunlight slapped me in the face through my window sheers. I had forgotten to close the heavy over-curtains the night before. My face felt puffy and swollen. Eyelids pasted shut. I forced one eye open to read the wall clock. It said it was twelve-thirty.

Great. I slept way too long. I'm going to be groggy all day.

Pure will alone forced me to roll out of bed. I needed to apologize to the Ballios' for sleeping in so long. No one was in the kitchen or the living room. I went outside to check the gardens. They were nowhere to be found.

Returning to the living room, I closed the front door.

Phaidra rushed out of her bedroom in her little white nightgown. Dio staggered behind, still dressed in his nightcap. Their faces were pale as death.

"I'm so sorry we left you alone all morning." Phaidra rubbed her eyes.

"Looks like we all needed some extra rest," I groaned. "And, truthfully, I could sleep for another eight hours."

When Elka got sick she used to say, she was rolled over by a gravel truck. That is exactly what this felt like.

"I had a crazy dream too," I recalled.

"Oh," Phaidra questioned. "What was that?"

"I was wandering in a forest," I said, "collecting brightly colored jewels from a path and placing them in a basket. The strange thing was, the basket never got heavier. I just got stronger."

"That sounds like a nice dream," Dio commented.

"It was, until this snake slithered into my path," I continued. "The serpent transformed into a woman. She had a forked tongue, which flicked out through a white porcelain mask. She wanted my jewels and when I told her she couldn't have them, she hit me. I punched her back, and it became this never-ending wrestling match."

"Oh dear," Phaidra commented.

"That's all I remember," I said rubbing my arms. "Feels like we were fighting for real, all night long."

"My old friend Fi Fi Quinn used to say jewels in visions represented our talents," Phaidra said.

Fi Fi? That's the second time I've heard that name? First it came from that blonde dancing girl in the forest? Does everyone know everyone here?

"So, some doll-faced snake woman is going to steal my talents," I half-laughed. "I'm pretty good at basketball, even though I don't particularly like it. She can have it."

"I'll have to give you a lesson on symbolism." Phaidra patted my arm. "Only not today."

Stretching his arms over head, Dio yawned. "It's lunch time. Maybe we'll feel better if we have something to eat."

"We have some soup in the icebox from last night. I'll heat that up," Phaidra said.

Phaidra trudged to the stove and added a few pieces of wood. Dio wearily staggered to the low cupboard and pulled out some bowls. Watching them struggle made me tired.

"I'll go pick some berries from outside," I murmured. "Hope you don't mind me going out in my gown. Energy is not a friend of mine right now."

"You go right ahead, dear." Phaidra's voice was muffled because her head was inside the icebox.

After grabbing two small baskets from the garden shed, I made my way to the backyard. Warm moist grass felt wonderful on my bare feet. It almost made me forget how sick I was.

Glorious sun shone upon my face, giving me enough strength to grab a couple handfuls of blueberries. I made up my mind that after lunch, the bench at the back of the house would be mine. I would lay down on it and let the sun love me.

"Sophia, lunch is ready," Dio called from inside.

We ate quietly at the table.

"Sunshine feels wonderful," I mentioned, taking a spoonful of soup.

"Yes. I'll do some weeding after lunch. It would be such a shame to waste all this wonderful weather," Phaidra said, her face becoming even more lifeless.

Dio lovingly cupped his wife's cheek. "You don't look so good, dear."

"Neither do you," Phaidra replied.

"Maybe you should have some berries." I reached for the basket from the counter behind me and placed it in the middle of the table.

"No thank you, Sophia. I'm going to lay down a little longer." Dio withdrew to his room.

"I'll have some." Phaidra reached for the berries. Out of exhaustion, her hand fell down on the corner of the basket, spilling berries all over the table.

"Oh no, what a mess." She unknowingly squashed some of the berries, creating purple stains on her wrist and on the side of her hand.

"Phaidra, I'll take care of it." I clasped her tiny wrist and lifted it off the smashed bits. "Why don't you go lay down?"

Trying to clear her head, Phaidra blinked before joining her husband.

Breathing accelerated. I became hot and sweaty. Cleaning the table was quite a chore. It had to be done though. Dear Phaidra did not deserve to wake up to such a mess. I popped a berry into my mouth. It made me feel worse.

Maybe I should go sit on the couch and rest a while. No. My bed would be more comfortable.

Dragging myself, muscle by muscle, I went to my room.

This sucks.

After flopping down on the bed, I managed to draw the covers over my body...

CHAPTER 39

Sunday morning started the same as the day before, only, the clock read eleven-thirty.

Can't believe I slept another day.

Slogging past the empty kitchen, I went out the front door, and straight to the backyard.

Unsure if I stumbled, or plopped down on the grass of my own accord, it was of no consequence. It is where I longed to be. Muscles still ached and the fresh air relieved me. It was so stifling indoors.

The new day was warmer than the day before. Thankfully, that left the grass dry. I could enjoy sitting without worrying about getting my nightgown soaked. Lying back, grass tickled my neck and feet. Birds in the trees chirped so sweetly. I imagined they were singing for me.

Phaidra wandered out to the yard and sat at my side.

"How are you feeling?" she asked.

"Better now that I'm out here in the sun. It may sound strange, but it's like the ground and air gives me energy." I sighed.

"That's not strange at all. All creatures draw energy from nature. Beings like gnomes, elves and faeries, especially, get their power from the elements," Phaidra explained.

Opening one eye to look up at her, I asked, "Not witches and wizards?"

"Yes, they do, too, but they have to call upon it to wield its power. For us, it's almost as natural as breathing."

After Phaidra brushed back a strand of blonde hair that blew over my face, she rested her small hand on my shoulder.

"Are you and Dio feeling better?" I asked.

"We're doing about the same as you, right now." She forced a smile. "Are you hungry?"

"No, just super thirsty." My tongue wanted to stick to the roof of my mouth.

"Did someone say water?" Dio tootled over with a bucket from the well and three tin cups. After dipping each in the bucket, he offered a mug to Phaidra and me. We gulped it down.

Phaidra exhaled and let her arms rest in her lap.

Dio filled the cups a second and third time, and then the bucket was empty.

"I'll get some more if you need it," Dio offered.

"That's enough for now," Phaidra said.

We all reclined in the grass and let the air move through us. Rays of light charmed my eyes closed before affectionately massaging my eyelids into a peaceful near doze. The sound of hoofs galloped on the nearby roadway, but I could not be bothered to move. A shadow passed over me. It was Phaidra who sat up to see who it was.

"It's young Saban," she announced.

A burst of gusto shot through me.

Saban slowed his horse and was squinting to view the yard.

"Oh no," I groaned. "I'm lying on the ground in my nightgown, and my hair hasn't been done in days. He's really going to think I'm a freak now."

Could I manage the strength to run into the house and avoid the horror of him seeing me?

"He's coming to the fence, Sophia. You should go say hello," Phaidra recommended.

"I'm not even dressed!" I screeched.

Phaidra shook her head. "You're wearing more than you kids wear to school. Besides, you don't have a choice, he's already seen you. Go on."

Saban dismounted, and was pulling his horse by the reigns to the fence. I got up from my resting place and walked warily towards him. Tugging at the tail of my braid, I thought about ripping out the band, and shaking it, to allow my strands to fly.

Yes, that would be totally inconspicuous.

His appearance went from a greeting, to a look of concern as I got closer, "What's wrong Sophia? You look terrible."

I managed a fractional smile and peered up at him through one eye. The sun was bright overhead.

"You know, if I wanted to be insulted, I would go to school."

His rich-coffee colored horse was quite stunning. My attention was drawn to the magnificent animal. I desperately wanted to stroke his mane.

But, I'm afraid it might talk to me. . . What? Why did that crazy thought enter my mind?

More insistent, Saban examined my face. "No really, what's the matter?"

"Don't know, just sick. We all are."

I tried to concentrate on Saban's beautiful face, as I gripped the wooden fence to steady myself. I must have wavered. His hand darted across the fence to my shoulder helping me to stand. Blood whooshed through my ears, the same way it did every time he was near, only it was much louder.

"Hope you haven't picked up my mother's illness from when you were at the house," he said with a pang of guilt.

His face became blurry, and I am sure his horse asked me if I wanted a pickle.

I know you can talk horsey. Does Saban know you can talk?

"Dio and Phaidra were feeling ill before that." A rush of heat sweep over me. "It'll pass. How is your mother doing?"

"She's not well. I'm off to Larrant to get my father. And . . ." He cleared his throat, and reached for his jacket's breast pocket. "I guess, it's good I've run into you. I have your necklace."

"He's been carrying it around all day," said the horse without even moving his lips.

I squinted in disbelief.

I can't friggen believe you talked. Are you for real? Am I for real? I don't feel very good.

"It must have slipped off when you were at the house," Saban continued. "I wanted to fix it before I returned it to you."

"That's a clever story, Saban," the horse chuckled.

Did you really just laugh, I asked the horse.

He winked at me.

Saban did not see it.

Under normal circumstances, I would have really questioned my sanity. In this situation, I prayed that my stomach would not feel inclined to erupt all over Saban. My grasp tightened on the fence.

"Why are you outside? You should be in bed." The classic Saban lecturing-attitude returned.

"I feel better outside, and don't use that tone with me," I scolded, before the ground rushed up to meet me.

My brain must have banged against both sides of my skull as I hit the ground. Boots scraped along the fence and landed hard beside me.

"Sophia!" Saban called.

I wanted to answer him. Sadly, my lips refused to move.

Arms reached under and scooped me up. He held me against his body. A heart pounded in my ear, but it was not mine.

"Can you bring her in here?" It was Phaidra's panicked voice.

I heard the familiar cottage door as it opened. Feet scrambled on hardwood floors. I was being placed in my soft cozy bed. Layered scents of bath oil, lavender, rose, and chamomile that had previously transferred from my skin to the sheets wafted up into the air and filled my lungs. Although, aware of the sounds around me, I was paralyzed with an overpowering exhaustion.

"I'll get Dr. Holbrook!" Saban's voice pulsed up my spine.

I envisioned being Frankenstein's bride, lying on a table, while my beloved sent volts of electricity through me, to bring me life.

"You need to retrieve your father, Saban. I'll go," Dio said hurriedly.

"You're too ill, Mr. Ballios, you should be in bed," Saban protested. "I have a horse. I'll be faster."

Saban's insistent voice grew further away as my consciousness began to fade.

At first there was nothing. Then, I saw green. Everything was green. I felt myself rising, floating horizontally. The green became grass as a forceful rush of cool air entered my lungs. I immediately moved upright, feet firmly planted on the ground.

Where am I? I think I'm dreaming.

CHAPTER 40

I was standing to the side of an unknown house. Voices came from the front yard. I followed them until I saw three girls crouched behind some bushes.

A brown-haired girl and a blonde poked their heads around one side of the opening that allowed access to the yard. A red-haired girl stooped on the other side. They were all quite captured by whatever it was they viewed.

Angry male voices shouted in the distance. A thunderous crack of lightning shot up into the sky. I jumped in fear. Tripping over my feet, I backed into a lilac tree beside the front porch. The girls in the yard remained unaffected by my blunder as they kept their attention fixed on the show outside the yard.

Two girls standing together did not even try to conceal their pleasure over the scene they watched, laughing hysterically. The red-haired girl clasped her hand over her own mouth in fright.

Brushing some broken twigs from my nightgown, I crept closer. I recognized the two girls standing together as Daphne and Wisteria. The other girl was also someone known, very well in fact. It was Divina!

What is she doing with these girls? She told me, her parents had forbidden her to hang out with them. Divina said they were trouble makers, and that she did not know what she was getting herself into when she started to hang out with them.

"Divina, what are you doing? What have you done to your hair? It looks ridiculous." I commented on the blunt cut of her bangs, about a half an inch above her brows. She ignored me as if I were not even there.

"Please, we have to do something! They're going to get hurt," Divina pleaded with the other girls.

"Whatever, Divina! I knew you were as simple as a Goliath," Wisteria snapped.

In school I overheard certain students murmuring about Goliaths. I gathered from the prattle that they were an unusually large-statured race, not known for intellect.

The sound of cracking startled me. It must have been something large and heavy breaking from the Earth, because the ground began to rumble.

Standing behind Divina, I poked my head over the bush.

A lanky man levitated and hurled a tree stump across the street. It smashed through his neighbor's stained glass window.

Divina shot up and ran into the streets crying, "Stop, it was me. It was me!"

Wait a second. This already happened. It's the story of how Divina got grounded from hanging out with those terrible girls.

The man clutched Divina roughly by the wrist. He proceeded to authoritatively guide her to the sidewalk, and down the street. Daphne and Wisteria whizzed past me, racing down the side of the house to disappear into the backyard.

"Who cares about them?" I grumbled. "Divina's in trouble."

I stepped out to follow Divina when I felt a tap on my shoulder. I turned to see the most beautiful faerie woman hovering about a foot off the ground. Emerald eyes glittered like jewels.

Her sapphire mini-dress flattered her tiny frame. A shimmering barely-there, cape rested upon it. Reaching out, she gently brushed my cheek. I felt a warm tingle along the trail of her fingertips.

I knew her, sort of. She looked much older, but it was the same singing faerie from my forest dream.

Why isn't she talking?

Spinning around, she glided along the path that the wicked girls had taken. Thin, opaque wings fluttered. It was hard to believe they were strong enough to propel her.

"Alright," I said to myself. "I'll follow. Divina's story has already been written. Let's see what's behind door number two."

I followed the golden-haired faerie around the corner, almost crashing right into the menacing pair of witches. They were crouched down in consultation.

"She'll be sorry for this!" the blonde named Wisteria snarled.

"Wait till they see what else we have in our little book of tricks." Daphne sneered, "Let's go."

The girls took off toward the back gate. As I twisted to trail them, the faerie woman pulled a willow branch from behind her back. She flicked it at the ground, and a giant mushroom sprouted up in my path. Before stopping myself, I tripped and fell flat on my face.

"Hey, what did you do that for?" I spun around to confront her. She was gone.

Vision zeroed in on a basement window. Curiosity overcame me. I crawled nearer to see what was inside. Below the window, a long table held a tower of books, various bowls, and a pot of flowers.

Hey that's odd. How did they get those bright, purple flowers to grow in a dark, dusty basement? I'll have to ask the Ballios about that.

I made sure to get a good look at the flowers, so an accurate description could be given. It was more of a fuchsia bulb, set atop a green stalk. It had waving black leaves on it.

"Hey, wait a second," I said aloud. "Druaudidon! The outlawed plant that makes magics sick is growing right here. I've got to tell Dio and Phaidra!"

Leaping to my feet, I raced to the front yard. Not knowing where to go, I curved towards Saban's house. I rationalized that the griffin guards, Sam and Able, could get a message to the Ballios, or maybe, Gerard.

Gerard could help me with anything. Then again, I should go straight to the RBI . . . but I have no idea where that is.

Searing pain burned on my shoulder. The scar's image radiated red. It started with the etch of a triangle, and then the X lit up. Now that it was glowing, they seemed more like flaming's wings. A blazing ring enclosed the preceding symbols.

"So, this is why you're so weak," a rancid voice grated from behind.

Even before I turned around, I knew it was the disgusting demon from earlier. For some reason, his presence made the mark on my skin burn. It happened the last time he was around too.

The sight of him still stole my breath. There was no mistaking his mangled appearance.

Rolled-up cuffs and an unbuttoned shirt exposed gaping cuts and sores. He grabbed my arm and pulled me into him. With my back pressed into his chest, he entrapped me. Cold, sticky wounds rubbed against my bare-arms. The stink of rot filled my nose.

"You've had poison eating away at you all this time." He panted at my collar. "Lucky toxin. I wouldn't mind having a bite myself."

CHAPTER 41

His rough tongue lapped against my neck. Jagged teeth grazed the skin.

Do demons eat people? Is he going to tear a chunk out if my neck? Am I going to die? Or will he leave me as disfigured as he is?

I heard myself whimper. It scared me more.

Gerard said the demon wasn't that powerful. He seems pretty friggen strong to me.

"What's your problem?" an unexpected growl of defiance rumbled through my cry.

Before he could answer, the faerie woman appeared in front of us.

Her mouth opened to scream, but nothing came out.

This made the demon laugh.

"Look, it's a little faerie," he scorned. "Even as magnificent as you once were, it will take too much energy to rip through the planes. You've ascended too high, doll. Your voice can't even make it through."

Her face twisted with wrath.

Does she want to help me?

"We've got to be going now. Azdor is waiting to meet your little gal. Don't bother following. Faeries aren't allowed in my realm. Sayonara."

We disappeared and re-emerged on the dark sidewalk of a quiet city neighborhood.

The demon stumbled, his feet tangled in a trash bag. Someone must have put it out after he left from this spot. He released his hold on me to free his feet. I took the opportunity to run.

Fresh air replaced his stench once a few yards came between us.

A thin space between two stores revealed itself as the quickest way to disappear. It ran the length of the buildings and exited on to a back ally. I was well acquainted with the area. It was Swan Street back in Gettysburg.

Slipping into the safety of darkness required caution. It was well known to the neighborhood, as a spot used by drunks who needed to relieve themselves. I watched my step to avoid any manner of human waste.

Broken glass littered the ground. I barely began to wonder why it was not cutting my shoeless feet, when something snapped against my neck. It pulled tight and began to block my airway. Gasping, I spun around trying to remove whatever had snared me.

Black teeth grinned as he drew me towards him. The demon had lassoed me. In an act of viciousness, he jolted the strap, slamming my head into a concrete building.

Vision blurred. I could not tell if it was the blow to the head or the lack of air that triggered it.

Blood trickled into my eyes. With one last tug, he had me back in his clutches.

I did not struggle as he hauled me down the sidewalk. I was too scared he would impede another one of my senses. He brought me back to the spot we originated from. It was in front of the textile factory. A memory of the Asian girl from my childhood flashed.

She warned me with her eyes to stay away!

With a tight hold on the leather strap, the demon shoved me through the front door. I was dragged down a stairwell into the basement. He tossed open a heavy metal door. Roaring from the rampant blaze made it hard to hear. Walls themselves were on fire.

I drew back from the flames and the demon laughed. He pushed me, and I fell to my knees. Peering through the sweaty tangle of my own hair, I inspected the walls. They were not truly burning. It was an illusion, but the intense heat was real.

A deep, abysmal voice from behind a newspaper grated my eardrums. The beast sat at a mammoth, grey metal desk, well-suited for a dingy, basement office in a slum building.

"Reef, that is no way to treat my guest," the voice boomed.

When he lowered the paper, I forced myself not to scream.

Glistening red from head to toe, this monster had no skin.

The demon named Reef dropped to his knees and obediently held my tether out to the skinless one. I fixated on the bones in the master demon's feet as he approached. They resembled bloody organ keys, as the bones lifted and fell with each step. I wondered if they would bust through what little flesh he had left to encase them.

Grasping my forearm, he forced me to my feet. His hand was hot and slippery. It left a blood congealed handprint on my skin when he let go.

"I'm glad you are joining us, Sophia." He smiled, a lipless sneer, showing exposed jaw muscles. "I am Azdor. You can call me Master. I've waited a long time to add you to my collection."

"What are you talking about?" I took a step back, not that it mattered. While the slight extra distance gave me some comfort, it was not going to benefit my cause in any way, trapped in an inferno with demons.

"Your time has come," Azdor said, confident of his mastery over me. "I grant you the honor of becoming part of us."

"Join you? That doesn't happen until death. Are you saying I'm dying?" I stammered. "I'm not dying! I'm just sick."

Both demons laughed with an empty, soulless screech that echoed off the burning walls.

Azdor pointed to a line of seats made from concrete blocks. Nothing more needed to be said. Reef scampered instantly to the nearest chair.

The head demon waved his hand and chanted, "By the power of obsidian, open a window to the deathbed of my newest servant."

A movie screen lowered from the ceiling. It played with a scene of my bedroom. Dio and Phaidra wept at either side of my bed. My body lay unconscious between them.

"Blossom," Phaidra whispered an endearment. It rolled off her tongue as though it were a childhood nickname spoken a million times before. "I can't lose you. Fight it. Oh, great guardian," she sobbed to the ceiling. "Please help her fight this."

Dio swabbed a wet cloth against my reddened face. I could actually feel the cool stroke here in my captivity.

Gerard stood at my window, looking in.

"It won't be long now," Azdor declared with the confidence of absolute authority. "Death comes shortly. All I need is your submission to proceed."

It took time for what he was saying to register. I was so engrossed with my impending death being played out before me on a screen. Then comprehension came.

"Are you crazy?" I snapped back to reality. "I will never join you."

"Resist and die, or live forever with me, pet," Azdor replied.

"Yeah, sounds like a plan," I mocked him. "Do I get to look forward to being as mutilated as you two? No thanks."

"Fool," Azdor roared. "You will cease to exist."

Admiring his biceps, he said, "I am excellence. Can you not see the years of dedication I invested, transforming my body into perfect form?"

His physique was rather large with layers of rippling muscles. But I was so distracted by the slimy, skinless mess that I could not appreciate the things he revered.

"You did that to yourself? Took off your own skin?" I asked in a mix of contempt and disbelief.

"Someday, I will rule all realms. Everyone will see my perfection."

"You're revolting."

"No!" he raged. "It is you, humans, who are revolting." He yanked my tether, choking me. "Join me now, or I will prolong your death."

Through choking sputters, I laughed at him. "Isn't that a good thing?"

Honestly I was not sure why I was being so cocky. Maybe it was the swagger of hopelessness.

Azdor pointed to the scene in my bedroom. "They will suffer much longer than necessary. It will make their bodies weaker-- fragile enough for the toxin to takeover. Those tiny creatures will be ravaged . . . and they will die."

The evil one grinned at his prophecy. Unfulfilled by his initial abusive outburst, he jerked my strap once more, sending me tumbling across the floor and wheezing for breath.

Phaidra cried out.

My ailing body twisted in the bed beside her, the same way I did while crumpled on the inferno floor.

Azdor laughed. "Rule number one. Bodies feel the spirit's suffering."

Dio reached across the bed for his wife's hand but was unable to ease her anguish. She tucked her hands into her stomach and expelled a tortured cry.

Something tugged at my hair, reefing my head sideways as Azdor dropped his face close to mine. A gory disembodied hand hung from the end of my hair. A stump at the end of Azdors arm revealed one of his evil attributes. Sending body parts across the room must have come in handy for stealth attacks on victims.

"You are killing them," Azdor shrieked. "Don't you care? Do you care about no one but yourself? You selfish girl?"

I knew he was manipulating me to his own ends, but it did not matter. He was right. The Ballios's were both very sick and getting worse. It was a miracle they were not already in the same state as me.

For whatever reason, they care for me. They love me.

Azdor screamed over and over. Each word cursed seemed to spill through me onto Phaidra like vats of acid. It deepened her cries.

Screams grew louder. My senses overwhelmed. All I could think was how they took me into their home, how Saban referred to Phaidra as my mother.

I haven't known them long, but, somehow, we are connected. I love them. I can't let them die!

"Alright," I conceded through tears. "Take me."

CHAPTER 42

Azdor did not hear my submission. He had become sadistically distracted by the misery playing out on screen.

"What the hell is that outside the window?" The bloody muscle-head monster moved closer to the screen.

"Looks like that nosy queen, again," Reef replied.

"Interesting." Azdor rubbed his chin.

"That the faerie is still hanging around, draining her energy?" Reef asked. "Doesn't she care that it will incapacitate her for months, being so far from her proper home?"

"No," Azdor replied, "interesting because the obsidian spell should not pick up spirits."

"She's not technically a spirit, Master."

"Which makes it even stranger." Azdor tapped his finger to his cheek. "I must remember to complement my warlock minion for the extra feature in the incantation."

The faerie reached for Gerard's shoulder. He was crouching to see inside my window. His distraught expression over the tragedy unfolding in my bedroom melted when saw who was behind him.

Bowing deeply, Gerard lowered his head in respect, as if he had not seen her in a long time. She must have been very important to him.

Quiet discussion between the two became oddly animated. We could not hear what was being said, but any joy Gerard initially felt in seeing her quickly faded. His posture stiffened. Fury twisted his stone face.

What are they talking about?

Gerard shot straight up into the air and disappeared. The force visibly shook the Ballios's house. Whatever news the faerie gave him demanded immediate action. Dio and Phaidra took little notice of their home quaking or the down rush of air from his enormous rate of ascent.

The faerie assumed Gerard's vigil at the window. Lips pressed into her delicately clasped hands as sorrow consumed her.

Who is she? Why does she care what is happening to me? Unless... could it have nothing to do with me at all? Does she know the Ballios? Perhaps, she cannot bear to see them so upset.

"Argh! That damn gargoyle," Azdor snarled. "Mobile statics are the most unpredictable. Put my newest trinket in a cell. We need to contain the situation."

Fearing Reef was going to yank me up by the neck, I forced myself to my feet to avoid any more violence. He caught my arm and part-shoved, part-pulled me down a short, blazing hallway.

No surprise, he thrust me into an empty room with the same flaming, hellhole motif as the rest of the place. A metal door clanked shut behind Reef. I could hear the lock engage. The assumed safest part of the room was in the middle, away from the walls. I huddled on the floor. Concrete felt cool against my skin.

It doesn't make sense.

Even though the fire neglected to consume the building, it gave off insufferable heat. *Why was the floor so cool?*

Agitated by the strap around my throat, I pulled it free and flung it across the room. It took a great deal of energy. Sweat dripped from my nose.

More skin needed to be cooled. I tugged at my nightgown. Once my legs were exposed and pressed against the soothing concrete, a fevered cheek collapsed and found solace there too. I tried to find comfort in the rhythmic beat of a heart that hammered dangerously fast.

Thoughts stopped forming for a time. What was there to think about? There was no way out. I was seventeen and dying. The only thing suckier was knowledge that I was harming the people who were unfortunate enough to care about me.

Faces began to flicker in my mind. They belonged to everyone I ever loved. Caleb smiled at me. He was missing a front tooth. Mrs. Tifton held out a cranberry muffin. Elka and Edwin pointed at my first car. Many images of Phaidra and Dio rushed through in a blur. Even Gerard, as a stone monolith in the park across of the school, slipped into my thoughts. Emotions from events, both happy and horrible, filled me. I remembered that I wanted to do stuff with my life.

I don't want to die!

My mouth had become so dry. It hurt to breath.

I don't want to leave Phaidra and Dio. I want to see them again.

"Please don't leave us, blossom," Phaidra's voice suddenly cried out from nowhere.

What!

Pressing up onto my hands, I searched the ceiling and room for the source of my gnome mother's voice.

Maybe I'm hallucinating, I thought. Under the circumstance, it would not be unreasonable.

"Sophia is strong," Dio reassured. "She'll find a way."

A projection of my bedroom formed on the concrete floor. Phaidra lay, inconsolable, across my stomach in bed. Dio stroked her back in helpless repetition.

A dark, hooded figure loomed behind the faerie. She was startled when she noticed him standing there and backed away in fear.

That must be death. He's there to take me.

Contempt spread across the faeries beautiful face, while the creature who had arrived to escort me from life advanced to the window.

Silken wings drooped and shoulders slumped, but the cloaked-man did not acknowledge her distress. She might as well have been invisible to him.

Death observed from behind the glass. I could not see his face. If he resembled these demon freaks, I was glad he could not be seen. Did he have any emotions?

Does he feel joy from watching misery? Is he a monster or simply an impassive entity?

I was soon going to find out.

Oxygen in my fiery prison had nearly burned up. Short intermittent pants were all I could get in. It would have been helpful if I had the power to blow off the ceiling and get some air.

"Her lungs are shutting down," Dio whispered from the image.

"Nooo," Phaidra sobbed.

I reached for the depiction of her on the floor, but she could not feel me. It was just a hologram.

The cloaked-one at my window flinched. His pale, white palm pressed against the glass. This reaction seemed to confuse the faerie. She inspected him from behind, strained to see his face around the hood.

What she saw brought her relief. She smiled momentarily before being reminded of the suffering inside the window.

Iridescent tears trickled down the beautiful faeries face. She closed her eyes.

Past exhaustion, I slumped flat to the floor. From that vantage, I could no longer see the Ballios, but my heart brought me closer.

Hard to breath . . . I need air. Now!

A wall quaking clap sounded above, followed by an immediate an overwhelming squall of wind. The ceiling exploded. Debris blasted upwards, as if detonation came from the room I was in.

In preparation of ceiling particle return-fall, I covered my head.

Uncontrollable vibrations pulsed through me. Without knowing what to expect from impending death, I figured my spirit had started to dissolve.

The entire building shook.

Is my consciousness beginning to shift?

Something crashed above.

I squirmed on the ground. Terror enveloped me.

Enough Sophia! If death is coming, face him. He will not get the pleasure of seeing fear.

With the last remnants of life-strength, I tossed up to my side. It was enough to let me collapse onto my back.

An altered landscape above came into focus. Shock at the ones who hovered up top was enough to kill. I shook forcibly.

CHAPTER 43

Gerard, and dozens of stone-bodied sidekicks, had torn off the building's roof. They must have also blasted the massive perfect circle over the ceiling I was trapped in as well.

Weird. How did they cut a hole in the basement ceiling where I was, and return to the roof without me knowing?

As easily as tossing a hay bale, the team heaved the roof to one side. It crashed on the street below, making a strong quake, one that surely would have been felt over several neighborhood blocks.

Enormous tree-creatures leaned into view and took positions around the newly demolished skylight. Glowing rods they held illuminated the room like an ethereal sky.

I can't believe it. There are so many of them . . . all here to help me.

Sam and Able from Saban's home swooped in. They spotted me at the same time. After pointing me out to one another, in a comical "I saw her first" performance, they landed.

"Sophia!" Gerard yelled from above.

The metal door to my prison flew open. Demons, Adzor and Reef, rushed in.

"Minions arise. Defend my kingdom!" Azdor's voice filled the vacant chamber.

Dark mist wafted out from all walls. Floating upward, the mist formed into shadowy masculine figures. Tormented moans of varied tenors merged into a dismal symphony.

Once the murky creature came into contact with Gerard's army, they transformed into an exact duplicate of them. It startled the gargoyles to be faced with themselves.

Oh no! That can't be good.

The element of surprise proved an advantage for the hell creatures.

One perfect replica of Able caught him around the neck, ramming him against the wall on the main level. Both disappeared through the hole they created in solid concrete. Chaos of ferociously flapping wings prevented me from pinpointing how the mid-air brawl was going with Sam and his double.

Gerard barely got out the words, "They can't--" out before his demon doppelgänger crashed into him.

Boulders rammed. Debris shattered. My bones quaked with every close impact by falling parts of concrete and stone wall.

Creatures, good and bad, delivered blow after blow. They showed no withhold, but not a move could be made, that was not foretold. Mirror images matched exactly.

I lost track, of who was who, as they wrestled in-flight and on the ground. Finally, Gerard roared the loudest and I understood that he was the one who kept glancing at me in concern.

Tree men, remained in place along the top of the building and bashed their twins with light rods. Originals had white poles, while the fake's had blue. The color of the pole was the only thing that could not be duplicated.

Moving in sync, every twisting impact formed an X of light, and an explosion of sparks in the sky. From where I laid the display was extraordinary.

Rock-hard oblique's flexed with precise movements against her equally exquisite female gargoyle adversary. From the main floor level, she shielded blows from her twin with ease. Who was this stone lady?

The hard bodied good-gal squatted with a smirk. Bracing her hands to the floor, she ducked under the evil chicks legs, and launched her in the air.

"You may look like me, honey," good-gal taunted, "but you lack my panache."

Nasty twin bashed her head on a beam. A murmured chuckle escaped me.

My new favorite superhero readied herself with a club worn on her back. While nasty twin descended, superhero heaved upwards with the weapon, meeting her in the mid-section. The demon exploded into a black haze and vanished.

Alright! Score one for super chick!

"How did she do that?" Azdor roared in anger before bolting from the room.

Reef followed him.

Pleased with her triumph, the stone-lady turned to the match above her. It was between two scrawny, bent-back beings with pointed ears. One might consider their features grotesque. I thought they were beautiful. Well, the ones that belonged to my team, that is.

I hoped the lady gargoyle was better at deciphering her comrades than me.

She circled behind the scuffle, to determine friend from foe. She settled on one. Seizing the base of his wings, she yelled, "You can't fly without wings, dude. Believe it!"

She ripped both wings off.

Outstanding!

The demon's face dropped faster than he did. He fell from the roof level headed straight for me. I could not move.

With my forearm, I shielded my head. Not that it was going to make a difference. I was about to get crushed.

Seconds before impact, the demon's impersonated body dissipated. A shadowy form whooshed over me and away.

"You help them," the woman gargoyle told her comrade and pointed to the roof. "I'll get the girl."

Bent-back nodded and rocketed upwards. She-goyle swooped down and scooped me up. I felt so feeble in her hard, granite arms.

"So, you're Sophia," she greeted with a friendly welcome.

Closing my lids to acknowledge, I could scarcely laugh when I said, "And you are?"

"I'm Panache."

"That wing tear off thing was pretty cool." I managed a weak smile.

"I know, right."

With a stroke of her wings, we elevated past the former ceiling of the basement to the main level.

Reef was waiting with his leather lasso. He twirled it over head.

With a snap of the tether, he caught Panache's ankle and yanked her toward the wall.

She released me so I would not crash with her.

Even though it was a short distance to fall, it hurt when I landed. Feeble and winded, I curled to my side.

"It's all in your head, Sophia," Gerard bellowed from overhead while tightly engaged by his rival duplicate.

I don't understand? What's in my head?

Gerard slammed into the anti-Gerard with a stone cracking impact. Despite the fight to the death, only one of the Gerard's strained to keep eye contact with me.

I wish he would kick that jerk's butt, so he could tell me what the hell he means. That could take forever. How do you win in a fight against yourself? You can't . . . although, Panache managed the impossible. Judging by Azdor's reaction, her victory was unprecedented. Could she repeat it? More importantly, can Gerard?

Every combat had its own version of smash and bob, yet neither side appeared to advance toward victory. I had little knowledge of demons or gargoyles, much less those weirdo animated trees. I wondered if either side would ever fatigue.

Can they battle for eternity?

"You can't win," I uttered mostly to myself. "You can't fight them."

By some marvel, Gerald heard me.

"What would you suggest I do?" he asked as they wrestled.

"I don't know. Give up?" I spoke into the air.

"Not an option, Sophia."

My brain raced for a solution. Nothing was coming.

"Fighting won't work," I said. "He's just as strong as you, and knows every move you're going to make. You've got to do something . . . unpredictable . . . like the opposite of what you would do normally."

"The opposite?" Gerard questioned as he ducked a right hook.

With his expression in full out confusion, he straightened and wrapped his enemy up in his arms. "Come here, buddy," he grinned through a clenched jaw.

The doppelgänger thrashed to no avail in Gerard's stronghold. This made my friend laugh. The sound lessoned the pressure felt in my chest.

Gerard's rock-tight embrace must have weakened the demon. The struggle subsided. Faux-Gerard started to moan, lonely, drawn-out cries. Even withstanding my deathly state, the wail brought me a deep sadness.

Long blades sprung from Gerard's knuckles. Rolling his wrist inward, he jabbed them into his enemy's back.

Relief, not the scream of defeat I expected from the demon, washed over as he was torn in two. The rock replica dispersed into a shadow and vanished.

The rest of the gargoyles followed Gerard's lead. Most were too involved in their own fights to see what had happened, but they all mimicked Gerard's attack. It was like they had a telepathic connection to one another.

It seemed to be working. Once embraced, demon attackers became docile. Gerard took a deep breath. His chest heaved in reprieve.

Helpless on the narrow lip of the main floor, I watched him descend. Seeing him gave me comfort, even though I knew there was nothing he could do. I was still dying.

At least, now I can go peacefully . . . Dio and Phaidra can recover.

Fright replaced Gerard's calm expression.

What's wrong now?

Bloody hands slipped under my shoulders, curled around my arms, and dragged me to my feet. Repositioning, muscled arms clasped me around the ribcage. I was little more than a lifeless doll.

"Let her go, Azdor," Gerard demanded as his feet touched down.

Long claws ejected from the demon master's knuckles, the same way they had on Gerard. Steel clanked as the glistening blades crisscrossed around my ribcage.

CHAPTER 44

Gerard's stance locked. He knew the efficiency of the weapon held on me.

"I admire certain attributes about you, rock-head," Azdor mocked. "These blades are ingenious. And, the way you ripped my man apart up there really got my blood pumping, you know. I'd like to see that done again. Wouldn't you?" He pressed his bloody cheek to mine.

"Sophia, he can't hurt you," Gerard said. "None of this can."

"Of course we can," Azdor snapped. "We've already done a magnificent job of hurting her. How does your head feel, sweetie?"

How the hell do you think it feels? It got smashed into a brick wall.

I said nothing.

Azdor whispered in my ear. "How do you think it's going to feel when I lodge these blades around your sternum and rip you open like a lobster?"

Liquid ran down my face. I was not sure if it was sweat, tears or his blood.

"Sophia, he can't do that." Gerard assured with a calm that did not match the urgency of threat.

"Gerard," I whimpered. "I've enjoyed living in the world of illusion, but this is reality."

"No, Sophia. You're in spirit form. Your body is in Desta."

"I know," I replied. "I saw the whole thing on TV. You were outside my window with that faerie."

"Did you hear that, rock star?" Azdor sneered. "She has all the information she needs to make an informed decision. We've discussed it, and I'm pleased to say the girl already came to a decision. You and your Neanderthals can go."

"We go nowhere," Gerard growled. "Sophia," he softened, "if you saw it, than you should understand. You are not your body."

"Why am I so weak?"

"Because you think you should be," Gerard explained with a simplicity I wanted to believe. "Your body is very sick, so your spirit easily separated, and began to wander. Without knowing it, you travelled into a past event. Those can be tricky to get out of. Especially if you think you're dreaming. But a guardian followed you."

"Guardian? Who?"

"Queen Calista," Gerard said with deep reverence.

That must be the singing blonde that tripped me with the mushroom.

"Why would she care what happened to me," I panted.

"You're one of her people," he explained. "She feared you might get lost, so she tripped you into the present. Travelling in spirit can be confusing. Deception becomes difficult to distinguish from reality. That's why Reef was able to lure you here. You believed he could hurt you, so he did."

Thoughts drifted back to the broken glass stepped on in the alley.

It should have cut me, but it didn't. Can I believe that it's because I did not have time to give it power over me?

I touched my neck where chafe from Reef's tether rubbed my skin raw.

I felt Reef's lasso around my neck . . . I know I did! But I feared he would catch me. Is Gerard saying I could have stopped him? What about the fire? This has got to be hell. The building's still blazing.

"This is a version of hell," Gerard replied to my thoughts. "You're creating the fire. Sophia, a high fever is ravaging your body. You've incorporated that feeling into this setting, and explained it to yourself as a burning building. These slum lords knew you would be more vulnerable with this illusion."

"You can read my mind, Gerard?" I muttered.

"Yes, Sophia. We all can," Gerard replied. "We statics can only read your mind while in spirit form. All you need to know, now, is that this is your true form and you are strongest when you're in spirit."

A haunting choir howled from above. Minions of this hell returned to their former murky selves, before vanishing into nothing.

Panache stepped out from a large hole in the wall beside us.

"Dentro de demonio," she said to Azdor. "I've tangled with these beasts before, and they have no authority over me. I'm always true to myself. I forgive every mistake I've ever made, cause, that's how I got to be so awesome."

Azdor lampooned, "You're one in a million, my dear."

The bloody creature tossed me toward the ragged edge of the busted floor. Panache anticipated such an act and was poised to catch me. It was a little like being tossed into a brick wall, but the inherited protection she offered softened her embrace.

Why did Azdor suddenly let me go? Is it really that easy? His hold on me is broken simply because, I know?

Gerard set an arm across us both. The rest of the gargoyles, including Sam and Able, sailed down and created a formidable army surrounding us.

"We'll be going now." Gerard fixed his glare on the demon.

"I caught that," Azdor grumbled. "That one," he pointed to me, "won't make it much longer, anyway."

Something scuttled at my chest, making its way up to my collar bone. Azdors smarmy hand emerged from beneath my gown and clutched my throat. Digging his glare into mine from several feet in front of us, he concealed to everyone else the rounded stub. Even under my protector's care, he was able to attack me again.

"No," I roared through my gasp.

Panache flinched. All eyes turned to me in question.

As everyone realized what Azdor was doing, I ripped through Panache's stone arms.

"Don't touch me." An unanticipated force raged inside as I threw myself into the vile trespasser.

Gerard's heavy foot scuffed along the floor as he advanced to aid me, but his lady held him back.

"She's got this one."

Panache assured with more confidence than warranted. I was no match for a demon. My only aim was to go out fighting. Compliance with the world of beasts, who stole whatever they desired, was no longer tolerable.

Both hands seized his neck. If killing him was the plan his slick body would have made it difficult. I just wanted him to look me in the eyes. Show him I had enough.

Azdor laughed to ridicule, but it did not bother me. I was instantly captured by my reflection in the black of his eyes. It was a tiny silhouette, but then it disappeared because of a radiance that shone upon his face.

The monster's grin faded. Features warped. Although the unexpected light displeased him, perhaps even repulsed, he could not turn away.

"Her eyes are glowing," Sam spoke in awe. "I didn't know she could do that."

Is he saying my eyes are creating the spotlight?

Through sputtered breaths Azdor rasped, "Even oblivious to who you are, you still found a way to stumble through."

Convulsions ensued. He was dying.

"What does that mean?" I questioned. "Who am I?"

At first, Azdor's response seemed flippant, or at the very least ambiguous. Despite its origin though, coming from the mouth of evil, I sensed his answer held great truth.

"Maybe if you stop asking, you'll figure it out."

Flames ignited around his feet and swiftly consumed his deviant form. Gerard pulled me into him. Since my last tank of energy had to be drained, I collapsed into his arms. He scooped me up, and we watched as Azdor burned by the fire from his own hell.

"And that takes care of the last sack of rubbish," Able jested.

"Well done, baby girl," Panache brushed her hard palm along my arm.

"Azdor's clean-up crew should be arriving shortly," Gerard said. "Let's get out of here."

"Shouldn't we stick around and take care of them too?" Panache protested. "They broke *a lot* of laws. We're perfectly justified in--"

"In time," Gerard interrupted. "The inferno filth needs to reset balance in the neighborhood, first. I project construction on the roof will begin in about ten minutes."

"Reset balance?" I muttered. "I don't understand. Are you saying demons care about what happens to the local people?"

"No," Gerard replied. "Azdor owns the building. He's got it veiled with some pretty heavy demon mojo. No human is able to see the real form of any supernatural as long as they are in a certain radius of the structure. I'm not sure how far his power extends, but we made sure the roof didn't fall on any human when we tossed it off."

Yeah that's right, the roof. How could I forget?

I regarded beautiful stars through the opening above.

"Rebuilding will be complete before morning," he explained. "It will look as decrepit as it always did. They will also spread their influence throughout the community to whitewash anything that can't be covered up by magic."

"I thought demons relied on chaos?" I asked.

"Yes, but demons fear that too much, too soon, will cause humans to turn to their chosen God."

"I see." Breathing still hurt. "So, I'm wandering around in spirit form. Does that mean this is all in my head? And what about you?"

"We're in our bodies." Gerard indicated him and his clan. "Demons are in their rotting meat sacks. And, you, Sophia, are really here, in Gettysburg, Ohio."

"Are you ready to go home?" Panache asked.

I nodded.

Dozens of wings belonging to my savior-army began to swoop. We rose through a brilliant yellow film created by the tree's light rods, which momentarily blinded me. When next I could see, we were surrounded by buttery light with sparkly flecks floating down around us.

Holding my palm out, I collected some flecks. When I had a handful, I blew them away.

Gerard's chest vibrated against my side when he smiled.

"Sophia, I want you to know that some things are forgotten when you return from spirit form," he said. "Memories will come back, in time. As they do, you'll have questions, and I want you to come to me."

I hummed to acknowledge.

"You can return to your body from here," he said.

"You're coming with me, aren't you?" I asked.

"No," he replied. "We must go back to Earth. There are matters we must attend to. Don't worry. I'll be back. I've watched over you for a long time, even when you were a little girl."

His head hung. "I haven't been able to protect you from everything. For that, I will never forgive myself."

"Gerard." I reached up and stroked his hard face. I wished to ease his guilt.

He shook his head, not wanting to be consoled. It seemed to make him feel worse.

"Now," his voice cracked with emotion, "you have many to watch over you. Soon, you will discover how powerful you truly are."

I wanted to ask him what he meant, but could not bring myself to speak. His despair took my words away.

Phaidra's voice echoed in the distance. "I can see your eyes fluttering, darling. Are you ready to come back to us?"

CHAPTER 45

Upon opening my eyes, the first thing I saw was the wall clock. It read quarter after nine. Judging by sun shining through my bedroom window, it must have been morning. I slept almost another whole day.

In my waking mind, I had a sense of Gerard, however I could not be sure why. He was not anywhere.

Maybe I had a dream about him?

I remembered seeing Divina, Wisteria, and Daphne. I recalled a faerie woman. Flashes of bloody men, and shadow creatures were a haze. Their identity or what they wanted faded as I looked around my room.

The window caused me pause.

What happened here?

Holding my wrist was a silvery-haired man wearing a stethoscope. I felt a sting in my forearm. He was drawing blood into a syringe.

"Dr. Holbrook?" I asked.

Since we had never met, he looked at me oddly.

Before he could question me, I said, "Divina showed me a picture of you . . . and a cow."

A blush grew over his cheeks as he replied, "I see. How are you feeling, Sophia?"

I took inventory of my previous ailments and answered, "Muscles aren't sore anymore. The heaviness in my chest is gone. I think I'm better."

Phaidra was standing on a chair, peeping over the doctor's shoulder.

"You look much better," I said.

Phaidra brightened, "We're all better, thanks to you."

"Me? What did I do?" I sat up on my pillows.

"You discovered what was making us sick," Phaidra informed.

"What the heck are you talking about?" I asked.

Before Phaidra could explain, Dr. Holbrook started talking.

"Fever is finally down, and your heart rate has returned to normal. The antidote has done its job. I think you got so much sicker than your guardians did because of your age. Your magical immunity hasn't had a chance to develop fully, yet."

"She's human," Phaidra replied.

"Human? Oh?" He scratched his head.

I found his lack of knowledge concerning my genus interesting.

Surely, he had already heard the gossip about the Ballios taking in a human. It had to have been the talk of the town. Perhaps, he doesn't get out much. Maybe, he just isn't much of a gossip, and citizens respected that enough to keep their tittle-tattle to themselves. Even so, Divina, or Mrs. Holbrook, would have mentioned it, unless they don't register me as being different from them.

"Well, I'll test this blood to make sure the toxin has fully left her system, but I think Sophia should be able to return to school tomorrow," Dr. Holbrook said while folding up his blood pressure apparatus.

Phaidra placed clasped hands over her mouth. "That's very good news."

"I'll check in again this evening to give you the final word on school." Dr. Holbrook patted my hand before he got up to leave.

"I'll walk you out," Dio said from the doorway.

I had not even noticed him standing there. He really did look so much better. Both of them did.

"Thank you for all of your help, Abraham," Phaidra said.

I was interested to know if she gushed over the man because she was so happy we were all okay, or if it was because Dr. Holbrook was a very distinguished-looking man?

Standing with Dio at the doorway, Dr. Holbrook turned and smiled. "I couldn't have done it without, Sophia."

After the men left the room, I asked almost frightened, "What is going on?"

Hopping from the chair to the side of my bed, she sat down. She certainly must be feeling better to move about with such agility.

"So much has happened, Sophia. Where do I begin? After you lost consciousness, young Saban carried you to your bed. He rushed back into town to get Dr. Holbrook."

"Oh no, Saban was on his way to get his father," I cried.

"Yes, after he delivered Dr. Holbrook to the door, he set off to Larrant. Dr. Holbrook checked you over."

Grabbing my hand, she cried. "It didn't look good, Sophia. We were so frightened that you might not make it. I thought for sure, that when you started babbling nonsense, the fever had completely taken over, and it was going to be too late."

"What was I babbling about?" I asked.

"At first, you mumbled about bad haircuts and tree stumps. It was rather incoherent. You were upset about a mushroom that you tripped over, and then, out of nowhere, you shouted, Druaudidon."

Mimicking my rant while unconscious, she leapt up. It was a little dramatic. I was in no position to be leaping.

"That got us all thinking. We started to get sick after eating the mushrooms from Eve."

She put her hands up as if she were posing a question.

"Could it be that she had poisoned us with Druaudidon?"

"But, she was sick too," I added.

Sweeping her pointing finger to the ceiling, she said, "Yes, she was. She had just received a shipment of mushrooms, from Crandall."

The pieces of the puzzle started to fit.

"Somebody in Crandall wanted to poison Mrs. Chariot?" I concluded. "They couldn't have known she was going to share the mushrooms. We just ended up being collateral damage. What would have happened to Mrs. Chariot if she hadn't shared the mushrooms with us?"

"I suppose she would have eaten more, and would have died," Phaidra replied.

"Who would want to kill her?" I gasped.

"Anyone who has met her, I suppose," Phaidra replied in jest. "Actually, you answered that for us, too. You told us there was Druaudidon growing in Daphne Wilts basement."

I brushed the cobwebs from my memory.

"I had a dream about an incident Divina told me about. It was as if . . ." I rolled my fingers at my temple, "I was replaying the story in my mind. There was a faerie woman who tripped me."

I paused, recalling that the faerie part of the dream was most vivid. "Why would Daphne want to poison Mrs. Chariot?"

"She probably wouldn't, but her mother, Iris, might."

Phaidra jabbed at the bedspread.

"Iris and Lee Chariot had a 'thing' long ago. He ended up choosing Eve. That man sure does have terrible taste in women."

"How would Iris get poison in the mushrooms going to Eve?" I asked.

"We don't know for sure since she hasn't been located yet. We do know that Iris is engaged to an accountant at the mushroom factory," Phaidra said.

There were accountants in Celsus realm?

"Poor Daphne, does that mean she's all alone?" My heart went out to her.

"After the RBI confiscated the Druaudidon, they had Daphne contact a friend to stay with," Phaidra eased.

"I can't believe this all happened yesterday." I slapped my hand on my forehead. "And I slept through all of it. How is Mrs. Chariot doing?"

"I didn't think to ask Abraham. I'm sure she is doing much better. She got the antidote the same time Dio and I received it. We felt better within an hour."

"I got so sick because I'm human, I suppose," I rolled my eyes.

"You got so sick because of your age, my dear. We all have had years to build up a resistance to these kinds of things."

Phaidra hopped down to the floor. "Are you hungry?"

"I'm starving!"

"I'll get you some soup . . . chicken soup."

CHAPTER 46

Unbelievable! I was so close to Saban, but too sick to enjoy it.
Regarding myself in the bedroom mirror, I watched my cheeks became flush while thinking about him.

Why do I feel such a longing for him? It couldn't be because he is so incredibly good-looking. I never considered myself to be that shallow. Who am I kidding? Of course, I am.

Maybe I'm drawn to the subtle command he has on people and situations. Maybe, it's his composed, calculating manner. Or maybe I just have a thing for smart guys.

Whatever it was, it was difficult to think of anything else. I prayed Dr. Holbrook would okay me for school. I simply could not bear to go another day without seeing him.

After reviewing my schoolwork, I joined the Ballios outside. Since they were out of commission for so long, they were anxious to get back to their yard work. Dio was making adjustments to the fountain in the front. Phaidra worked in back.

"Can I help you?" I asked Phaidra.

"No dear. You're on the mend, but still recuperating. Have a seat," her demand was tender.

After picking a pear, I moved to a sunny spot in the middle of the lawn. Plopping myself down, I sat cross-legged on the grass, watching Phaidra pick some unruly vines from the tomatoes.

Something cold plunked around my neck. It felt like someone had put my necklace on for me.

"What the . . .?" I felt for my throat.

Phaidra chuckled. She must have placed it around my neck, the same way Dio had when he gave it to me. It was nice to see her powers had made a comeback.

"Did Saban give this to you?" I asked.

"No," she replied. "I found it on your window sill earlier."

"My window sill? That's an odd place for it to be." I took a thoughtful breath. "So, what was the antidote to the Druaudidon toxin?"

"The antidote was the plant itself." She did not look up to answer. "You grind the black leaves with the stem sap, and ingest it. That's why we're confident it was the Druaudidon toxin which poisoned us, and that Iris was responsible."

"Because not many people would have the outlawed plant in their possession, unless they needed it for something specific?"

"Precisely." She nodded.

"Minor question . . ." I started with hesitation.

"There are no minor questions," Phaidra corrected.

"What if it wasn't Druaudidon that poisoned us?" I rolled the pear around in my fingers.

"We would have died."

My face fell. That's an awful lot of faith to impart upon a delirious girl. A chill ran up my spine.

Why would they do such a thing? They pretty much put their life in my hands? Did Mrs. Chariot know the remedy to her illness was inspired by disjointed ramblings of little-old-me? I hope nobody told her. She might lose her mind.

Taking a bite of the sweet, juicy pear, I zoned off into Phaidra's weeding. She seemed bothered. I guess it was understandable with everything that had happened. Sitting back on her heels, Phaidra shook her head at the heavens.

Was she searching for an answer?

I took another bite of the pear.

Phaidra straightened with a swift intake of breath. Realization had struck. She must have found a solution to whatever was bothering her.

I took another bite.

She snatched the cherry-filled, wicker basket beside her, and jumped up. With eyes wide and wily she said, "Dio and I are getting our powers back."

"That's great. I bet the Holbrooks will be happy to hear that too. They can finally get rid of that silly patio carpet." I cheered.

"Yes, about that." She eyed me. "Dio and I have never seen patio carpet before."

"Hmmm," I carelessly took another bite.

Speaking every word with an eerie precision she said, "And, Divina and Alary have never been to Earth."

I paused to consider the situation.

"What's wrong, Phaidra?"

Taking a measured step, the little woman snapped and pointed her fingers at me.

By some unseen force, my wrists pressed together. The pear fell from my hand.

With a crash, the shed door across the yard slammed open. Phaidra had magically done it from where she stood. A cord of rope floated out. It was coming right for me.

CHAPTER 47

"Phaidra, what are you doing," I laughed.

She said nothing as the rope came nearer. It wrapped itself around my wrists, until my arms were cuffed in front of me.

"Is this a joke," I asked. "The rope's kind of tight."

"Can't you get yourself out?" she taunted.

"Uh, no. I can't."

I pulled against the rope.

Picking a cherry from the basket, she whispered, "Come on, you can do it."

She threw a cherry. I heard a plunk as it bounced off my forehead.

"Hey, what's that for?" I grumbled.

What the heck has gotten into her?

Coming closer, she tossed another cherry. It hit me on the shoulder.

"Well, do something," she ordered in a mothering tone.

"Like what? You tied me up." I held my hands up in case she needed a closer look to be sure.

Phaidra snorted. "I see you need more incentive." Reaching into the basket, she threw another cherry at my chin, one at my head, and another at my knee.

"Do something!" she demanded.

I sat quietly for a moment.

"I don't like this game, Phaidra."

Just as the gnome lady puffed in exasperation, cherries started flying off the tree. Like tiny red missiles, they blasted me. I held my hands to my face in defense. Unfortunately, that left my entire body as fair game.

"Dio," I shouted, looking down to see red splotches all over my white nightgown. "Oh great, this is never going to come out."

"I know you're a magic!" Phaidra cried. "I just don't know what kind!"

Cherries kept flying. They hit the back of the house, leaving wine colored splats, before becoming running stains.

"Dio, she's wrecking the house!" I bellowed.

"What in Desta's bluff is going on here, woman?" All of the missiles halted mid-stream, and fell to the ground as Dio rounded the corner.

Cherries dripped from my hair.

"It took you long enough. I just had a bath, you know."

Phaidra exhaled in defeat. A tear rolled down her wrinkled cheek.

"I'm so sorry, Sophia," she said. "I was sure you were a magic. I thought if I pressed you hard enough your powers would reveal themselves."

With my hands still bound, I rose to my feet and tried to console the little woman.

"But, I'm not a magic. You just proved it, didn't you?"

She looked up at me with guilt stricken eyes.

"Can you forgive me?"

"Yes, if you never, ever do this again."

I held out my bound hands so she could release me. Phaidra did her snap/point thing. The rope unraveled and fell to the ground.

"I have to go have a bath now. Please, stay out of trouble."

Dio held his arm around his wife. As I started for the house, I heard him whisper, "What were you thinking? She knows you would never hurt her."

Her head was hung when I turned to view them. Dio embraced her tighter.

They love each other, so much. I wish I could be blessed with a love like that one day.

~

We had a lovely mushroom-free dinner with glazed orange cakes for dessert. Dr. Holbrook returned after to give me the go ahead for school. Once in the seclusion of my bedroom, I burst out into a celebratory jig.

Even after my slumber-filled weekend, I still went to sleep at nine. The last thoughts before my eyes closed were of Saban, and how I would get to see him the next day.

CHAPTER 48

Everything was running on schedule with my morning routine, until I took one last look in the bathroom mirror. I had missed a cherry stain behind my ear. Since it had all night to set in my skin, I had to scrub extra hard to remove it. This would make me late.

The yard was empty when I arrived at school. I had an appointment to see Head Mistress Aristotle on Monday. I hoped she would forgive me for coming a day later. Upon opening the office door, I came face to face with Eve Chariot. She was seated at the reception desk behind the counter.

"Good morning, Mrs. Chariot. You're looking much better," I said with a pleasant respect.

"Thank you. I understand you were near death," she replied in her usual detached bluntness.

I released a short uneasy laugh. "That's what they tell me."

Mistress Aristotle came out from her office.

"Good morning, Sophia. Please come in."

Thank goodness she came along when she did. I was not sure what the follow up would be to a conversation that ended with, "I understand you were near death."

Mistress Aristotle secured the door and motioned for me to sit. She did so as well.

"You got one hundred percent on the herbs test you took on Friday. After discussing things with Dr. Akin, we feel it would be a waste of time to put you through the paces of junior classes. You will go directly to advanced magic, starting today. We call it AM for short."

"I'm honored that you would consider me knowledgeable enough to join the class, but isn't it a bit pointless?" I asked.

"Pointless?" She raised a brow.

"Yes, I can understand those other classes. They concern practical things, such as stones, plants, and herbs. They are things I can work with. AM class deals with actually performing spells. Using the natural abilities that magics are born with. I'm human, hence, no naturally born magic at my fingertips."

"Even so, you are living here, now," Mistress said. "It will be beneficial for you to learn what our people do. It can only enhance your understanding of our way of life. Besides, even humans can perform certain spells."

"We can? Which ones?" I asked eagerly.

"You'll have to find that out for yourself once you get to class," she answered. "It has been pushed back to the second to last class of the day. Magi Wilder is taking his masters in sorcery, and Sage University is completely inflexible with their course schedule. Now, off you go. I'm sure Miss Updar is looking forward to your returning to class."

Head Mistress stood and reached for the door.

"I'm glad you're feeling better, Sophia."

"Thanks, me too." I smiled over my shoulder.

Mrs. Chariot was purposely not looking in my direction.

"Have a nice day, Mrs. Chariot," I said in my most pleasing tone.

She rolled her head in my direction. I sensed it took a great effort on her part. It amused me.

~

Blood raced as I approached Miss Updar classroom. Before I could knock the door flew open.

"Sophia, I'm glad you are back," the little teacher chimed.

In appreciation of her warm welcome, I nodded before searching the room for Saban.

As hoped, his beautiful head popped up from the book he was reading. His dazzling eyes expanded at my presence. I felt a smile begin as our eyes locked, although I tried to hold back a bit, so as not to appear overly excited.

Sarah sat with a smug expression. When she realized where my sights were, she promptly whipped her head around to her brother, sending him some sort of icy reminder glare.

Saban flared his nostrils in acknowledgment of his sister's message, before returning to his book.

Nasty little witch, I grumbled in my head as I made my way to my desk.

After class, Sarah deliberately knocked into me as she marched past. She headed straight for Shea and whispered something in her ear before they scurried out.

Saban witnessed our encounter, but did little more than clench his jaw in annoyance of his sister's less than dignified behavior.

Contraptions class was equally frosty. I sat back and stared mindlessly at the wall while the teacher gave his introductory lecture on the next chapter. Cell phones.

What have I done to make Saban dislike me, again? Not that I thought he was falling for me or anything, but surely, he must have some friendly regard. He did help save my life, after all.

Asher's booked slammed on the floor and jolted me out of my daze. I realized in that instant, it must have looked like I was staring directly at Saban all this time. Maybe I was. I hoped nobody saw me. I did not need anyone to think I was a crazy, pathetic-gawker.

I met up with Divina at our usual lunch table. Before I could sit down or say hello, Saban came up behind me with Asher and Harris at either side.

"My mother has enlisted me in a competition," Saban stated coolly, wasting no time with frivolous greetings. "I will need a great deal of preparation. As such, I will be unable to attend final period, or help you with math."

Harris scrunched his face and stared at Saban. Asher shook his head.

My teeth clenched. I wanted to shout, *what the hell is your problem, jerk? Could you be any more bipolar?*

"I see," was all I could say aloud.

"I'm glad you're doing better, Sophia." Asher smiled. "It wasn't the same without you yesterday."

Saban slowly turned to his friend and looked at him as though he had just stolen the last slice of pizza, not that they had pizza here.

"Thank you, Asher," I answered. "*Your* consideration is very much appreciated."

Asher returned the loveliest white-toothed smile. I brightened at the unexpected sight while Saban stood back, evaluating my response to his friend.

I puffed lightly and turned my back to him, taking my seat with Divina. I heard their footsteps as they walked away.

Divina let out the breath she was holding and pointed past me.

"That doesn't make any sense," she said.

"So, we're back to everyone hating me. Awesome," I growled, while wishing there were some chocolates close by.

I flipped open my lunch basket and pulled out a banana, a piece of buttered rye bread, and a jar of . . . chocolate candies. I sighed happily.

"Phaidra must have known these would be needed today. Want some?"

I unscrewed the lid and offered it to Divina.

"Yeah," she sang as she reached into the jar. "You know, it looks like not everyone hates you."

She expressed the cutest double brow lift.

"What do you mean?"

I grabbed myself a candy and set the jar on the table between us. I took a bite.

Mmmm. Strawberry cream.

"It's true you have made some enemies, Daphne and Wisteria, to be precise. And Shea and Sarah were never fond of you," Divina began.

I rolled my eyes.

"But it seems you have found friends in Harris and Asher," Divina said. "And I still like you. Oh, Sophia, I can't believe you were so sick. We were so worried. I know we haven't known each other for long, but I don't know what I would do without you."

Divina reached across the table and clasped my forearm. "You're the best friend I've ever had."

"Thanks Divina, that really does means a lot." I returned her pat.

"My father never fully explained how you knew the Druaudidon was in Daphne's basement? And, how did you know it was even dangerous?" Divina asked. "I've been down there lots and never paid any attention to it."

"I had a dream. I think my mind was recreating the story you told me about the night you guys were playing those pranks. I saw Mr. Jasper send a tree through Mr. Beatty's window. The dream was so real, like I was actually there. Only, you guys couldn't see me. It must sound crazy."

I grimaced.

Divina sat back and crossed her arms over her chests. "That doesn't sound crazy at all. That's how my mother sees things. However, she doesn't have to be near death to do it."

"That would be easier. Unfortunately, I'm not a witch."

I popped another sweet, silky candy in my mouth. This one was a decadent, chocolate-covered, orange sherbet.

Divina looked at me in surprise.

"That's right. You're not a witch, so how did you see everything?"

She acted as though she were just now remembering I was human.

"We humans have some tricks in our bag, too, Divina," I was mildly defensive. "Some humans see visions . . . of stuff. I can't say that I have ever done it before, but I've heard, in extreme circumstances, it becomes more possible."

"Really?" Her eyes widened. "Do a lot of humans have this ability?"

"I don't know. I don't think so." I pondered. "Then again, maybe. It's not readily spoken about." My answer was ambiguous.

"How do you know these so-called humans are not actually witches?" Divina posed.

"What! No. Of course, they're not," I declared absolutely. Although, her question gave me pause.

"They couldn't be . . ." I trailed off in thought. "Forget about it. Anyway, back to the story."

"Yes, your dream. What happened?"

She leaned forward.

"After you ran into the street to stop the men, Daphne and Wisteria ran to the backyard. I followed them and noticed a window to the basement . . . and the Druaudidon plant. I was curious how they were able to get the beautiful flower to bloom in the dark. It's the strangest thing. I had just read about that plant in a text book that Dr. Akin had given me. It didn't mean anything at the time."

I shook my head at the coincidence.

"That's when your sleep-jabber alerted my father!"

Divina brightened as the story started to come together for her.

"You know," she picked out another chocolate from the jar, "I answered the door when Saban came to retrieve my father. I have never seen such a fright on anyone, certainly never on the unwavering Saban. He looked like death."

Like death . . .

Her last statement struck me, although I could not be sure why.

"You would never know that, now." I glanced over my shoulder to his table, and watched as Daphne and Wisteria approached and took a seat. "And, what's with that? I haven't been here long, but I didn't realize they were all buddies."

Divina snorted, "That is a recent development."

The boys seemed less than interested in their new lunch companions. Saban took out a book and began to read. Asher turned his back ever so slightly to the girls, and continued his conversation with Harris. Daphne seemed to consider this a snub, and she looked down on Asher with an acidic glare.

"That witch better watch her attitude with Asher," Divina growled.

She was obviously seeing the same interaction. I chuckled. I had never heard such aggression from her.

"Divina, do you have a thing for Asher?"

"Of course not." She straightened. "It's not his fault that his mother was the one to confiscate the plant and put out the arrest warrant for Iris. Somebody had to do it. If it wasn't Agent Griffiths, it would have been someone else."

I knew her dispute was not with me. She obviously had strong feelings about the situation.

"That's right. Asher's mom is an RBI. Do you think Daphne will hold it against him?" I asked with some apprehension of my own.

"I wouldn't put it past her. They're vindictive little imps," Divina replied. "It doesn't matter. The noble has triumphed over the wicked."

"Yes," I agreed, "Agent Griffiths has saved the day. She's quite the superhero. I like strong women."

"Me too," Divina laughed, "and she did a commendable job, only, I was talking about you."

"Me?"

She nodded. "You, my human friend, were the one who set things right."

A shiver went up my spine, and memory traveled back to the first day I met Eve Chariot. The hunched-back, Latin spirit who spoke through her said, "Soon to be set right."

Could I believe the spirit was talking about me?

"Father says, the Ballios probably would have pulled through the Druaudidon poisoning, but Eve would be dead. Wizards are not as resilient as wee folk, especially at the dose she received. Everyone knows that, including Saban."

She glanced past my shoulder. "That's what makes his attitude toward you even more obvious."

"What do you mean, obvious?"

"He likes you."

"Yeah right," I scoffed.

"Come on, Sophia. Aren't you listening? You saved his mother's life, and the day you return from your own deathbed, he brushes you off? No way! He's trying to hide his feelings." She laughed. "Everyone is. But it's getting increasingly difficult with you around. Face it, you changed this place. Whether you know it or not, Calista is your home. Can't you feel it?"

CHAPTER 49

Exiting the stall in the girl's washroom, I rummaged through my basket to find lip-gloss. In front of the mirror, I smiled. Besides the granite floors, silver faucets, and majestic oak décor, the bathrooms were the same as at home, on Earth.

Rubbing my lips together to smooth freshly applied gloss, I came to the conclusion that Divina was right. Setting aside my near-death escape, and Phaidra attacking me, in a sweet, albeit, erroneous attempt to bring out dormant supernatural powers, Calista did feel like home.

A shiver went up my spine. I had the sense someone was watching me. Too scared to turn, I glanced at the reflection in the mirror. I gasped so hard I thought I might choke.

Saltwater filled my mouth. It always happened before I puked.

Drunken eyes, seething with an indecent desire, fixed onto mine.

Panic set it.

"Max!" I cried.

Laughter met me when I whirled around–a baneful, female teenaged mirth. The newly developed girl posse stood before me, Daphne, Wisteria, Sarah and Shea. Pleasure regarding my fear was shared by all.

Setting a hand on her hip, the blonde named Wisteria sneered, "Who's Max? Is he a lover of yours?"

"He couldn't be a lover," Shea grumbled. "The incantation was intended to expose her fears."

"What are you talking about?" I struggled to steady my breath.

"We were beginning to think you were some sort of high level sorcerer in disguise," Daphne said. "None of the spells we cast on you worked."

"Up until now, that is." Sarah smirked.

"Yes," Daphne smiled and glanced at Shea. "We used an ancient spell—it was a raven—that let us watch you through its eyes to gather information about your powers. You weren't supposed to fall in that hole. We didn't even know it was there."

"Although," Shea sneered. "I certainly enjoyed watching that happen."

"You have caused us quite the fluster," Daphne continued. "We were ready to throw our hands up in defeat."

I didn't know we were fighting.

"Then, you got sick," Shea grinned. "Guess you're not as indestructible as we thought."

I never claimed to be indestructible. Where are they getting this stuff?

"This morning we decided to give it one more try," Daphne explained, positioning herself as the leader of the mob. "If nothing else, your defenses would be down after your brush with death."

Backing into the counter I replied, "I don't have any defenses. I'm not some undercover magic."

"We know," Shea squawked as Sarah held up a jade pendent.

Feeling for my neck, I realized Dio's gift to me was gone. "How did you get my necklace?"

"It must have slipped off," Sarah replied. "Shea saw it under your chair in the commissary when she discovered you ogling my brother, again. I brought it to Saban. He has sort of a flair for detecting enchantment in objects. After he demanded we return it to you at once, he advised that it held no magical charge."

"What does he know?" Daphne resumed her charge and ripped the necklace from Sarah's hand to examine the stone. "I'm sure I've seen this pendent in one of my mother's ancient books. I know it's been protecting you all along."

She fixed her eyes on me.

"I imagine that's true." I swallowed hard. "Can I have it back? Please."

I held out my hand hopefully.

"Are you crazy?" Daphne laughed. "This is just the beginning of the fun . . . for us."

She tossed my necklace into the toilet behind her and flushed. My stomach sank when the Ballios gift disappeared from the bowl.

Taking a pace forward, Daphne moved her face within a hand width of mine and said, with all the venom her voice could carry, "Welcome to Calista's Court–human!"

Made in the USA
Charleston, SC
07 August 2014